SHARPENED BLADE

The Story of Dinah Clark

Joseph J. Swope

Black Rose Writing | Texas

ISBN: 978-1-68513-707-6 (Paperback); 978-1-68513-734-2 (Hardcover)
LIBRARY OF CONGRESS CONTROL NUMBER: 2025945616
PUBLISHED BY BLACK ROSE WRITING
www.blackrosewriting.com

Printed in the United States of America
Suggested Retail Price (SRP) $21.95 (Paperback); $26.95 (Hardcover)

Sharpened Blade is printed in Garamond Premier Pro

*As a planet-friendly publisher, Black Rose Writing does its best to eliminate unnecessary waste to reduce paper usage and energy costs, while never compromising the reading experience. As a result, the final word count vs. page count may not meet common expectations.

Dedicated to all those who overcame oppression
and made a positive mark on the world.

PRAISE FOR
SHARPENED BLADE

"A proud retelling of a proud black woman's incredible life."
–Tracy A. Ball, International Bestselling, Interracial Romance Author

"An engrossing read. It's the way history deserves to be taught. Highly recommended."
–Karen K. Brees, Amazon #1 best-selling author of the *WWII Adventures of MI6 Agent Katrin Nissen* series

"Swope deftly weaves Reading, Berks County and American history around the life of this interesting African-American woman. The author successfully tiptoes between fact and fiction, bringing this memorable tale to life. Definitely a keeper!"
–Paul A. Druzba, Berks County historian and author of four books on local history

The only known photograph of Dinah Clark

"*I know why the caged bird sings, ah me,*
When his wing is bruised and his bosom sore,—
When he beats his bars and he would be free;
It is not a carol of joy or glee,
But a prayer that he sends from his heart's deep core,
But a plea, that upward to heaven he flings —
I know why the caged bird sings!"

Paul Laurence Dunbar (1872-1906), the son of African parents who had been slaves prior to the Civil War. Dunbar achieved fame and success as one of the first internationally popular African American poets.

SHARPENED
BLADE

CHAPTER 1
THE INTERVIEW

December 1871

The young reporter sat down on a chair in Dinah Clark's humble home and greeted her warmly, maintaining eye contact as much as possible. He wanted to ensure Dinah saw a friendly face. As he settled in, he looked about the room to get a sense of Dinah's life. He saw no luxuries or decorations. Dinah had neither the time nor the money for anything pretty that failed to serve a function.

"I've heard so much about you," he said. "You've lived quite a life, becoming quite famous about town."

"I don't know anything about that," Dinah said, now in her late seventies. "I just went about doing what work I could find to make a living. Along the way, I made quite a few acquaintances, both white folks and colored. Many of them were very kind to me."

"But you were born an indentured servant. . ."

"A slave," Dinah corrected him. "Whatever you want to call it, I was a slave." She shifted in her seat as if the memories of those days still seared through her brain like a hot iron.

"Yes, a slave," the reporter corrected himself. "But then you became a sawyer . . ."

"Before that I met my husband, William Clark," Dinah again cut the reporter off. "He taught me to saw wood. I did many jobs, but cutting wood was always my favorite."

A loud bang from the other room interrupted their conversation. Dinah twisted her head toward the sound.

"Are you hurt?" she asked. "You didn't trip over something, did you?"

"I'm all right, Momma," a voice said. "Don't you worry about me. You keep talking. I don't want to meet no reporter. I've got nothing to say. You tell him whatever you want. I'm staying right here."

Dinah turned back toward her visitor, shaking her head. "That's my daughter, Mary Ann," she explained. "She's three-quarters blind, can hardly see. She must have banged into the dresser again."

The reporter nodded in understanding. "Do you need to check on her?"

"No, she's fine. She'd only give me sass if I did."

"Well then," the reporter said as he put his pen to paper, "shall we begin?"

"I'd be glad to," Dinah said. "Where would you like to start?"

"From the beginning. Tell me who you are and where you were born, then tell me about your life. I want to hear everything you can remember."

Dinah searched deep in her memory for a moment then began to speak.

"I was born a slave many years ago—I don't know how many—on the farm of Gabriel Hiester on the Tulpehocken creek, in Bern township, Berks county, Pennsylvania. My parents' name was Bell..."

CHAPTER 2
THE LENAPE

1638

The Lenape hunters hid silently in the trees, waiting for their prey to wander into their path. The grove of tall oaks and red maples stood in a meadow along a strong-running creek. With the arrival of early fall, the leaves already displayed a kaleidoscope of colors. The hunter's clothing blended into their surroundings, disguising them to their quarry. One hundred yards to the north, a bank rose sharply to higher ground. The forest provided both shelter for the Lenape's presence and the perfect feeding ground for those they hunted. The hunting party waited patiently, unseen and unheard. Through many generations, these Native Americans had learned to become one with nature.

Just a little longer, the leader of the Lenape hunters thought, *he will come. He always does.*

A short while later, a full-grown deer moved casually into view, feeding on the bountiful food around him. The impressively sized twelve-point buck showed no recognition of those who watched him cautiously, and the animal eventually moved into an open clearing. The deer sensed no danger, though imminent peril lay all around him.

Two members of the Lenape suddenly shot their arrows, hitting their target from either side. The deer staggered forward for several steps, then summoned whatever energy it had left to attempt an escape. The deer began to run, but two more arrows tore through the air, dropping the animal to the ground. Once more, the deer staggered to get up, struggled a few more steps, then fell in the meadow, the life draining from his body. In just a few seconds, the Lenape surrounded the buck, and one of them mercifully put it out of its misery with a slash of a knife through the neck.

"This is a healthy and fine-sized *achtu*," the leader of the hunt said as he inspected the deer. "He will feed us well for many days."

The Lenape elder checked the animal one more time, then looked at two of his companions who had less hunting experience than the others. "You take this back to the village so it can be skinned and carved," he said. "You know what to do. The rest of you, we still have more hunting before we return."

Native American tribes typically did not prepare a deer in the field for transport using the same methods as hunters that followed them. Later hunters turned the deer onto its back and cut from the groin to the top of the rib cage. They removed the stomach, colon, intestines, lung, esophagus, and male genitals, as well as the tarsal gland on the hind legs. This ensured the meat would remain unspoiled and allowed them to move the deer more easily out of the forest.

Instead, the two young Lenape followed the tribe's traditional practice. They pulled out their knives, one made of animal bone and the other shaped from deer antlers. The hunters had meticulously sharpened the blades and tied them snugly to wooden handles. Using precise cuts, the Lenape men removed and washed the internal organs. They partially skinned and separated the buck into nine pieces, allowing them to carry the animal to their camp on their backs. The front legs were removed, followed by the back legs. The hunters excised the sinew and sliced along the deer's backside and along the ribs. They cut off the head last.

With the process complete, both men mounted the deer parts on their backs and began their trek back to the village nearby. As they did so, an arrowhead that had downed the creature and been retrieved by one of the hunters fell unnoticed to the ground. The men continued on their path, unaware of the lost arrowhead.

Once they returned to the village, the Lenape completed the butchering process. The buck provided a hearty feast for the community. The tribe often used stone boiling, where they covered chunks of venison with water and then added hot stones until the water boiled and the meat cooked. Fresh deer meat was also baked in clay pots or cooked on spits on an open fire. The tribe consumed even the liver, pancreas, and kidney. The women cut the meat not immediately consumed into strips and salted and dried it for the oncoming winter. Many Native American tribes made a dish called pemmican by pounding dried venison into powder and mixing it with melted fat and dried berries, including blueberries or cranberries.

But the fallen deer would provide much more than food. The tribe wasted no part of the animal. The Lenape used marrow to make tools such as hoes, arrows, and knives. The deer's skin would be tanned and made into clothing and moccasins, while deer hair often decorated the tribe's apparel. Bones and antlers became pendants, combs, tools, dishes, arrowheads, and fishhooks, while sinew was fashioned into bow strings and sewing thread. Hollow bones were made into musical instruments and whistles. Jaw bones were used to remove corn from the cob to make succotash. Bone slivers became needles. Deer tallow made various ointments and candles.

The eyes? The Lenape used deer eyes in their headdresses and breast ornaments for men, as well as headbands for women. Deer and other wild game of this area sustained the tribe in innumerable ways.

The Lenape's territory, known as Lenapehoking, encompassed much of the Northeastern American Woodlands, including a present-day section of Delaware, all of New Jersey, the Lehigh Valley and Northeastern Pennsylvania, New York Bay, western Long Island, and the lower Hudson Valley in New York State. On the western border, the Lenape lived in small towns along rivers and streams, sharing the hunting territory along the Schuylkill River and its tributaries with the Iroquoian Susquehannock. The Lenape had inhabited this region of America for more than ten thousand years. Their oral history told many great tales.

On this day, the Lenape hunted on the southwest border of their traditional land, in what later was known as Berks County, Pennsylvania, about sixty miles west of a region that eventually became the City of Philadelphia. They had established their own village on the northern side of the Tulpehocken Creek, on a gently rising hill bordering the wooded meadow serving as the location of their hunt. In Lenape, *"Tulpehocken"* meant "land of turtles," a sacred animal to the tribe and the name of one its familial clans.

The entire Lenape party eventually returned to their homes and immediately began enjoying the spoils of their foray. Besides two bucks, the haul also included several rabbits and a number of fish caught in the nearby waters. The day of hunting had proven productive. Together with the recent harvest of corn, beans, and squash, the catch provided hearty meals for the tightly knit community then and in the future. The hunters would leave the village each morning until they filled their coffers with enough food for the cold weather to come. No member of the tribe would go hungry that winter.

"You have done well," one of the elder mothers of the tribe said. "You make our village proud."

The first recorded contact between the Lenape and the Europeans took place in 1524 when local Lenape greeted Italian explorer Giovanni da Verrazzano as his ship and crew entered the Lower New York Bay. Verrazzano had become the first European to explore the Atlantic coast of North America between Florida and New Brunswick. As the years progressed, more and more Europeans settled in the Lenape territory. For a considerable amount of time after that, the Lenape and the European immigrants lived side-by-side in a relative but ultimately tenuous peace.

The Lenape maintained a tightly knit culture, focused primarily on their immediate family, friends, and the village unit. Among the Algonquian tribes along the East Coast, the Lenape held the honor of serving as the ancestors from which other Algonquian-speaking peoples emerged. Each member of the tribe took their heritage seriously.

When the Europeans first settled in North America, the Lenape had three clans, each of which historically included twelve sub-clans. The Lenape family and society were based on a matrilineal clan system. Children belonged to the mother's clan, the basis of their social status and identity. The mother's eldest brother was generally a more significant and influential figure to the male children than their father, who typically belonged to another clan. This practice effectively prevented in-breeding and ensured the continued health of the tribe. Leadership passed through the maternal line, with homes and agricultural land controlled by women. Newlywed couples lived with the bride's family. Lenape men hunted, provided food, cleared fields, built houses, and protected the clan.

However, by the time William Penn arrived in American in 1682 to claim his Pennsylvania Commonwealth, a combination of forces had seriously reduced the Lenape population. Some of these had proven self-inflicted, as the Lenape and other Native American tribes declared war on each other. A serious famine also affected the Lenape population. Finally, and perhaps most detrimentally, the European influx brought diseases such as smallpox, for which the Native Americans had no immunity and suffered grievous losses.

With segments of the traditional Lenape societal framework collapsing and having few alternatives, the sub-clan mothers merged their families into the main clan family. Because of this, William Penn always believed the Lenape clans comprised only the Turtle, Turkey, and Wolf clans. In reality, more than thirty Lenape clans had inhabited the eastern seaboard prior to the arrival of the Europeans, their numbers already greatly reduced by the time of the mass entry of newcomers.

The eventual fate of the Lenape had already impacted their clans by this day of hunting, though the full effect would not occur for many more decades. On this occasion, however, the Lenape went about their traditional lifestyle, one that effectively supported a complex and long-surviving culture. The demise of their authority over their traditional territory did not cross their minds. The familiar hunting ground they traversed provided a bountiful harvest for the local village and had sustained a culture for hundreds and even thousands of years.

The meadow where the buck had fallen became strewn with used arrowheads over the years, along with other remnants of the hunt. Little did the local Lenape realize that these halcyon days would soon end, and they would no longer claim this terrain as their own. The Lenape now celebrated the last days of their empire, though they failed to realize their fate, which would arrive far sooner than they expected.

CHAPTER 3
THE UNCOMFORTABLE ARRANGEMENT
WITH SLAVERY

1681

William Penn may have been a prominent member of the Religious Society of Friends, better known as the Quakers, but he also possessed a strong helping of political realism. Thus, the issue of slavery proved both vexing and inconclusive during the early days of the colony that bore his family name.

In 1681, King Charles II deeded a large piece of his North American land holdings to Penn to pay the debts the king owed to Penn's father, the admiral and politician Sir William Penn. The younger Penn founded the Province of Pennsylvania as a colony of England. Pennsylvania literally means "Penn's Woods," an apt name for a territory known for its seemingly endless forests and hills.

In many ways, William Penn implemented surprisingly progressive policies for his colony. Penn proved to be an early advocate for a democratic government and religious freedom, and he maintained good relationships and negotiated successful treaties – at least from the British perspective — with the Lenape Native Americans. But when addressing slavery, his stance proved significantly less enlightened and more restrictive.

In 1684, just three years after Penn established Pennsylvania, the slave ship, the *Isabella*, docked in Philadelphia and delivered one hundred and fifty-four Africans condemned to involuntary servitude. Local Quaker settlers immediately purchased them to address the dire need for workers to help clear the heavily wooded land they now struggled to tame.

A year later, Penn unhesitatingly defended the institution of slavery, claiming he preferred African laborers on his own farm rather than white indentured servants, because *"a man has them while he lives."* His words remain chilling.

Penn's comments confirmed the common belief that Pennsylvania's slaves and indentured servants in the late Seventeenth Century had no path to freedom and remained "property" their entire lives. This acceptance of slavery in Pennsylvania remained established well into the Eighteenth Century. In fact, by 1700, Pennsylvania's colonial lawmakers passed *An Act for the Better Regulation of Servants in this Province and Territories* that created formal distinctions between the treatment of white indentured servants and black African slaves. Lifelong servitude became legally sanctioned for Africans, and penalties such as being *"severely whipped, in the most public place of the township"* for *"offences"* were enforced with regularity.

Despite the legal sanctioning of slavery, vehement opposition to the practice arose soon after enslavement came to the province and did not abate. Opponents may have made up a minority, but they ensured their voices rang loudly and persistently. Shortly after the colony's founding, four Quakers from Germantown in northwest Philadelphia authored the first resolution against slavery in colonial America in 1688. Converts from the Mennonite congregation, the Quakers' petition claimed:

"Now though they are black, we cannot conceive there is more liberty to have them slaves, as it is to have other white ones. There is a saying that we should do to all men like as will be done ourselves; making no difference of what generation, descent, or colour they are. And those who steal or rob men, and those who buy or purchase them, are they not all alike?"

Despite ongoing opposition, however, slavery continued to exist in Pennsylvania, failing to find a crack in the political landscape for more than a century. Only in 1780, with the passage of the Commonwealth's *Gradual Emancipation Act*, did that foundation finally begin to crumble. While the Act served as the first of its kind in the colonies and steadily decreased the slave population, it hardly proved an all-encompassing elixir. Rather than providing immediate freedom, the legislation provided for the gradual abolition of slavery. The act permitted Pennsylvania slaveholders to keep the enslaved individuals they already owned, mandating that owners needed to register their slaves annually. Slavery explicitly ended only if the owner had either freed the slave or died of natural causes. The Act did not free existing slaves, only their children born after March 1, 1780, and even then, far past their date of their birth. Slave owners did not immediately lose their "property," an ongoing economic benefit for those who counted African Americans as part of their assets.

Part of the Act read:

"From and after the Passing of this Act, shall not be deemed and considered as Servants for Life or Slaves; and that all Servitude for Life or Slavery of Children in Consequence of the Slavery of their Mothers, in the Case of all Children born within this State from and after the passing of this Act as aforesaid, shall be, an hereby is, utterly taken away, extinguished and for ever abolished."

However, the Act continued, adding an important distinction:

"That no Covenant of personal Servitude or Apprenticeship whatsoever shall be valid or binding on a Negroe or Mulatto for a longer Time than Seven Years; unless such Servant or Apprentice were at the Commencement of such Servitude or Apprenticeship under the Age of Twenty one Years; in which Case such Negroe or Mulatto may be holden as a Servant or Apprentice respectively, according to the Covenant, as the Case shall be, until he or she shall attain the Age of twenty eight Years but no longer."

Unscrupulous slaveholders soon found loopholes around these restrictions. In response, the Pennsylvania Assembly amended the legislation in 1788, prohibiting slaveholders from transporting pregnant enslaved women out of the state in order that their child was born into slavery elsewhere. This had served as an insidious scheme by some slave owners to skirt freeing children once they reached the age of twenty-eight. The amendment also declared that enslaved individuals owned by people who intended to move or settle in Pennsylvania became immediately free.

From the time of the passage of the Act, the slave population slowly but steadily decreased, until only sixty-four slaves were recorded in 1840, the final year the census designated a column to record that status. Despite its serious flaws, the Act served as the first piece of legislation abolishing slavery in a democratic society. This legislation eventually became the model for abolition laws across the Northern states.

A simple reason may exist to explain the gradual abolishment of slavery rather than a definitive end. Coincidentally or not, many slaveholders worked in prominent government positions in Pennsylvania. For example, during the time of the enactment of the Act, Gabriel Hiester, part of the prominent Hiester political dynasty of the Eighteenth and early Nineteenth Centuries, served as a Justice in the Court of Common Pleas. Earlier, he had been a delegate to the Pennsylvania Constitutional Convention and served as a colonel in the Pennsylvania Militia as an American Revolutionary War Patriot. Hiester continued his public service throughout much of his life, later serving as a member of Pennsylvania's unicameral Assembly, a delegate to the Commonwealth's second Constitutional Convention, a member of Pennsylvania's House of Representatives, and eventually a member of the State Senate.

Hiester also owned slaves, a fact confirmed by tax records. In fact, on at least two occasions, he offered a reward for runaway slaves.

The *Lancaster Intelligencer* published Hiester's advertisement in the September 20, 1800, edition:

"Ten Dollars Reward RAN-AWAY from the subscriber on Wednesday, the 10th inst. a Mulatta lad, named SIGHE, about 19 or 20 years of age, 5 feet 8 or 9 inches high, stout made, light complexion and generally wears his hair queued. Had on and took along with him 2 shirts, 1 pair gray tow trousers, 1 pair do. stripe, 1 pair [two unintelligible words], small clothes line with leather, 2 wool hats, 1 pair shoes newly patched and soled, besides sundry other clothes which cannot be ascertained. Whoever apprehends said runaway and secures him in any jail shall have the above reward and reasonable charges if brought home. GABRIEL HIESTER. Barn township, Berks county. September 11, 1800. P.S. All persons are hereby notified not to harbor said runaway."

Several years later, Philadelphia's *Aurora General Advertiser* published yet another advertisement from Hiester on the front page of its June 24, 1806 edition:

"TWENTY DOLLARS REWARD. RAN AWAY from the subscriber, living in Berne township, Berks county, state of Pennsylvania, on the night of the 7th inst. a mulatto man named LISH, about twenty-five years of age, five feet 8 or 9 inches high, stout built, smooth face, has a scar occasioned by a cut on his instep; is fond of spiritous liquors and when a little intoxicated his eyelids appear heavy, and his tongue thick; a great boaster of his activity, strength and capacity for working; his wool is short, being fresh shorn excepting a little on the back part of his head — Had on and took with him, a dark brown cloth coat, swansdown jacket, ribbed velvet pantaloons, and other clothes not known. Whoever takes up and secures said runaway, so that the subscriber gets him, shall have the above reward, and reasonable charges paid if brought home. GABRIEL HIESTER. Berne township, Berks county, June 21, 1806."

Gabriel Hiester clearly did not represent the only well-heeled member of public service who worked diligently to maintain possession of what he considered his "property." Thus, in a compromise to abolitionists that still protected their assets, legislators passed an Act that abolished slavery–for the next generation- yet protected their own holdings.

Freedom never came easily or quickly for those shackled by the bonds of slavery.

CHAPTER 4
GABRIEL HIESTER

July 1770

Gabriel Hiester's luck began at his birth, and he never seemingly lost it.

Born on July 17, 1749, Gabriel was the son of German immigrants Daniel and Rosanna (Hager) Hiester. Daniel Hiester operated a brick-and-tile making business in Sumneytown, Montgomery County. At some point, the Hiester family moved west to Berks County. Ultimately, Gabriel Hiester settled into a comfortable life in the southeastern Pennsylvania county.

The Hiester political dynasty played a critical role in both Colonial America and the early days of the country's independence. In addition to Gabriel's own public service, his brother, named Daniel after his father, served as a brigadier general of the Pennsylvania militia during the American Revolution and later served as a member of the Pennsylvania General Assembly and the U.S. House of Representatives. Gabriel and his siblings were second cousins to Joseph Hiester, who served as the fifth governor of Pennsylvania under the Commonwealth's current Constitution from 1820 to 1823. The Hiester family's political affiliations continued well into the Nineteenth Century, with both a William Hiester and yet another Daniel Hiester serving in the U.S. House of Representatives.

But much of that would come in the future. In the mid-to-later Eighteenth Century, the Hiester family had only begun establishing themselves in America. They arrived as part of the English empire but soon found themselves at the forefront of the battle for an independent nation.

As Pennsylvania grew in prominence and population, the Hiester family set their sights on the still-developing Bern Township in Berks County. Founded in 1733 mainly by German settlers and named after Berne, Switzerland, Bern Township offered a fertile, hilly environment ideal for farming. The Tulpehocken Creek sliced through the land before emptying into the Schuylkill River. Reading Town served as the centerpiece and economic lifeblood of Berks County, with the municipality founded by William Penn's sons, Richard and Thomas, along with Conrad Weiser in 1748. Weiser had his own unique history: a German pioneer who served as an interpreter between the Pennsylvania Colony and the regional Native American nations, he gained a reputation for fairness that transcended the years since his death and produced a school district named after him. With the establishment of Berks County in 1752, Reading became the county seat.

Not surprisingly, when young Gabriel Hiester purchased a two-hundred-acre plot of land in Bern Township in the western part of Berks County, the few residents already living there welcomed their new neighbor. The Hiester family was proving to be good stock. All welcomed his residency.

Gabriel did not disappoint those expectations. His farm exuded a fair air of elegance for the time, a charm and dignity which he insisted upon. Gabriel aspired to greater things in life, and his residence needed to personify that ambition.

"This home should appropriately represent our station in life," Gabriel told his wife, Elizabeth. "I have hired the best craftsmen I could find to build it and secured only quality materials. Our home will be a fine and sturdy structure."

"I'm leaving that up to you," Elizabeth answered. "Just make sure we have a comfortable home for us and the children. Fancy is fine, but we still need to live here."

"I will ensure our home is as functional as it is beautiful," he assured his wife.

Eschewing the typical stone construction of most Berks County farmhouses, Gabriel secured brick from his father. It represented the only brick home in the area, but the family business made such construction inevitable. Gabriel built a classic four-cornered farmhouse that featured elaborate hand-carved woodwork painted in the Colonial green popular at the time. Crown molding highlighted the woodwork as well as an intricate fireplace mantle and a corner cupboard with glass cabinet doors. A triangular design decorated the top of the doorway in and out of the main living room. The woodwork survived the demolition of the farmhouse two centuries later and became part of the Hiester Room in the Berks History Center.

The first floor included a living area and dining room, both twenty feet by twenty feet, with ceilings that rose more than nine feet high. The thick outer walls, designed to insulate the home as best as possible, created wide window ledges that could easily hold decorations, household necessities, and even plants if so desired. An oversized hallway and the main entrance sat to the right side of the building when looking at the structure from the passing dirt roadway created to accommodate the horses and carriages of the day. A summer kitchen and hand-pumped well stood detached from the principal home, a building that would be repurposed in the future when later owners expanded the farmhouse.

The second floor featured two larger bedrooms and a smaller one. All rooms but the small bedroom had their own fireplace. The main bedrooms were spacious, the same size as the rooms below them on the first floor.

The third floor, however, proved more uninviting. The area was cut into an oversized entrance hall and three rooms, large in dimension but constructed of unfinished rough lumber. No fireplace provided heat. No paint decorated the walls. Someone walking up the stairway would turn left at the landing, then reach the open area after another set of steps. One door led to a room on the right and the other two stood side-by-side straight ahead. The angled roofline gradually reduced the height of the rooms on each side.

This area–far less elegant than the rest of the home–represented the quarters of the slaves owned by Gabriel Hiester. Slaves also likely occupied the basement of the house, one that provided ample room and enough heat to survive a brutal winter day.

Though the house boasted a generous size for the Eighteenth Century, it housed a plethora of occupants. Besides eleven slaves at any one time, Gabriel had married the former Elizabeth Bausman. Together, the couple had six children: Gabriel Jr., Jonathan, William, Jacob, Mary, and Elizabeth.

In some ways, slave ownership in the Eighteenth Century provided both a status of wealth and a means to complete the work on a large farming operation. A 1767 report shows that forty-four percent of all slaves in the province were owned by the wealthiest ten percent of the population. Only five percent were owned by the poorest fifty percent.

History has forgotten the names of most of the slaves held by Gabriel Hiester. Birth and death records were scanty and inconsistent, and the recording of marriages was virtually non-existent. Certainly, those souls lost to history deserved better than that fate, but time has erased the existence of many of those involuntary servants. But at least one name has survived, and her story is recorded for posterity. In truth, she was never a "slave," but was born an indentured servant. To her, there was no difference, and she referred to herself in later years as a former slave. Her birth name was Dinah Bell. Today, most people who have heard her story know her as Dinah Clark.

Dinah's parents gave birth to her in 1794 or 1795. Even Dinah didn't know for sure. Nor did she remember her parents' first names in an interview many years afterward. That is perhaps not as surprising as it first appears. It's likely she became separated from her parents as soon as she could function somewhat independently to not create any unnecessary family bonds. Such kinship proved an inconvenient hindrance, with slaves often bought and sold. Perhaps Dinah witnessed her parents sold away from the Hiester farm during her time there. Dinah never revealed her parents' fate, if even she knew it.

Dinah also had two brothers and one half-sister, though she *"don't know what became of them but I supposed they were sold out."* Familial ties proved mostly a nuisance to a slave owner and clearly were strongly discouraged.

By her own account, Dinah saw her one brother, 'Lij, many years later, sometime around 1850. He said he *was then roving about the country, came to see me at Reading. He didn't say where he came from or where he was going."*

Dinah likely never saw him again and knew little about her brother and his life.

In many ways, however, Dinah defied the odds. She eventually became free from her servitude, and despite never learning to read or write, emerged as perhaps the most well-known African American woman in Reading and Berks County in the Nineteenth Century.

Her journey was never easy. Yet she persevered, and history at least remembers her name.

CHAPTER 5
DINAH BELL

1794

"I was born a slave many years ago–I don't know how many–on the farm of Gabriel Hiester, on the Tulpehocken Creek, in Bern Township, Berks County, Pennsylvania. My parents' name was Bell; I don't know their first (Christian) names."

Dinah Clark, "What She Did and Saw," Reading Eagle, December 23, 1871

"Push, Mamie, push," the midwife exhorted the pregnant woman. "We're almost there."

The midwife, an enslaved African American woman from a nearby farm, had hurriedly travelled to the bedside of the pregnant woman on Gabriel Hiester's farm. She had no formal medical training but had assisted in other births and had derived her knowledge from those experiences. In a day where physicians were still scarce and lacked many medical advances and where slaves rarely received professional care, the midwife served as the best practitioner for the woman in labor.

"I am pushing, Granny," the woman cried using the familiar term for African American midwives. However, listening as best she could, she strained harder than she thought possible one more time. The midwife cradled the baby's head as it emerged, and a few minutes later, she cleaned the newborn and placed the baby in the mother's arms.

"It's a girl, Mamie," the midwife said, "a healthy baby girl. Congratulations."

The birth had taken place in the basement of the Gabriel Hiester home in late 1794. Her parents named the baby Dinah, which means "judged" in Hebrew. The parents' names remain unknown. Perhaps they were called Jacob and Leah, who, according to the Book of Genesis in the Old Testament, were the parents of Dinah. It would serve as an elegiac aspect of Dinah's life, and many African Americans received Biblical names in the pre-Civil War era.

It's not terribly surprising that Dinah failed to remember or even knew her parents' names. Both served as slaves on the Hiester farm and had duties that kept them busy during their waking hours. Once she grew old enough, Dinah had her own chores. Dinah's parents were healthy, able-bodied adults and needed to perform work on the farm. Gabriel Hiester did not own slaves for them to raise children. He kept them to work in the fields and perform household chores. As an infant, a combination of older children and elderly adults who lacked the endurance and strength of the young reared Dinah. Dinah became another body in a collective of slaves who operated the farm based on their owner's directives.

As Dinah grew old enough to follow directions and complete tasks, she became less of a child and more of a working asset. At an early age, she assumed her own duties, many of which involved performing some assignment required on the substantial farmland. The labor proved hard, but it turned Dinah into a powerful woman whose slender frame belied her strength.

"I never went to school, and never learned to read or write," Dinah recalled later. *"The most I was taught was work. I used to hoe corn and potatoes, pitch hay and grain–I could stand aside of any man a-pitching hay–I took two rows in hoeing corn, and two swaths in raking and binding grain.*

"I helped to spread dung, pick stones, and I carried lime out of the limekiln until sometimes my back was as raw as a fresh piece of beef," she continued. *"If I had as many dollars as bushels of grain I thrashed with the flail and carried into the granary, I would never want for anything more."*

Despite the hard work that Dinah and her fellow slaves endured each day, their diet proved less robust. How they continued with their backbreaking labor each day testified to their inner strength of will and hope in the face of adversity.

"We were fed rye bread as black as a hat, a few potatoes, and cheese mixed with water," she recalled. *"You didn't see an ounce of butter on the table in two years. We drank rye coffee without milk."*

Dinah's life on the Hiester family remained difficult throughout the time Gabriel kept her. Her memories revolved mostly around the endless chores that needed to be completed, no matter what the conditions. She had few, if any, childhood memories to cherish. While her view of Gabriel was mixed, those of Elizabeth were kinder than they might have been.

"Mr. Hiester was a good natured man when he wasn't intoxicated," she said, *"and Mrs. Hiester was a splendid woman. She was very kind to the poor people."*

Gabriel apparently liked his whiskey and drank at times to excess, but his own bouts of drunkenness were the least of the slave's concerns.

"Mr. Hiester kept a barrel of whisky upstairs, and made pretty sharp use of it himself," Dinah recalled. *"He gave liquor to the slaves, who would sometimes get drunk in the field. When the slaves wouldn't behave themselves, they were taken in the large kitchen. . . ."*

Here, Dinah's recollection of these times took a dark and violent turn. According to her, Gabriel and other family members stood in each corner of the room. Dinah crouched tightly along the wall, trying desperately not to be seen. Once the Hiesters herded the inebriated slaves into the kitchen, Gabriel bolted the door behind them and the family members forced them to dash awkwardly around the room, according to Dinah, *"like horses on a thrashing floor."*

As the slaves reached each corner of the room, family members beat them with cowskin whips. The slaves screamed in pain as the weapon of punishment ripped across their skin. More than one felt their skin open under the assault.

"Have mercy, master," one female slave shouted. "We have learned our lesson."

"Not well enough from the last time," Gabriel Hiester replied. "If you had, we would not be here again. How many times do I have to tell you before you understand?"

Gabriel answered her plea with another strike of a cowskin.

After a few minutes, Dinah closed her horrified eyes. She could no longer bear to watch the carnage. The lashing went on for some time longer until both the farm owners and the slaves grew exhausted. The slaves, however, had endured far worse, and they tried to help each other dress the fresh wounds as they slinked away, hobbling from the room of punishment.

Jonathan, the oldest son of the Hiester family, looked down at Dinah as he left the room.

"I hope you learned from this," he said threateningly. "You watch yourself and stay out of trouble. Then you won't be getting the cowskins like these did. I hope you remember the lesson from today."

Dinah wondered why Gabriel provided alcohol to the slaves in the first place if he knew they *"wouldn't behave themselves"* after drinking too much.

Maybe that's what he wanted all along? Dinah wondered. *Was this just a form of entertainment?*

Dinah never received a definitive answer to that thought, but she always maintained her suspicions.

•　　•　　•

When the Hiester family members had left the room, Dinah ran from the scene and hid behind an outbuilding as her body shivered, tears running down her face. She struggled to make sense of the event she had witnessed. Clara, a black girl a few years older than Dinah, eventually found her and sat down next to her on the ground.

"It's a fearsome sight, isn't it?" Clara asked.

Dinah could only nod her head affirmatively, her body still shaking from what she had witnessed. She had a hard time understanding such wanton cruelty.

"In times like this," Clara said, "we must trust in the Lord. One day, God will take us to a better place, away from such torment and punishment. You must always believe that."

Dinah looked tentatively at Clara, a faraway glimpse of hope in her eyes.

"The Lord will look after us?" Dinah asked skeptically.

"Of course He will," Clara assured her. "He always does, even in times like this. Do you want to pray with me?"

"Will that help?"

Clara nodded, and Dinah clasped her hand. The older girl closed her eyes and recited a prayer from memory.

"Oh yes, fix me, Jesus, fix me.
Fix me so that I can walk on a little while longer.
Fix me so that I can pray on just a little bit harder.
Fix me so that I can sing on just a little bit louder.
Fix me so that I can go on despite the pain,
The fear, the doubt, and yes, the anger,
I ask not that you take this cross from me, only that you give me the strength to continue carrying it onward 'til my dying day.
Oh, fix me, Jesus, fix me."

"Now this time, you pray with me," Clara said and slowly repeated the prayer. Dinah added her voice as best she could, trying to remember the words as she recited them.

Clara finished and let silence fill the air. She finally stood up, helping Dinah to her feet.

"Now you remember to pray whenever you need to," Clara said. "The Lord will always bring us peace. He will be the one to give us eternal life. If you can't remember the words, you can always make up your own prayer. God will always listen as long as you mean what you say."

Dinah nodded, feeling the strength of Jesus filling her soul. In the days that followed, she avoided Mr. Heister's whiskey and did her best to escape his wrath. She worked hard and kept to herself. She acknowledged her mother and father on the few occasions she saw them but was not particularly close to either. Each day she seemed to grow emotionally farther and farther from them. Her parents maintained a peculiar mix of warmth and distance. They knew Dinah would always be their daughter. But they also realized she could be ripped away from them at a moment's notice. Staying close would only tear out their hearts at some point in the future.

After this incident, Dinah prayed, long and often, as hard and with as much conviction as she could. More than a few days needed as many prayers as she could muster as she witnessed or endured senseless acts of cruelty. Clara taught her a litany of invocations Dinah could recite. She soon found prayers helped her find the solace she needed. Dinah held onto her faith for the rest of her life, leaning on it whenever she needed guidance and direction to move forward.

CHAPTER 6
THE HIESTER FARM

1800

The Gabriel Hiester farm represented a significant tract of fertile land that provided many advantages. Dinah and her fellow slaves never lacked work. The farm stretched from the northern edge of the Tulpehocken Creek through land that gently sloped upward. Gabriel built the farmhouse and outbuildings several hundred yards north of the creek on a relatively level area next to the rudimentary road carved out of the wilderness. A large cold cellar preserved food well enough to feed a household that included both the Hiester family and their slaves.

The farmland continued on the other side of the roadway, climbing consistently several hundred more yards before diving sharply into a valley where a small stream ran through the land. The land rose on the other side of the stream to a series of fields tilled for farming. Altogether, Gabriel Hiester's farm offered rich soil, abundant water, and a temperate climate ideal for agriculture.

"Take this down to the cold cellar," Gabriel Hiester barked in a familiar refrain, handing the slave a basket of apples. "And I don't want to catch you eating any along the way. I'll be watching you."

"Yes sir," the slave dutifully replied and hurried to complete his task. He knew he did not dare steal an apple. If caught, he would face the painful consequences.

Gabriel also found his farm strategically located. Running along the Tulpehocken Creek, the tract sat along the proposed path of the Union

Canal. Transportation across the young United States proved a vexing and all-consuming challenge. Moving goods from their production point to population and manufacturing centers loomed large in the minds of many business leaders and legislators. The construction of canals linking one creek or river to another became an ever-popular topic.

First envisioned in 1690 by a contingent led by William Penn himself, a proposed canal provided a shipping link from the Schuylkill River to the Susquehanna River in central Pennsylvania. Development of what would eventually become the Union Canal initially began in 1792 during George Washington's administration but stalled four years later because of both financial difficulties and engineering challenges. Initially, grandiose plans called for a series of canals that would connect the Atlantic seaboard with Lake Erie. The Pennsylvania portion of the proposal included a 426-mile canal route connecting Philadelphia and Pittsburgh.

Dinah possibly witnessed the early attempts at the canal construction, since part of it cut through the meadow to the east of the Hiester farmhouse. If she did, one can only wonder what a young girl thought of such a monumental effort in the days before most mechanized equipment. But more than likely, even if construction had started near the farm, Dinah's chores would have kept her too busy to notice much of the work taking place.

The canal, albeit one less ambitious than the original design, breathed new life shortly after the War of 1812. Urban centers on the East Coast faced a critical energy crisis as harvesting had eliminated large swaths of forest in easy proximity to cities to deliver wood for fuel and charcoal production. What woodlands remained to cut and use as fuel required long days of transportation by wagon, a cumbersome, often unreliable, and time-consuming task. The bituminous coal imported from England and Virginia proved both smoky and sooty, mostly unusable in many commercial settings. Mills and manufacturers ended up closing for days because of a lack of fuel.

The discovery of large deposits of anthracite coal within a hundred miles of Philadelphia around the turn of the century in Northeast Pennsylvania offered the promise of an additional energy source. Industrialists discovered how to burn anthracite properly in 1808. But overland transportation by mule train proved both slow and costly, leading to canal construction resuming in 1821.

One of the most daunting challenges for the completion of the canal was the construction of a 729-foot tunnel through the ridge separating the headwaters of Quittapahilla Creek and Clarks Run between Reading and Harrisburg. Workers completed the drilling of the tunnel primarily by hand, using gunpowder to blast through the slate and veins of limestone below the summit of the ridge. They completed about fifteen feet of tunnel each week and required more than two years to finish the effort.

While the initial design of the canal mapped a path from the Susquehanna River in Central Pennsylvania to the Delaware River, the rival Schuylkill Navigation canal opened in 1825, providing a route from Reading to Philadelphia. Because of this, the Union Canal Company focused solely on the Middletown to Reading portion of the waterway. The Union Canal finally opened to provide a much-needed transportation alternative in 1828, enhancing the importance of Reading as a hub along the way.

Part of the completed Union Canal did indeed run directly through the meadow owned by Gabriel Hiester, though he never saw the canal's completion, having died in 1824. Dinah also failed to see that part of the canal in action, since she had left the farm years before it opened. But if she had remained, she could have easily walked to Lock Number Forty-Two, one of the hundred-and-two locks constructed as part of the canal system.

In 1832, builders completed construction of a twenty-two-mile branch canal northward from the waterworks along the Swatara Creek, a tributary of the Susquehanna River, to the town of Pine Grove. The branch canal served as a feeder that allowed the transportation of anthracite coal from the mountains further north, which became the principal source of revenue for the canal operation.

The charter of the canal company allowed it to build railroad lines from the canal to nearby coal mines. Completion of a three-and-a-half-mile line from the end of the branch canal and Lorberry Junction in Schuylkill County occurred in 1830. The Swatara Railroad later leased the line and extensively refurbished the facilities and converted the horse-powered system, operating it by steam locomotive by about 1850.

Storm and continuous water damage, along with the advancement of locomotive technology, eventually doomed the Union Canal. Facing declining revenue, the canal closed in 1881, the locks left to decay over time.

Over time, the Lebanon County Historical Society took over the operation and refurbishment of the Union Canal Tunnel, the oldest existing water transportation tunnel in the United States. They also created a one-hundred-ten-acre recreational area surrounding the tunnel and the last remaining five-eighth mile section of the original canal.

•　　•　　•

Less than a mile east from Gabriel Hiester's home stood a mill, a familiar site in agricultural settings. In truth, the mill bordered a meadow owned by Hiester, but one that had considerable usage in the Nineteenth Century. In addition to a segment of the Union Canal, a mill race provided hydropower to the facility.

Originally built in 1741, the mill's handsome stone construction clearly indicated it pre-dated the arrival of Gabriel Hiester and his brick-making father. The mill provided a convenient location for local farmers to have their crops ground into food for both families and their animals. The facility produced products such as flour and cattle feed in equal abundance. For a time, the mill also housed the local post office, so residents could have their crops ground and collect and send mail all at the same time. In many ways, the local mill served as a center of commerce and everyday life in early agricultural America.

At some point, Gabriel Hiester purchased the mill and changed its name to Hiester's Mill. Whether or not he constructed the waterfall on the Tulpehocken Creek and the millrace that powered the turbines that ran the mill's equipment, the falls bore the name "Hiester's Dam" until well into the Twentieth Century.

Hiester's Mill provided Gabriel with both a valuable asset to enhance the operation of his own farm, as well as another source of income from other farmers in the region. It also likely furnished an additional use for his slaves. Undoubtedly, Dinah Clark was no stranger to Hiester's Mill, at the very least helping to harvest the raw material used in production of the mill's products. Certainly, some of Gabriel's slaves worked at the mill running the machinery, hauling bags, and loading and unloading wagons.

Gabriel Hiester, always the entrepreneur, had built a thriving enterprise centered around his Bern Township farm, partly on the backs of his slaves and indentured servants.

CHAPTER 7
YOUNG DINAH

1802

The difference between a slave and an indentured servant bore little meaning for Dinah Bell in her daily life. As soon as she was able, Dinah assisted with the daily chores of the household, ranging from cleaning to cooking to harvesting. Dinah found few opportunities to enjoy the wonder of childhood. She spent far more time in the fields working than playing with any toy or doll, and she had precious little time to enjoy the creative imagination of a young girl.

This day proved to be the exception. It was a warm Sunday in late spring and the Hiester family had departed to attend a family function. With the chores on the farm completed for the moment, Dinah took a walk from the farmhouse down the hill to the meadow along the Tulpehocken Creek as she enjoyed a brief respite from her chores. The journey proved an unusual treat, as the demands of the farm and the constant oversight of the Hiester family rarely allowed such a leisurely escape.

Dinah walked down the lane toward the flat field below. An occasional boat would skim by in the middle of the creek, carrying goods to whatever market those directing the craft could reach. Cattle grazed in the clearing, paying no mind to the young girl. Dinah stood by the waterway for a few minutes, putting her hands and even her feet into the cool water. Occasionally, she would look back toward the farm to make sure her absence remained unnoticed. So far, she had not heard a voice beckoning her.

"This is a beautiful and peaceful setting," she said to herself. "If only we could enjoy it more. We should never waste the beauty of the Lord's creation."

Dinah said a silent prayer thanking God for this moment and sat down along the bank, allowing the sounds of the creek, the breeze rushing through the leaves of the trees, and the wildlife on the ground and in the air to lull her into a brief serenity. Finally, she stood once again and took a circuitous and unhurried path through the meadow.

Along the way, she looked down and saw a strangely shaped stone lying on the ground. She stooped down and picked it up, closely inspecting it.

"It's in the shape of an arrow," she said and studied it more carefully. She remembered the stories she heard around the farm about how the "Indians" had once hunted this land using bows and arrows. Only when the Europeans arrived did the Native Americans equip themselves with firearms and replaced many of their traditional weapons with muskets. Here, she had found an arrowhead from one of the Lenape hunts prior to the influx of the English, German, French, Spanish, and other immigrants.

"Wait until I show this off," she said proudly and slipped into a pocket in her ragtag dress.

Dinah wandered about the meadow for a few more minutes, looking at the flowers and making faces at the cattle. None reciprocated. She skipped and ran in a circle, chasing dandelion seeds as they floated from the flowers she held as high in the air as she could.

Eventually, she heard someone shouting "Dinah" and recognized the voice of her brother Elijah, better known as 'Lij.

"What in the world are you doing all the way down there?" he said at the top of his voice as he walked further down the lane. "I've been looking all over for you. It's time for the afternoon chores."

"I'm coming," Dinah said. "Don't catch your pants on fire."

"Well, next time don't go so far as you wander about," 'Lij said. "I'm near out of breath traipsing this far from the house."

"Now you just relax," Dinah said smartly. "A big, strapping boy like you doesn't tire out walking down a lane. Don't you try to sass me. I've seen you run about the farm for hours on end without wearing down."

'Lij smiled and the two headed back toward the farm and its outbuildings. Dinah knew her free time had ended. She pirouetted once around the meadow, then ran back up the hill toward her home. As she did so, the arrowhead fell out of a hole in the pocket of her dress and settled once more in the field where it had called home for nearly two hundred years prior to her discovery.

When Dinah returned with 'Lij, other older slaves scolded her for running off and wasting time. She quickly went back to work. The memory of the lost arrowhead slipped from her mind.

•   •   •

One day became the next. Dinah's life remained relatively static, only the change of season and the different duties expected as spring turned into summer marking a change in her routine. Several months later, a torturous day in mid-July exhibited all the characteristics of a typical Pennsylvania heat wave. The sun burned in a cloudless sky, delivering an uncomfortable warmth by late morning. The temperature reached well over ninety degrees by noon. Accompanied by high humidity, the day felt even hotter, bordering on oppressive.

Berks County had not seen rain for more than a week. The ground lay dry and hard. But despite the nearly intolerable conditions, Gabriel's Hiester's slaves received their assignment for the day. The snap beans had matured and needed to be picked before rotting or ending up on the menu of the voracious bugs and insects living in the fields.

Just as many others with land, the Hiester family planted an impressive array of fruits and vegetables in the spring. The bounty of those harvests provided food not only when they ripened, but throughout the fall and cold winters. Besides beans, the expansive garden included strawberries, blueberries, peas, potatoes, and, of course, sweet corn. Sweet corn, unknown to the Europeans until the Iroquois taught the settlers how to grow, harvest, and prepare it in 1779, quickly became a staple of the meals of European settlers. Earlier, the Oneida tribe delivered more than six hundred baskets of white corn to the Continental Army at Valley Forge in the spring of 1778 that staved off starvation and helped ease the severe food shortages faced by George Washington's troops. Corn, originally found in Mexico and called maize, quickly spread across the Americas and became a dinner table necessity.

Later in the year, the harvest included pumpkins and squash as the farm season stretched nearly to the first fall freeze. In addition, the workers would pick apple and peach trees clean when they ripened.

But on this day, Dinah and many other slaves picked the snap beans from the long rows of plants. The group formed a ragtag parade as they crossed the dirt road between the Hiester home and outbuildings to the tilled fields. They each carried multiple wicker baskets, which they would fill and return to the house in order to preserve the vegetables.

Dinah selected a row of beans to harvest and crouched down to begin her task. The beans did not surrender easily. For every bean that quickly came off the plant, another would resist leaving its comfortable home. Others had become tangled in a mass of leaves and stems that needed to be separated before capturing the wayward bounty. Dinah soon remembered the challenge of picking beans.

"I hate this job," she muttered under her breath. "So much work for what? A basket of beans. Whenever I leave this place, I hope I never have to pick or eat another bean again. I don't know why God would create such an abominable plant."

Dinah looked up momentarily. "I'm sorry, my Lord, for questioning your wisdom," she said. "I'm sure someone appreciates beans."

The task soon became far worse as the sun beat down on the laborers. Within just a few minutes, sweat poured down Dinah's face and body. Soon, Dinah's dress and the rest of her clothes soaked through with perspiration. As Dinah continued her work, her throat burned from thirst, but she knew no water would come until the crew broke for lunch.

By the time that arrived, Dinah and the other slaves had already picked many baskets of beans with even more to come before they finished. They staggered off the field and drank copious amounts of water once they arrived at the hand pump outside the building that housed the summer kitchen. They pushed the handle down vigorously, each filling whatever container they could find to hold the refreshing water that now flowed freely. The next worker pulled the handle back up and pushed again, renewing the supply of fresh liquid. Several of them at a time snuck down into the cold cellar to catch a precious few minutes to cool down. The slaves were careful not to consume any of the food, since the Hiester family meticulously monitored their stock. Missing food would lead to repercussions. After a brief break and a simple meal, the workers returned to the field, continuing their task until well into the late afternoon.

The drudgery in the field was only the first task in the process of preserving the food for use from that point until the next harvest. As the slaves picked whatever assigned, the kitchen became a veritable assembly line as fruit and vegetables endured drying, jarring, pickling, and other processes to ensure their long-term freshness. The slaves who did not spend time in the fields picking or working the farm labored instead in the hot kitchen toiling on the spoils of the harvest. The cold cellar and the basement became filled with food, jarred and otherwise, for later consumption. Throughout the harvest season, meals included freshly picked produce to be used before it rotted.

•　　•　　•

Some days later, Dinah worked for hours in the yard, pulling weeds and picking up stones in front of and on the side of the farmhouse. She eventually stood up to stretch her back and stared at the east side of the home. As she did, she noticed a feature she had never seen before, and her young mind tried to make out what exactly she now examined. She stood there for several minutes until she heard a voice that made her jump to attention.

"What are you looking at, girl?" Jacob, a teenager and one of Gabriel Hiester's sons asked, curious at what had caught the young slave's attention.

Dinah pointed toward the third floor, where several slats in the bricks were clearly visible. "Did the house break?" she asked.

As Dinah spoke, she squinted to identify several small holes drilled through the brick under the window facing the eastern side of the house. Unbeknownst to her, the holes fit the barrel of a musket perfectly.

"Silly nigger," the son said, chuckling. "We'd use those if we ever have to protect our home."

"Protect the home from what?" Dinah asked.

Jacob looked at Dinah with a look of wonder on his face. He decided to take a few minutes to educate her, though he surmised it likely would be a futile effort.

"You've never heard of the Indian massacres?" he asked.

Dinah shook her head, indicating she had not.

"I don't know how you didn't. I guess you didn't learn nothin'. Well, that's why my father built those into the house. Let me tell you a story . . ."

CHAPTER 8
THE HOCHSTETLER AND BLOODY SPRINGS MASSACRES

1757

The tale Jacob spun centered on two notorious incidents in Berks County during the French and Indian War. Both took place within ten miles from where Gabriel Hiester eventually built his home only a few years after the conflict ended.

The French and Indian War represented one segment of the larger Seven Years' War between the British Empire and France. Fought from 1754 to 1763, the conflict here pitted the British colonies in North America against those of the French, with each side supported by various Native American tribes.

The French and Indian War reached into Berks County on multiple occasions, the most well-known episodes remembered as the Hochstetler Massacre near the Northkill Creek on the eastern edge of the Blue Mountains and the Bloody Springs Massacre at a spring near the modern-day town of Strausstown. Both attacks involved the Lenape tribe, who had sided with the French in the conflict.

"The Bloody Springs Massacre caused the water to run red with the blood of the family," Jacob said earnestly, repeating historical lore repeated through the ages. "It was a terrible affair, one that people will always remember."

Dinah shuddered at the thought as she pictured the scene in her mind.

The Hochstetler Massacre occurred at a farm that was part of the Northkill Amish Settlement. After arriving in Philadelphia from Switzerland in 1738, Jacob Hochstetler and his family soon settled along the Northkill Creek and helped to establish the first Amish Mennonite Church in America.

The Northkill Amish Settlement laid on the edge of the legal boundary between the European settlers and Native Americans. This area had been the traditional home of the Lenape, who had unwillingly relocated through several one-sided land purchase agreements and the growing European population. The influx of new residents also severely reduced the availability of wild game on which the Lenape depended for food, adding to an already tense relationship. This animosity found a natural outlet when war broke out between the English and the French. The Lenape had little care for world events or whatever issues drove the larger conflict, but they resented the loss of their traditional homelands and way of living.

On September 19, 1757, the Hochstetler family and local neighbors gathered to pare and slice apples for drying. After the guests departed, the family dog began barking, leading Jacob's son, eleven-year-old Joseph, to open the front door. Lenape warriors immediately shot him in the leg. The Lenape had entered the settlement under the command of three French scouts. Joseph, recognizing the attack on his family, managed to lock the door before the warriors and scouts could enter the house.

The Hochstetlers had firearms in their home they used to hunt. Joseph and his thirteen-year-old brother, Christian, loaded their guns to defend their family. Both were excellent marksmen, as was their father. But adhering to the Anabaptist Christian doctrine of nonresistance and nonviolence, Jacob refused to allow the weapons to be used against the Lenape. That decision had dreadful and deadly consequences.

At dawn, the Lenape set fire to the house and stood guard for some time so the family could not escape without risking their lives. One by one, the tribe members eventually left. The Hochstetlers initially fled into the cellar, using apple cider to wet the floorboards above them. But the billowing smoke from the fire threatened them with asphyxiation. They attempted to escape out the cellar window. Since they could not see their attackers, they presumed the Lenape warriors had departed.

One Lenape, however, whose name history records as Tom Lions, remained nearby to feast on a supply of peaches left near the home. When he saw Joseph's wife, Anna, stuck in the window during her escape attempt, he called back the other warriors. Anna–who sources described as *"a fleshy woman"* — was stabbed in the back and scalped. The Lenape also killed a daughter and another son, Jacob Jr., while the warriors took Jacob Sr. and Christian captive. Joseph initially escaped but was later recaptured.

The Lenape apparently considered Jacob a "safe" prisoner since they held his children captive. The tribe members gave him a gun and assigned him the task of bringing meat to the camp when the warriors were away. He slowly stashed a bullet or gunpowder in a spot in the woods on each foray and eventually made his escape. He found a river and built a raft and drifted downstream. By the time settlers found and rescued him near present-day Harrisburg, his feeble condition prevented him from standing. Eventually restored to health, he travelled to the British stronghold, Fort Augusta, on the Susquehanna River in May 1758. He requested assistance from Governor James Hamilton in getting his sons back.

Following the negotiation of a peace treaty with the Lenape, Joseph returned from captivity and arrived at Fort Augusta. His Native American family encouraged him to visit in the future and to consider them "brothers." Reportedly, he returned to the Lenape village frequently. Throughout the rest of his life, he maintained that if their father had allowed them to shoot in self-defense, the Lenape would have fled and his mother's life spared.

"That's why we keep guns," Jacob said to Dinah. "And if we ever get attacked, we can defend ourselves from the attic. No Indians are ever going to scalp any of us. They won't take us captive either. We'll make sure of that. There will be plenty of dead Indians in front of the house if they try."

According to the Hochstetler family tradition, Christian lived in a village in Ohio and did not return to Pennsylvania until 1765. Legend claims Christian arrived at his family's home during dinner and they offered him food, not recognizing him because of his own physical maturation, his

Native American dress, and his haircut. Later, as Christian sat outside the home, Jacob Hochstetler approached him, and Christian finally told him his name in broken German. Christian rejoined his family and his community, later married, and eventually converted to the Schwarzenau Brethren faith and became a minister.

"And that was only one incident," Jacob told Dinah. "There was still another."

"Another one like that?" Dinah asked, somewhat terrified at the tales. "Lord help me. I never heard of such terrible things before."

The Bloody Springs Massare took place just a few miles away from the Hochstetler Massacre and involved the Spatz family and other settlers on October 1, 1757. Conrad Weiser, Pennsylvania's ambassador to the Six Nations of the Iroquois, directed the construction of multiple forts along the northern region of Berks County to protect German farm families. One of these was the nearby Fort Northkill, built in early 1756. However, despite its designation as a "fort," the structure hardly proved imposing. The small stockade covered only thirty-two square feet and was poorly and hastily built, offering little cover for refugees in inclement weather. The unimpressive fort also failed to serve as an impediment to attacking forces.

Various versions of the Bloody Springs Massacre exist. No military journals or reports to colonial authorities from that time have survived. Without official records, local and family sources handed down differing and often contradictory renditions of the events. In one of the most popular accounts, someone in the Spatz family killed a Lenape and in retaliation, his companions killed the entire Spatz family of six.

After killing the first family, the Lenape went to the nearby Degler home and ransacked it. They broke open a cedar chest with tomahawks, thinking Frederick Degler was hiding inside. Degler had maintained a good relationship with the Lenape and shared food with them. But when the attacks threatened his home, Degler and his family took refuge at Fort Northkill and the Lenape assumed he had joined their enemy.

When Degler returned home and re-engaged with the Native Americans, the Lenape warriors apologized for breaking the chest. As a token of their renewed friendship, the Lenape repaired the chest top and carved two fish as an acknowledgement of the food Degler had provided, a heart as a symbol of friendship, and crossed canoe paddles which represented an emblem of peace. Degler also carved his initials and the year on the chest top. Since that time, the Degler Chest has resided in the Degler Family Homestead, with the deed to the property stipulating the chest remain with the house.

Altogether, more than one hundred and fifty Berks County residents lost their lives and another one hundred fifty suffered kidnapping by Native Americans during the French and Indian War. Many Amish, who did not believe in violence, perished when the Lenape attacked their homes. Women and children often became victims of kidnapping. Some returned after payment of a ransom, but a number of captives remained with the tribes because they had integrated themselves into their community.

Because of the relative lawlessness of the northern frontier, the Amish eventually moved further south and established their thriving community in and around Lancaster County. Ultimately, it was there, rather than their original home in Berks County, that became the heartland of the Amish community.

• • •

"So that is why my father built those slats into the wall," Jacob Hiester continued. "He needed to protect us from Indian attacks."

Jacob paused for a moment and examined the slats himself. "And then," he continued, "a few years later, the Revolution broke out, so we had to keep an eye out for the British wandering about. We had to be ready to defend ourselves again.

"You know," he added proudly. "Father served in the War for Independence. He was a colonel. And the tent that George Washington stayed in during the war was made right here in Berks County, in Reading."

"George Washington?" Dinah asked. "Who's he?"

"You don't know nothin', do you?" Jacob said. "Ain't your fault. Niggers' just as dumb as dirt."

Jacob took on the air of an exasperated teacher working with his slowest student. "George Washington was the father of our county," he intoned. "He was the first President of the United States of America. During the Revolution, he commanded all our troops against the British. And he did it living out of a tent made in Reading."

Jacob's claim was indeed true. The manufacturing of George Washington's tent–or at least the replacement to tents he wore out in 1776 and 1777–had occurred in Reading and delivered to him during the Valley Forge encampment in the spring of 1778. The marquee tent measured twenty-three feet long, fourteen feet wide, and twelve feet high and took the shape of a long oval when pitched. Constructed of sturdy flax linen with red scalloped edges, the tent served not only as his military headquarters but also as Washington's sleeping chamber. The tent comprised three sections–a central office, a half-circle sleeping area and a small area for luggage, and sleeping quarters for Washington's valet, William Lee. The tent served Washington through the end of the war in 1783, including the Siege of Yorktown in 1781, the last major battle of the Revolution. At the end of the war, it quickly became a national treasure. While the tent was verifiably made in Reading, no record exists of who actually deserves credit for its construction.

Jacob finished his tale and looked at Dinah, assuming his history lesson had no lasting impact on the African American girl.

"You've wasted enough time now," Jacob admonished Dinah. "You get back to work. There's more than enough weeds to pick."

Dinah nodded her head and resumed her task. Dinah's work allowed no more curiosity on this day. But she committed as many details as she could remember to memory. It became a useful exercise later in life as she travelled through town sharing news and anecdotes along the way.

CHAPTER 9
TIME MARCHES ON

1803

Sometime after the sun fell on a day in late fall, Dinah and two other young African American girls lay on the bank to the west of the farmhouse making up stories about the moon. This served as their version of a game called *"Ole Molly Bright"* that gained popularity among black children on southern plantations. When it came to Dinah's turn, she had run out of new moon tales, so she recited a well-known Negro folk rhyme called *"Ole Molly Cottontail."* Though most African American children in servitude could not read, they had memorized poems and other tales using rhyming and other language cues to more easily remember.

"Ole Molly Cottontail,
At night, when the moon's pale;
You don't fail to turn tail,
You always give me leg bail.
Molly in the bramble-briar,
Let me get at little nigher;
Prickly-pear it sting like fire!
Do please come pick out the briar.
Molly in the pale moonlight,
Yo' tail is sho' a pretty white;
You takes it fer way out of sight,
"Molly! Molly! Molly Bright!"

Ole Molly Cottontail
You sets up on a rotten rail!
You tears through the graveyard,
You makes them ugly haints wail.
Ole Molly Cottontail,
Won't you be sure not to fail
To give me yo' right hind foot,
My luck, it won't be for sale."

The others in the small group softly applauded, and the stories and rhymes continued for a short while longer. Bedtime soon called. They needed to go to bed early that night so they could wake in time to complete their morning chores. Slave children never had permission to sleep late.

• • •

The next day, Dinah and the other girls were working in the yard, raking leaves and piling them in a fertilizer heap for use the next spring. They moved at a steady pace, working hard enough to not attract the attention of a Hiester family member.

About mid-morning, Dinah and the others heard a gunshot coming from the valley just beyond the tilled fields. They stopped and looked that way for a moment, but with no further activity, soon resumed their task. About an hour later, they saw two male slaves dragging a ten-point buck down through the field toward the house. A proud Jacob Hiester followed, holding his rifle with one arm and allowing it to rest on his shoulder. The land had proven just as rich for hunting by the settlers as it did for the Lenape for many generations prior to their arrival.

"I imagine we best get the butcher shop ready," Dinah said. "It looks like it's about to get a good use. Young Mister Hiester got himself a deer."

The girls agreed and set down their rakes. They would return to this task once the men had started butchering.

•   •   •

Dinah likely stayed on Gabriel Hiester's farm until sometime around 1806. In the early years of the Republic, the United States experienced remarkable progress and growth. However, that progress often came in fits and spurts as the young country grappled with the issues of financing, governance, and competing visions of the future. Much as Dinah grew from a youthful child to a near adolescent during this time, the surrounding country experienced its own growing pains, sometimes smoothly and at other times more chaotically.

Perhaps no single event illustrated the potential and the challenge of building the United States than the Louisiana Purchase in 1803. When the United States negotiated the purchase of five hundred thirty million acres of territory from France for fifteen million dollars, it completely changed the face of the nation and its future.

As the country expanded over the Appalachians, the Mississippi River soon became a critical transportation hub for America's West. When France acquired the Louisiana territory from Spain and took possession of it in 1802, many Americans expressed deep concern over the powerful French controlling the crucial port of New Orleans, as well as Napoleon Bonaparte's plan to revive the French empire in the "New World." Both statesmen and business owners expressed concern that the westward expansion of the United States would grind to a halt in the face of French resistance.

In response, President Thomas Jefferson adopted a two-prong strategy. While he prepared for a potential military conflict in the Mississippi Valley, he also dispatched James Monroe to France in an effort to purchase New Orleans and West Florida for as much as ten million dollars. Failing that, they were to attempt to create a military alliance with England to prepare for a seemingly inevitable conflict.

Unexpected circumstances, however, played in the favor of the United States. The French Army in Saint-Domingue was decimated by both yellow fever and a slave rebellion that ultimately created Haiti as a free nation. In addition, the potential for war between France and England still simmered. Faced with this adversity and additional potential threats, Napoleon gave up his plans for Louisiana and offered Monroe and the U.S. Minister to France, Robert Livingston, the entire territory for fifteen million dollars. Although this price far exceeded the directive they received from Jefferson, they agreed to the purchase. Apparently, Monroe and Livingston decided it was easier to apologize than ask permission.

The Louisiana Purchase included land from fifteen present U.S. states and two Canadian provinces, including the entire current states of Arkansas, Missouri, Iowa, Oklahoma, Kansas, and Nebraska. It also encompassed large portions of North Dakota and South Dakota, areas of Montana, Wyoming, and Colorado east of the Continental Divide, and the segment of Minnesota west of the Mississippi River. Finally, it comprised the northeastern section of New Mexico, northern portions of Texas, New Orleans and parts of the present state of Louisiana west of the Mississippi River, and small pieces of land within Alberta and Saskatchewan.

While the offer elated most citizens, Jefferson initially found himself in a bit of a quandary. Jefferson, always a strict constructionist to the Constitution, knew well that no provision empowered him to purchase territory, especially an acquisition of this magnitude. Given the overwhelming public support and obvious value of Louisiana, however, Jefferson decided to forego any legalistic interpretation and move forward. This decision ultimately contributed to the principle of implied powers of the federal government still in effect today.

An unintended consequence of the Louisiana Purchase was that the revolt that had freed slaves in Haiti ultimately helped spread slavery in the United States. Haiti served as one of the great sugar capitals of the world and provided forty percent of Britain and France's sugar and sixty percent of its coffee. Thus, the French colony served as a ripe location for a brutal slave trade, and Haiti's population prior to the revolt included ten African American slaves for every white resident.

Inspired by the ideals of liberty and equality, Haiti's small population of free African American people pressed for additional freedoms, and the French government gave some the right to vote in 1790. But the colonial government in Saint-Domingue refused to recognize the law, leading to violence and ultimately rebellion.

In 1791, the pending storm broke and thousands of slaves revolted. The revolution brought the colony to a state of insurrection and civil war. As slaves killed their enslavers and occupied and burned their plantations, white people tried to defend themselves mostly unsuccessfully, then inevitably fled. The social order of the island crumbled. In an effort to stop the violence, France abolished slavery. Under the leadership of former slave and military general Toussaint Louverture, slaves took over the entire island of Hispaniola, including Saint-Domingue and its neighbor Santo Domingo.

Napoleon looked at this development with dismay. He would not accept an island controlled by formerly enslaved people and plotted to take back Haiti and re-institute slavery. But the plan failed spectacularly. When French forces invaded Haiti with the goal of restoring the original order, the slave rebellion refused to budge. They burned cities, used guerrilla warfare, and killed thousands. The French army found themselves both outnumbered and outmaneuvered.

Napoleon soon realized the hopelessness of his dream of a French empire in the Americas. He had planned to send his army to Louisiana to take over the colony with the goal of using the territory as a trade venue for the sugar and coffee produced in Haiti. But if Haiti remained under control of the former slaves, his plan had no chance of success.

As France and the United States completed the Louisiana Purchase, Haiti became a free country, but while this development eliminated slavery in Haiti, it increased it in the country that Haiti had spooked France into selling. The Louisiana Purchase created a whole new dilemma for the United States. How much of the new territory should be open to slavery? Pro-slavery advocates argued the entire territory should be allowed to hold slaves, and lawmakers fought over the issue for years. In 1820, the Missouri

Compromise drew an imaginary line in the new territory that separated free and slave areas. As an example of the agreement, slavery became legal in Missouri, and the new state added pro-slave members to Congress. By 1860, Missouri held more than one hundred thousand slaves "valued" at over forty-four million dollars.

Dinah, of course, knew little or nothing at all about such international machinations. But ultimately, the Louisiana Purchase, while helping to create the United States known today, added fuel to the slavery debate that ultimately led to the Civil War, a conflict that Dinah lived to see. While never pointing the barrel of a gun in combat, Dinah and others played their own critical role during and after the war.

CHAPTER 10
JACOB SELTZER

1806

"Well, I don't know, Jacob," Gabriel Hiester said to the visitor as they stood together on Gabriel's front lawn. "We're awfully busy here on the farm. There's more than enough work for everyone, especially with the harvest season coming up soon."

"I understand that, Gabriel, I do," Jacob Seltzer agreed, doing his best to strike a deal. "But with opening the inn and all, I have more work than I can handle. I can certainly use an extra hand. I thought you might have someone you could spare."

Gabriel considered Jacob's plea and looked around at the various slaves going about their tasks. Finally, he came to a decision.

"Well, I'll tell you what," he said. "I have a young girl who is just coming to an age where she can be useful. Dinah is her name. Do you remember her?"

"Yes, I've seen her about the farm," Jacob said. "She would be just fine."

"Now remember," Gabriel cautioned. "She's indentured until she turns twenty-eight. But I suspect you're not concerned about that just now."

"That is a long way off," Jacob nodded. "I need the help now, and I know she's a hard worker. How much do you want for her?"

"Seeing you're family and all, I'll give you a deal," Gabriel said after pondering a moment. "You can have her for a hundred dollars."

Gabriel paused and gauged Jacob's reaction.

"I wouldn't sell her to anyone else at that price," Gabriel added. "She's much stronger than she appears, and she never tires. Goes all day and never complains."

"I'm sure she is everything you say," Jacob said as he considered Gabriel's offer. "Well, I need the help as soon as I can get it."

"You can take her along with you if you want," Gabriel added.

"Then you have a deal," Jacob finally conceded. The two men shook hands and Jacob paid Gabriel the agreed-upon price.

Gabriel motioned to one of the nearby slaves. "You go find Dinah and tell her to pack her bags and come out here," he said. "And tell her to be quick about it. She won't be coming back, so tell her not to forget anything."

The woman nodded and headed off to find Dinah. She did so a few minutes later, finding the young girl picking strawberries in the garden.

"You go pack your things now," the older woman told her. "You're going to Master Seltzer's house."

"Master Seltzer's house?" Dinah asked confusedly. "I don't understand. For how long?"

"Forever," the woman said. "You've been sold. You have a new home now. Now go get all your belongings and report to Master Hiester as quick as you can. You know how impatient he can get if you dally about. You don't want to get him mad as you're leaving. He'll take it out on the rest of us."

In that instant, Dinah's world changed. She had never left the farm, going only as far as the mill Gabriel owned down the road. All of a sudden, without notice, she was leaving everything and everyone she had ever known.

She walked up to the small bunk on the third floor of the house where she slept, her head spinning with such an unexpected turn of events. She packed her few possessions and wrapped them in a sack, and in a few minutes, stood before Gabriel and Jacob.

"You belong to Mister Seltzer here now," Gabriel said. "You serve him well. He paid a good price for you. I promised him you would be a good worker."

"Yes sir," Dinah said timidly. "I won't let you down."

"You best not, or Mister Seltzer will whip you into shape."

Jacob directed Dinah to the horse-drawn carriage that had brought him to Gabriel's farm and soon started travelling toward his own home. Dinah looked back at the world she had known one last time. Dinah left her parents, childhood friends, and the entire existence she knew as Jacob's carriage pulled away. She had no opportunity to say goodbye. She did not know what would come next.

• • •

Sometime around the time Dinah turned from a child into a young girl, or in her words, *"when I was old enough to sit on a horse,"* Gabriel Hiester sold her to Jacob Seltzer for one hundred dollars. Perhaps Gabriel owned more slaves than he needed, or perhaps the transaction was a friendly deal between relatives. Dinah never said and likely never knew. But she did her best to settle into her new home.

Jacob and Gabriel Hiester were brothers-in-law. Besides his farm, Jacob had opened an inn, a somewhat profitable enterprise, but one that had strained the family's workload. Jacob's farm sat next to the Berks and Dauphin Turnpike, three miles east of Womelsdorf, seven or eight miles from Gabriel Hiester's farm, and about fifteen miles from Reading. Completed in 1805, the turnpike primarily served farmers who needed a more efficient transportation system to move their crops to market. The turnpike bisected Myerstown, Lebanon, Annville, Palmyra, and other towns as it stretched from Harrisburg to Reading and further east. The Berks and Dauphin Turnpike eventually became a section of State Route 422.

Thus, Jacob found his farm positioned in a strategic location between the center of the state and the lucrative commerce centers of Reading and Philadelphia. The completion of the turnpike, with its promise of more passing traffic, clearly inspired the construction of his inn. In a time when travelling from the center of Pennsylvania to its southeast corner took days rather than hours, Jacob and his family expected to have a bustling and constant clientele.

Jacob lived in Womelsdorf since his birth in 1764. He and his wife, Catharine, raised eight children: William, John, Daniel, David, Jacob, Michael, Anna, and Elizabeth. Without a doubt, the Seltzer house remained a hive of activity. Whether slave or child, all remained fully engaged at both the farm and the inn, but the slaves clearly had the worst of it.

Dinah's chores included farm work as well as carrying water, cooking, and housekeeping. Her workload also included duties at the inn. She labored as a domestic servant not only for Jacob's family, but the string of guests who needed overnight accommodations. Her days were long and hard, especially under the brutal heat of the summer or the wintry conditions of January. Rarely did she receive a day off. The young girl on the cusp of adolescence grew up quickly.

Dinah had little to say about her time on Jacob's farm and inn. But in her strongest recollection, Jacob Seltzer had a suspect well serving his farm. This issue worked to Dinah's significant detriment.

"When the well was dry," she said many years later, *"I had to go two miles with the bucket to fetch water, and I had such poor shoes that I froze my feet. Sometimes the dog would put his nose in the water when I got back to the house, when the water was at once thrown away and I had to fetch another bucket full."*

It appears Dinah had good reason she never mentioned owning any pets.

• • •

While Jacob Seltzer did not have a reputation for being physically abusive to his slaves, he likely used a stern and threatening tone when he felt it warranted. More than once, after the dog despoiled a bucket of water carried in from the well or some other offense occurred, Dinah somehow received blame. Jacob glared at his servant.

"If you're not more careful," he may have warned, "you'll end up like Susanna Cox. You don't want that to happen now, do you?"

Dinah had only heard bits and pieces of Susanna Cox's story, but it made for an ominous admonition.

During Dinah's time with Jacob Seltzer, Reading gained a bit of national notoriety because of the controversial trial of Susanna Cox. Susanna served as a domestic servant for the family of Jacob Geehr at a stone mansion in Oley Township on the eastern side of Berks County. The twenty-four-year-old Susanna was born to a family of poor German immigrants and put out to work at an early age. She had worked for the Geehr family for eleven years and spent most of her time caring for their children. She spoke little or no English and had received no formal education.

On the morning of February 17, 1809, Jacob Geehr found the body of an infant wrapped in a piece of an old coat in an outbuilding closet that held a deep receptacle for rubbish. Susanna admitted the baby was hers but insisted that it had been stillborn. However, a subsequent medical examination found the baby's jaw broken and fabric stuffed down its throat.

At Susanna's trial, her court-appointed lawyers did little to defend her and called no witnesses. After she served a short imprisonment, her hanging occurred in Reading on June 10, 1809. She became the eighth woman in Pennsylvania since the state's founding to receive capital punishment.

After her trial and execution, Susanna's story gained such national sympathy that a ballad telling her story circulated widely in both English and German newspapers. More than eighty-eight editions of the ballad disseminated throughout the country in the Nineteenth and Twentieth Centuries. The reading of the ballad became an annual tradition at the nearby Kutztown Folk Festival, which was the oldest continuously operated folklife festival in America until its suspension prior to the 2025 season.

". . .Susanna Cox, a country maid, young, and of beauty rare,
In Oley as a servant had
Long lived with Jacob Gehr ...

Her neighbor, will remember we –
Merz was his second name –
He recklessly led her astray
By lust's unhallowed flame. . .

Though married, to seduce this girl
He did not hesitate –
He'll rue it when he's dead and gone,
But then 'twill be too late!

Fear of disgrace prevented her
From making known her state,
Which she by ev'ry means concealed
Despair did indicate.

The eighteen hundred and ninth year,
At half past four at morn,
The fourteenth day of February,
The unhappy child was born.

So far misled this sinner was
So much bewildered she,
That she her helpless infant's soul
Sent to eternity,

As soon as rumor did at her
Point as a murderess,
Off was she hurried to the Jail,
The foul deed to confess

A Jury then empannelled was
To investigate her case,
And to decide accordingly
What sentence should take place.

Although she supplicated hard
To pardon her great sin,
Of murder in the first degree
They, guilty, brought her in.

Ere long she in the courthouse was
Arraigned before Judge Spayd,
Where, shedding many scorching tears,
She learned her awful fate.

. . . Then to the Governor was sent,
Who lived in Lancaster,
The warrant which contained her doom,
For his own signature . . .

Just as the clock did strike eleven,
She straightways from the Jail
Was led to where the gallows stood,
Oh lamentable tale! . . .

She then was made to undergo
The punishment of death;
Scarce sev'nteen minutes had expired
When she resigned her breath.

. . . Short was, and sad, her pilgrimage,
Her youth mere drudgery,
Her age but twenty years and four,
Her exit – infamy."

Dinah never had a verse written about her. But nevertheless, she heeded the warnings of Jacob Seltzer and lived a hard but mostly uneventful life on his farm, far from the gallows endured by Susanna Cox.

CHAPTER 11
SMALLPOX

1808

Dinah woke suddenly in the middle of the night. Sweat soaked her thin bed sheets, and a fever raged through her body. Her body ached and overwhelming fatigue did not allow her to move. Her head pounded. She could barely think as her body felt ravaged by whatever illness had gripped her.

"What is wrong with me?" she whispered weakly. "I've never felt anything like this."

She lay sick for several days when flat red spots appeared. They began in her mouth and spread to her skin, covering her face, arms, and legs before radiating to the rest of her body. Soon thereafter, the spots turned into small blisters filled with fluid that later turned to pus.

Long before that, Jacob Seltzer's slaves realized Dinah had contracted smallpox and gave her a wide berth. Another woman on the farm had suffered from it recently, most likely catching it from a guest at Jacob's inn. Everyone knew the danger of the disease and how easily it could spread. In the Nineteenth Century and for hundreds of years before that, smallpox struck fear as one of the deadliest diseases faced by humans.

Egyptian mummies dating back three thousand years exhibited the earliest known evidence of smallpox. While the disease had been long known in Europe, it did not exist among the indigenous populations in the Americas and Australia. Early contact with Europeans and other foreigners devastated the Native American population. In many cases, tribes lost far more of their members to smallpox than they did to armed conflicts with settlers.

During the Nineteenth Century, smallpox ranked as the leading cause of death in the world. The disease killed about four hundred thousand Europeans each year, including five reigning monarchs.

During the Twentieth Century, smallpox claimed the lives of five hundred million people worldwide. In the early 1950s, over fifty million cases of smallpox occurred each year. Following a global vaccination campaign conducted by the World Health Organization, the smallpox vaccine finally eradicated the disease in 2011. But in the Nineteenth Century, most people became infected with smallpox during their lifetimes, and it proved fatal for about thirty percent of those who contracted it.

While Dinah lay suffering and mostly isolated, some of the older women in Jacob's farmstead offered what help they could. The slave who had survived smallpox recently came to Dinah's aid and continued to help her as she battled this deadly foe.

"I'll bring you what you need," the woman told her. "Now you listen, and with God's grace, you'll get better. I survived, and you are younger and stronger than me. I will pray for you every day until you heal."

"Yes, ma'am," Dinah answered meekly, vowing silently to add her own prayers to those of her benefactor. "Thank you."

The woman returned shortly with a basket of supplies and very specific directions for its use. Dinah later recollected her treatment.

"When I had the small-pox, I used a little sweet oil, and cold water out of the pump, and kept my face greased with hog's lard," she said.

Smallpox was highly contagious, transmitted through coughing or sneezing, contact with body fluids, and even sharing everyday items such as clothing and bedding. In places where people lived in close quarters, the disease spread quickly and efficiently, leaving a heavy toll in its wake.

Fortunately for Dinah, she recovered. Scabs form over the pustules after eight or nine days and eventually fell off. They often leave deep, pitted scars, though Dinah did not suffer from significant disfigurement, perhaps in her mind a nod to her use of hog's lard.

Whether hog's lard and sweet oil–typically another name for olive oil but also a moniker used for almond oil — provided any benefit remains open to debate. Perhaps the water from Jacob Seltzer's otherwise rickety well offered some curative qualities as an apology for all the grief it had caused Dinah over the years. In any event, Dinah soon resumed her duties on the farm and cataloged in her mind a treatment for smallpox with the other home remedies she had learned. No doubt she would use these in the future.

•　　•　　•

"Now you go mop the floors at the inn," Jacob instructed. "We had a crowd that acted up last night and the place is filthy. I had to charge them extra for all their wildness. Too much whiskey, I guess."

Dinah left and walked to the inn with her mop, sponges, and bucket, wondering why folks weren't responsible for cleaning their own mess.

"That's what white people think the colored folks are for," she muttered. "To clean up after their mess. I daresay they wouldn't make such a commotion if they had to pick up and scrub after themselves. No one cleans up after me, I'll warrant you that."

Dinah divided her time between Jacob's home and inn, rarely provided a moment's rest. Jacob may not have been a cruel master, but he was a demanding one. Between his family, his farm, and the many guests at the inn, Jacob constantly needed clothes laundered, food cooked, crops harvested, and rooms prepared.

However, over time, Jacob found himself stretched thin. Between eight children and an inn, Jacob's finances rarely hovered better than precariously, and he did not prove an effective money manager despite his various avenues for income. He fell into debt with multiple suppliers, and at some point, more than a few demanded repayments with interest.

On of the most vocal of those was Samuel Jones, another local farmer and shopkeeper. Major Jones, as he preferred to be called, proved most demanding and persistent in seeking his money, and more than once visited Jacob's home personally to settle the debt.

"I just don't have the money right now to pay you," Jacob said matter-of-factly. "Business has been slower at the inn lately, but the expenses don't go away."

"That's not my concern," Major Jones replied. "I allowed you to start a tab in good faith. I expect to be paid for my goods. My creditors want to be paid as well. If your circumstances didn't warrant your purchases, you shouldn't have made them in the first place."

Jacob conceded the major's point, though he didn't appreciate the attitude that accompanied it. With Major Jones clearly losing his patience, Jacob finally made him an offer.

"Listen," he said. "I don't have the cash to pay you. But I do have several slaves. I have one, Dinah, who is still young and strong. She works from morning until night without raising a fuss."

Major Jones considered the offer, then decided that could be the only way he would receive payment any time soon. "Well, let's take a look at her."

Jacob called for the servant he had purchased from his brother-in-law, and in short order, Dinah appeared. Major Jones examined her briefly, then turned back to Jacob.

"She doesn't give attitude, does she?" Major Jones asked. "I won't abide that in any of my niggers. I'll whip them bloody if they do."

"No," Jacob assured him, "she won't give you any back talk. She's a good worker. I hate to lose her, but the circumstances are what they are."

"I'll take her then," Major Jones concluded. "We'll consider your debt paid in full. But from now on, no tab. You pay in cash. I have no need to do business with you if you can't pay."

Jacob agreed and instructed Dinah to pack her things. Dinah was on the move again to an unknown place. Once more, she left behind all she knew.

CHAPTER 12
MAJOR SAMUEL JONES

1815

The cowskin strap came hurtling down again and again, thrashing Dinah across the back and now on the wrist. The whip opened Dinah's skin and caused a blood engorged welt that left a mark that would remain for the rest of her life. Dinah yelped in spite of herself. She knew any noise would generate more punishment.

"What did you say, nigger?" Major Samuel Jones hissed. "I don't need no backtalk."

"Nothing, master," Dinah answered. "I didn't say nothing at all."

"I best not hear a peep from you," Major Jones said and thrashed down his whip twice more across Dinah's back. Dinah forced her lips tightly closed as she focused on remaining silent during the torture. She did not want to incur any more of Major Jones's wrath than necessary. Her body already hurt enough.

"You goddam niggers need to learn your place," he hissed angrily. "I don't keep you to take advantage of my good nature."

He brought down his whip once more, then stopped. He wiped the sweat off his brow and stepped back, finally ending the punishment.

"Now next time I tell you to do something, be more careful," Major Jones admonished Dinah. "You make more work for me than you get done, and you cost me good money while doing it. Go and clean up the wreckage you caused. I want that floor so clean you can lick it with your tongue. I may make you do just that to make sure you get it spotless."

"Yes, sir," Dinah said softly and slinked away, her wounds still searing her skin.

•   •   •

Samuel Jones had proven himself a ruthless and sadistic master, inflicting punishment on his servants for even the slightest perceived transgression. Dinah had toiled under three men as an indentured servant, but Major Jones was by far the worst. He seemed to enjoy meting out pain and asserting his dominance. He left no slave unpunished and used his whip whenever he found himself in a foul mood. Even if his slaves had done nothing wrong, Major Jones still invented a reason to impose retribution. No one ever completely escaped his wrath.

Major Jones owned a large farm three miles west of Sinking Spring in Heidelberg Township, only a few miles from Jacob Seltzer's residence. He also operated an iron furnace, a grist mill, and a store. This made him both an active entrepreneur and a demanding and unrelenting slave owner. Hardly a moment went by when one of Major Jones's enterprises didn't need attention, and he expected his slaves to address every one of his whims immediately and without question.

Samuel Jones fought in the recently concluded War of 1812 around the age of thirty. He attained the rank of First Major in the First Regiment, Second Brigade of the Pennsylvania militia, commanded by Brigadier General John Addams. Coincidentally, Gabriel Hiester, Jr.–the son of Dinah's first owner — served as the Brigade Major of the Brigade Staff. Major Jones used his title throughout the rest of his life as a badge of honor and a symbol of his superiority to most of his peers. He also maintained his military ethos of driving those under his command incessantly and harshly. This made him a successful businessperson, but a despised master.

Major Jones had married his wife, Elizabeth Huey, in 1808. They had four children, Thomas, John, Margaret, and Mary. One of Major Jones's sons, Thomas, also became involved in the iron business in Leesport and at Windsor Furnace in Hamburg. It's more than likely Major Jones's involvement in that industry paved the way for his son's career.

Later in life, Dinah said that Major Jones's business partner was a *"Doctor Derry."* While *"Doctor Derry"* remains elusive, in all likelihood, this was actually Doctor James Darrah, who had married Major Jones's daughter, Margaret, and lived in Leesport. That would easily explain their business relationship.

The life of Dinah and Major Jones's other slaves consistently proved brutal and challenging. Their work ranged from domestic and farm chores to supporting the major's business ventures. That may have included helping to run the grist mill, where local farmers brought corn and grain and received ground meal or flour. Or it may have encompassed working at an iron furnace, a burgeoning industry where Berks County served as a critical national hub. Finally, slaves may have stocked shelves and cleaned the store frequented by residents for necessities–though certainly, the slaves would not actually check out or even speak to the customers. If they did, they would have faced the spiteful anger of Major Jones's iron fist and his hated whip. Major Jones's slaves lived under constant fear of his cowskin strap.

Dinah never forgot the cruelty Samuel Jones inflicted on her. Years later, she recalled that *"Old Sammy Jones used to whip me with a cowskin, and I'll carry a mark on my wrist to my grave."* Dinah showed the mark of the lash to the reporter interviewing her. Even then, the animosity in Dinah's voice as she spit out *"Old Sammy Jones"* still simmered. It clearly did not serve as a term of endearment.

Eventually, Dinah may have been the first slave manumitted by Samuel Jones. But she was not the last. Ironically, despite Dinah's depiction of the major's cruel nature, historical records claim he eventually freed all of his slaves. Perhaps at some point, he experienced a change of heart.

CHAPTER 13
INDEPENDENCE DAY

1815

"(Independence Day) ought to be solemnized with Pomp and Parade, with Shews, Games, Sports, Guns, Bells, Bonfires and Illuminations from one End of this Continent to the other from this Time forward forever more. You will think me transported with Enthusiasm but I am not. I am well aware of the Toil and Blood and Treasure, that it will cost Us to maintain this Declaration, and support and defend these States. Yet through all the Gloom I can see the Rays of ravishing Light and Glory. I can see that the End is more than worth all the Means. And that Posterity will tryumph in that Days Transaction, even altho We should rue it, which I trust in God We shall not."
John Adams, Second President of the United States, writing in 1776

Major Samuel Jones and his family celebrated the Fourth of July embodying all the enthusiasm of a youthful nation. Across the country, Independence Day began with an artillery reveille at dawn, followed by shooting cannons or muskets into the air. A parade followed in many towns and cities, ending with a speaker at the courthouse or a local church. The guest of honor was typically a lawyer, the mayor, or even a state congressman. The orations almost always blended a political stump speech with unbridled patriotism and often sounded more like a sermon rather than an address. But no matter the tone, the crowds reacted enthusiastically as they celebrated their commitment to freedom.

After the speech, the men typically travelled to the local tavern while women would serve the men in the establishment or go home with their families. The men would consume thirteen regular toasts in honor of the original number of colonies. Laid out in advance, these toasts varied somewhat throughout the young nation. But in the tavern frequented by Major Jones, the participants first toasted the current President of the United States – in this instance, James Madison - while the second was made in honor of George Washington. The toasts continued until the men's thirteenth regular toast, dedicated to the women in the men's lives–wives, mothers, and children. After gulping down thirteen drinks, the celebrants would then continue with voluntary toasts, since thirteen apparently did not suffice for such an important occasion. How well any of the participants reached their next destination remained unrecorded in any documents kept for posterity.

Major Jones enthusiastically took part in this ritual, then returned home in a somewhat inebriated state. Fortunately, his horses were less intoxicated than he and mostly knew their way to his residence. After sobering up as best he could, the major joined his wife in a late afternoon picnic, further extending the day's revelry. Mrs. Jones had recently lost a daughter in childbirth, but she did her best to join in the celebratory mood of her husband.

Mrs. Jones laid out an impressive spread for her husband and her children with the help of her domestic slaves. The meal included venison, cornbread, boiled potatoes, apples, and raisins. Pork pie proved a sumptuous dessert. The couple ate voraciously, with Major Jones providing an ongoing monologue throughout the meal as he resumed the drinking of alcohol he had temporarily halted.

Major Jones, in his ongoing state of intoxication, believed he was personally responsible for preserving America's freedom during the recent war, and he encouraged his wife and children to celebrate accordingly. The children were quite small and likely failed to understand their father's enthusiasm or any recounting of his military heroism. Nevertheless, they listened to a litany of stories, all of which they had heard many times before and would hear again many times thereafter. According to the major, he and his forces had repelled the British on many occasions, despite being outnumbered and outgunned.

Mrs. Jones tolerated the stories with kindness and a general feigning of attention. The children happily participated in the celebration, albeit with little concern for the tales being told.

"Bring me some more ale," Major Jones finally said to his wife.

"You can hardly walk. Don't you think you've had quite enough?" she asked.

"Not on Independence Day!" he proclaimed. "This is a day to toast our superiority to the British. We whipped their asses twice to get to where we are!"

History suggests a slightly different outcome to the War of 1812 than espoused by Major Jones, with most concluding the conflict ended in a draw with neither side fully achieving its pre-war objectives. Still, many Americans viewed the war as the nation's "second war of independence."

Nevertheless, recognizing she could not win an argument, Mrs. Jones reluctantly left to refill his husband's well-used mug, and the celebration continued until nearly nightfall. By then, Major Jones had moved to singing in a broken, off-key, drunken voice. But he belted the song loudly, one that he knew well and took much personal pride.

"O say can you see by the dawn's early light
What so proudly we hail'd at the twilight's last gleaming
Whose broad stripes and bright stars, through the perilous fight
O're the ramparts we watched, were so gallantly streaming
And the rocket's red glare, the bombs bursting in air
Gave proof through the night that our flag was still there
O say, does that star-spangled banner yet wave
O'er the land of the free and the home of the brave."

American lawyer Francis Scott Key, of course, wrote *The Star-Spangled Banner* as a poem called the *"Defence of Fort M'Henry,"* on September 14, 1814, after he witnessed the bombardment of the stronghold by the British Royal Navy during the War of 1812. The large flag of the United States, sporting fifteen stars and fifteen stripes that still flew triumphantly above the fort after the battle, served as Key's inspiration. Ironically, the poem was set to the tune of a popular British song written by John Stafford Smith. *"To Anacreon in Heaven"* had already gained popularity in the United States, and Key's new lyrics soon took over the tune. Naturally, the song became Major Jones's favorite, and more than once, he claimed he fought at the Battle of Baltimore and helped inspire the lyrics.

The Star-Spangled Banner was first recognized for official use by the United States Navy in 1889. On March 3, 1931, the U.S. Congress passed a joint resolution making the song the official national anthem of the United States. President Herbert Hoover signed the resolution into law. Despite the inability of most Americans to hit the highest notes, it has remained the national anthem since the passage of the resolution.

Major Jones continued to sing poorly until well into the night. By then, Mrs. Jones and the children were exhausted. Major Jones, well inebriated to the point of being pickled, soon passed out and eventually stumbled into his bed.

In the distance, sitting out of sight, the farm's slaves watched the festivities glumly. The food they ate was sparse and plain, and they had never experienced independence. To them, liberty remained a concept for which they had no reference. They had little to celebrate.

"Freedom," Dinah finally said to the woman next to her. "Something I fear we'll never see."

"It's nice the white folks can celebrate such a thing," came the response. "It's not a day for us colored people."

"I guess old Major Sammy Jones can celebrate anything he wants," Dinah concluded. "As long as it keeps him away from his whip, that's fine by me."

"Speaking of that," Dinah's friend said glumly, "Major Jones is likely to be in a foul mood tomorrow. He's usually ornery after drinking too much. His head will pound like a drum. We best keep our distance as much as we can."

The Joneses paid little attention to the slaves until the picnic ended. Then, they were called to clean up. That was the extent of their participation in the Fourth of July merrymaking. As time went on, African American leaders used Independence Day to advocate for the abolishment of slavery and freedom for the black population in the United States. But those entreaties did not provide any solace for Major Sammy Jones's servants this day.

• • •

Many years later, Frederick Douglass, the escaped slave turned renowned orator and fierce abolitionist, delivered an address called *"What to the Slave Is the Fourth of July?"* He insisted on delivering the speech not on Independence Day, but instead on July 5. In part he said:

"What, to your American slave, is your 4ᵗʰ of July? I answer: a day that reveals to him, more than all other days in the year, the gross injustice and cruelty to which he is the constant victim. To him, your celebration is a sham; your boasted liberty, an unholy license; your national greatness, swelling vanity; your sounds of rejoicing are empty and heartless; your denunciation of tyrants, brass fronted impudence; your shouts of liberty and equality, hollow mockery; your prayers and hymns, your sermons and thanksgivings, with all your religious parade, and solemnity, are, to him, mere bombast, fraud, deception, impiety, and hypocrisy – a thin veil to cover up crimes which would disgrace a nation of savages."

Douglass reportedly spoke in Reading on several occasions during Dinah's lifetime. It's possible, even likely, she attended at least one of his presentations.

• • •

As a postscript, John Adams wrote about American Independence Day in a letter to his wife, Abigail. But he referred to the historic event as being held on July 2. Adams served as a member of the Committee of Five charged with writing a formal statement to tell the world why the colonies cut ties with Britain. The document eventually served as the basis for the Declaration of Independence. Thomas Jefferson worked on a draft, which he gave to

Adams and Benjamin Franklin for their review and then incorporated their changes. On July 2, the Congress voted in favor of a measure calling for the colonies' independence introduced by Richard Henry Lee, a delegate from Virginia. That was the day John Adams wrote the letter to his wife.

Two days later, on July 4, the Continental Congress formally adopted the Declaration of Independence after removing passages critical of the English people and of slavery. From that point on, July 4 became the day celebrated as Independence Day, even though the actual vote for independence occurred on July 2. For the rest of his life, Adams believed July 2 was the correct date to celebrate America's freedom from the British. Reportedly, he turned down multiple invitations to appear at events on July 4 in silent protest. Coincidentally, both Adams and Jefferson died on July 4, 1826, the 50th anniversary of the adoption of the Declaration of Independence.

In a twist of fate, neither John Adams nor the slaves of Major Samuel Jones had anything to celebrate on July 4.

CHAPTER 14
WILLIAM CLARK

1816

William Clark was born in Virginia, most likely into slavery. His early life remains mostly a mystery. Along the way, he somehow earned his freedom and eventually moved to Pennsylvania. There, he learned wood cutting skills working in the Commonwealth's booming iron industry. Throughout the Nineteenth Century, the so-called "iron plantations" created a high demand for labor. The industry required ore mining, wood chopping, charcoal making, furnace stoking, and iron smelting, among many other tasks needed to keep the iron furnaces running day and night.

The demand for woodcutters proved especially high. The iron furnaces demonstrated an avaricious appetite in their need for constant fuel. As an example, Hopewell Furnace, in southeastern Berks County near Blue Rock – later to become the Borough of Elverson -- became perhaps the most well-known iron producer in the Berks County area. At its peak, the Furnace required over two hundred acres of wood each year to supply the plant with enough charcoal. Between 1835 and 1837, one hundred twelve of the Furnace's two hundred thirteen employees were woodcutters—more than half of its workforce.

Men and women, whites and free Blacks all found employment at Hopewell performing this arduous work. All earned equal pay. But not every furnace showed such fairness, and many operations also depended on the free labor of enslaved individuals or indentured servants.

What circumstances brought William Clark to the Samuel Jones farm we may never know for certain. Major Jones worked as an ironmaster affiliated with the Windsor Furnace and possibly other Berks County's furnaces. He may have hired William as a woodcutter to take down trees on his own farm to help supply his iron interests. In any case, William and Dinah met through Major Jones's hiring of the woodcutter.

The events that brought William and Dinah together would change the future of a young woman who had known only the existence of an indentured servant for more than twenty years. For the first time, Dinah would taste freedom and perhaps, just as importantly, love.

• • •

William walked through a path on the farm one day on his way to the task for which Major Jones had hired him, his woodcutting equipment slung over his shoulders. A young, attractive woman carrying water back toward the farm from the well caught his attention. He stopped hoping to get her attention.

"Good morning," he said. "My name is William."

Dinah looked up. William noted she stood taller than average with a strong build carved by many years of labor. "Nice to meet you," she answered perfunctorily. "I am Dinah. You here to cut wood?"

"I am," William said. "I hear Major Jones is quite the taskmaster."

"He is," Dinah said. "If he sees me dallying here with you much longer, he's likely to flail me good. He won't look kindly on your lollygagging either. He'll tell you to your face he doesn't pay you to waste the time of his slaves. You'll learn quickly not to get on the wrong side of the major."

Dinah moved away to continue her work, but William persisted despite her reticence.

"Can I see you again sometime?" he asked hopefully.

"We'll see," Dinah responded, looking back at him with a smile. She examined William more carefully, noting his broad shoulders and athletic build. He was not exceptionally tall–perhaps only a few inches more than herself — but he was solid and physically imposing. He appeared a good deal older than Dinah, but she decided on a whim to further the conversation.

"You'll have to do better than an axe and a saw to impress me," Dinah added. "I've seen many a man with those. And old Major Sammy Jones better not catch you or he'll whip us both."

"Yes, ma'am," William responded. "I'll remember that."

"You best do that," Dinah said, "and get to the work the major wants done. You've already wasted enough time in his eyes."

With that, Dinah continued on with her chores. She had a busy day and spending time chatting with a woodcutter she would likely never see again would not finish her work. William watched Dinah for a moment, then whistled happily as he made his way to the forest. Trees waited to be cut, and William had downed many in his lifetime. More would feel his wrath in the hours to come.

The next day, William arrived early and waited for Dinah to pass his way. He only hoped she followed the same routine. When she came by with buckets of water in her arms, he presented her with a rose and a small container of sweet pudding he had purchased from his neighbor known for her baking skills.

Dinah beamed. No one had ever given her a gift before in her twenty-one years. Dinah looked up at the sawyer and begrudgingly admitted to herself that William was very handsome, with a wonderful smile and caring eyes. Her heart and her mind raced. If possible, Dinah fell in love on the spot, perhaps reacting to the first man who had shown her genuine affection. Warmth radiated through her body as she experienced feelings she had never had before.

"Well, aren't you the charmer," Dinah managed to say, gathering back some sense of composure. "Are you going to do this for me every day?"

"As often as I can," William assured her.

"I better eat this pudding before someone sees," Dinah said conspiratorially.

"You go right ahead," William said. "I'll cover for you. I'll keep an eye out for Major Jones in case he comes walking around a corner."

As Dinah gobbled down the unexpected gift, William slipped the flower into her hair. When she finished her treat, Dinah looked back at the farmhouse and, not seeing anyone watching, allowed herself a few minutes to chat with her suitor. But before her absence became too obvious, she scurried off with her water buckets. Both William and Dinah promised to meet up the next day.

On cue, the two met in the same spot. William brought a small treat, again bringing a radiant smile to Dinah's face. Over time, the couple chatted about their lives and their challenges, but also their hopes and dreams of a better future. Dinah spent a bit more time "lollygagging" each day, hoping no one noticed her longer and longer absences. She thought herself quite clever.

Just as many others in the throes of an early romance, however, Dinah was not as sly as she thought. Soon, other slaves and farmhands noticed the interaction between her and William, and a week later, a woman a few years older than Dinah approached her surreptitiously.

"It looks to me like that new woodcutter Major Jones brought on is sweet on you," she said. "I've seen you two spending time together and making eyes at each other."

"I don't know what you're talking about," Dinah replied, but against her wishes, a slight smile crept across her face.

"Looks like you're sweet on him, too," the woman replied. "Well, you just be careful and make sure the major doesn't see you going on like that. He'll put an end to that right quick."

Major Jones, however, was not one to miss any development that somehow affected him and soon had more than an inkling that something was brewing between William and his property. However, he chose not to intervene as long as Dinah completed her chores in a timely fashion. He had plenty of other reasons to whip his slaves if he desired.

Surely, he thought, *they will do something to deserve it. They're stupid and lazy at the same time. I constantly have to keep an eye on them. Imagine what I could get done if I didn't have to spend my time watching them.*

It was no surprise to Major Jones, then, when William approached him some weeks later.

"Major Jones," William started, "I was wondering if I could have a word with you."

"Speak then, and don't take up too much of my time," Major Jones responded. "I'm paying you good money to chop wood, not talk all day with whoever you come across. I hope you're not here to ask for a raise. You hardly deserve what I'm paying you now."

"No, no," William assured him. "That's not it at all. You're very fair with what you pay me."

William could argue that, but there was no point. It wouldn't get him anything other than a sharp rebuke and the major's animosity.

"What is it then?" Major Jones pressed. "I'm a busy man."

"That you are," William agreed. "I appreciate you giving me a few minutes. I've come to talk to you about your servant, Dinah."

"Ah," came the reply, "I suspected as much. Seems to me you've paid her quite a bit of attention. I've seen you wasting her time every morning."

William turned his head momentarily. *Of course he knew,* he thought. *He misses nothing.*

"That would be true," William admitted. "And my apologies for that. But Dinah and I would like to get married."

"Is that so?" Major Jones said. "Well, you know she still owes me quite a number of years. She is my property."

"That is the case," William acknowledged. "I thought we might strike a deal for her freedom."

Major Jones's eye glistened. He had steered William to exactly the place he wanted. *Now,* he thought, *let's finally get down to business.*

"Freedom?" Major Jones asked in mock surprise. "You know I paid a considerable price for her. I'm not one to just give my property away at a loss."

In fact, technically, he had paid very little for Dinah. Jacob Seltzer gave her to him to resolve a debt. But Major Jones never let the facts impede a good negotiation where he held the upper hand.

Major Jones and William then worked out an arrangement, a transaction where the major held all the leverage and drove a hard bargain. William had little cash but was a dependable and productive worker. With promises of uncompensated labor–far beyond reasonable--Major Jones and William Clark finally settled on a price, though William could not claim Dinah's freedom until he completed the work they had agreed upon. Major Jones no longer sold on credit.

William never complained about Major Jones's demands, but he needed to take out loans to sustain himself during the time he completed the agreed upon service. This started a trend of William falling into debt for a variety of purposes, something that became a critical issue later in his life. But in his mind, whatever price he had to pay to secure Dinah's freedom and make her his wife was more than worth it. He and Dinah were truly in love.

CHAPTER 15
THE WEDDING

1816

When William Clark finally finished paying his debt to Major Samuel Jones, he whisked Dinah away from the farm as quickly as possible. He vowed never to return, a promise Dinah would make sure he kept. For the first time in her young life, Dinah Clark was a free woman at the age of twenty-one.

At first, she wasn't even sure how to act. Until then, her owners' whims and the demands of her tasks needing completion controlled her entire life. Now, with William by her side, she slowly adjusted to her new life. The couple settled into William's small and simply decorated rented room and planned to be married as soon as possible.

African American weddings in the Nineteenth Century typically were simple affairs attended by a handful of family and friends. Few churches catered to blacks, so most celebrations took place at a home or in an open field.

William and Dinah's wedding followed this basic formula. Dinah had not seen her parents since she left Gabriel Hiester's farm, and in truth, they did not grow close even when she lived with them. Coming from Virginia, William had lost track of his family years earlier if he had ever known them. In addition, seeing that Dinah had spent her entire life as an indentured servant, she had few friends to invite—or at least friends who could leave their duties to attend a wedding ceremony, something their owners would find trivial and a waste of time.

None of that deterred the young couple in love and intent on marriage. William and Dinah gathered at a park with a small contingent of guests. They located a preacher willing to perform the ceremony and assembled under an oak tree near a small brook.

"We are gathered here today to celebrate the marriage of William Clark and Dinah Bell and affirm their lifelong commitment to each other . . .," the minister began.

The preacher then conducted a short ceremony, extolling both the joys of matrimony and charging the bride and groom to ensure each other's happiness in the future. Both William and Dinah clearly proclaimed "I do" in vowing their love and loyalty to each other for the rest of their days. At the end of the ceremony, two of the guests laid a broom—well-worn and gnarled from years of use—in front of the bride and groom.

"I love you," William and Dinah said to each other, then jumped over the broom, figuratively leaping into the future and leaving their past behind.

African American slaves in the South had adopted the "jumping the broom" tradition, but they had not created the ritual. The oldest records of "jumping the broom" as part of the marriage rite date to about 1700 in Wales. The church did not recognize the marriages of the Roma people, commonly known as gypsies, and when the Roma married, they did so through non-church services. One of those became known as a "Besom Wedding," a besom being a type of broom. Couples jumped over the besom placed in a doorway. By the beginning of the Eighteenth Century, broomstick weddings were common in Wales and across England.

The tradition eventually travelled to America. Slave marriages rarely received legal recognition. Marriage certificates seldom existed. That lack of institutional acknowledgement came with tragic consequences. Slaveholders forcibly separated and sold families at their discretion, leaving couples and children never to see each other again. Unrecognized by the law, the family had no recourse to being torn apart.

Historians and folklorists offer different variations on how the tradition of jumping the broom became commonplace. Some argue that jumping the broom originated as part of a forced marriage ceremony for slaves. Rather than an ordained minister, slaveholders supposedly retrieved a broom and had the slaves jump over it as a symbol of marriage. Some of them reportedly forced slaves to jump the broom as a form of mockery.

Other historians, however, argue that owners did not impose the tradition on slaves. Many believe slave owners cared little about slave marriages as long as they bore children and added to the owner's holdings. In fact, some slave owners gave certain slaves elaborate weddings to show their "benevolence," a direct retort aimed at abolitionists who focused on the poor living conditions of slaves. By the 1830s, jumping the broom became a ritual that enslaved people understood as their own, no matter the origin. Communities recognized it as a way they could legitimately marry. William and Dinah, in a nod to their past, honored that tradition and jumped the broom, leaving their days as slaves behind them.

The marriage ceremony ended with a hearty round of applause. One guest handed Dinah a Bible as a wedding gift. Since neither William nor Dinah could write, the woman who had given the gift had written William and Dinah's name in the Bible, noting the marriage and the date and place of the event.

"You keep this as your family Bible," the woman said. "You record everything important that happens in your life here. Births, deaths, baptisms. All of those. If you need help, you let me know and I'll write if for you."

Dinah hugged her guest and held the book tightly. She instantly recognized the value of this gift, one that far exceeded whatever the price paid.

As the gathering dispersed, William and Dinah walked toward their modest home. They had neither the time nor the money for a honeymoon. William had already accumulated debt as he had labored to earn Dinah's freedom. He would be back at work the next day working his craft as a sawyer. They also needed to find employment for Dinah, most likely completing domestic chores and whatever other opportunities presented themselves.

Before they left the park, Dinah stopped and looked back at the spot of their wedding one last time. Tears welled up in her eyes.

"What's the matter, Mrs. Clark?" he asked gently.

"One day," she told William, "We are going to have a church of our own where colored folks can properly worship and marry. We deserve that. Every Christian family deserves that. We shouldn't be any different."

William nodded in agreement. Somehow, he knew Dinah would succeed in that commitment. Her strength belied her youth and stature. William knew she would relentlessly follow her dreams. He would be a passenger on that ride.

•   •   •

When William and Dinah Clark returned to their small home, William enveloped his new bride in his arms, holding her tightly with all his strength.

"My goodness, William," Dinah said. "I'm not going to run away."

William chuckled. "Let's dance," he replied. "We deserve a wedding dance."

"But there's no music," Dinah objected.

"We'll dance to the music in my head," William said. "Finding you has made me want to sing."

Dinah took William's hand and looked up into his eyes. "You can't sing a lick," she laughed. "I've heard you try. But I'll allow it this once. Don't make it a habit or the neighbors will complain we should put our dog out of its misery."

The groom smiled and began the song softly. William knew little music, but he had ingrained the words of Negro spirituals in his memory.

There is a balm in Gilead
To make the wounded whole;
There is a balm in Gilead
To heal the sin-sick soul.
Some times I feel discouraged,
And think my work's in vain,
But then the Holy Spirit
Revives my soul again.

William and Dinah danced slowly through the room to the unsteady rhythm of his song. After some time and a few more renditions of tunes of various merit, the newlyweds sat down on the two chairs in their home to relax for a few minutes before heading to bed. They had no time to celebrate any longer. Work beckoned the following day, and Dinah needed to establish herself in her new life.

Before they retired for the night, William pulled out his well-worn pipe and stuffed it with tobacco. As he lit it, he looked at his new bride.

"Do you want a puff?" he asked.

"What's it like?"

"Try it," William said. "It helps you relax. If you like it, we'll get you a pipe of your own."

Dinah tentatively took the pipe and put it to her lips.

"Now inhale," William instructed.

Dinah did so, coughing profusely as the tobacco reached her lungs. William chuckled and encouraged his wife to try again.

"The first puff is always the hardest," he assured her. "You'll get used to it."

Dinah put the pipe to her lips again. This time, she did not cough as she inhaled deeply. She then returned the pipe to her husband.

"Maybe you should get me one," she said as the couple retired for the night. "I can see where it's helpful."

CHAPTER 16
READING, PENNSYLVANIA

1815

William Penn's son, Thomas, founded Reading, Pennsylvania, and visited the site of the future city as early as 1737. Impressed by the land and its natural beauty and resources, he wrote a letter to his brother, John, proposing the development of a town and *"to name the place Reading in memory of our own beloved capital in Berkshire."*

In Thomas's eyes, Reading, Pennsylvania would become the American equivalent of Reading, England. Berks County received its name in honor of the ancient English county of Berkshire, itself named after a forest of box trees called Bearroc. *"Bearroc,"* in turn, was an ancient Celtic word meaning "hilly," and in that respect, Berks County well represented its roots.

Penn's land agent, Thomas Lawrence, drew a preliminary sketch of the new town in 1743, which received refinements from both Richard and Thomas Penn, along with Conrad Weiser, the well-known liaison between the Pennsylvania colonists and the Native American tribes living in the area.

The town of Reading finally became a reality in 1748 and became the county seat with the creation of Berks County in 1752. Despite Reading's very English origins, the large majority of early settlers emigrated from southern and western Germany. They had purchased much of the land from the Penn family.

It did not take long for Reading to show its strategic importance. The town became a critical location during the French and Indian War, becoming a military base for a chain of forts along the nearby Blue Mountain, including the infamous Fort Northkill.

Reading also quickly earned its keep as a center for the iron industry. By the beginning of the American Revolution, Reading's iron production exceeded the output of all of England. Reading became a critical supplier of cannons, rifles, and ammunition to George Washington's army and served as a major contributor to the fledging country's eventual victory.

Later, the young town also came within a whisker of serving as the nation's temporary capital. During the 1793 Yellow Fever epidemic, Philadelphia still served as the capital of the United States. President George Washington travelled to Reading and considered making it the emergency national capital but ultimately chose Germantown instead.

By the early Nineteenth Century, Reading grew at a rapid pace. Industry and commerce enjoyed continued success as the town served as a gateway between Philadelphia and settlements to the west. The completion of the Union Canal a few years in the future would only enhance Reading and Berks County's standing and further fuel its expansion. The county's population increased accordingly, from just over thirty-thousand residents in 1790 to over forty-six thousand in 1820. That population surge continued unabated throughout most of the Nineteenth Century, reaching approximately one hundred twenty thousand by 1876.

Into this environment arrived William and Dinah Clark. The newlyweds settled into William's small and sparse room he rented. Leaving the life of an indentured servant, Dinah had little to add to the accommodations. William worked as hard as he could to make Dinah feel at home, but in truth, nearly anything would serve as an improvement over the conditions Dinah endured as she had grown into a young adult.

For the newly married couple, both needed to focus on building a life where they earned enough to survive. William already carried a debt and had to seek work now that his long days under Major Jones had ended. Dinah needed to venture into a new world, one she had never experienced before—that of paid employment.

As an experienced sawyer with the ability to cut virtually any type of wood – from downing trees to cutting boards into firewood – William enjoyed a multitude of work opportunities. For both homes and industry, firewood proved an essential commodity for heating, cooking, and commercial applications. Woodcutting could lead to long days, especially if William needed to travel outside the confines of Reading. But it paid far better than most work available to African Americans in the early Nineteenth Century.

Dinah's work skills, on the other hand, were an entirely different matter. She was a young woman who had spent her life as an indentured servant and had completed a variety of domestic and agricultural tasks in her life. But being hired to complete household chores paid very little, and Dinah never had to look for a job before in her life. Until now, she always received assigned work with no accompanying pay.

"We're going to have to find you some work once you get settled in," William said.

"How do I go about doing that?" Dinah asked earnestly, having no experience in seeking a job.

"Let me ask around," her husband answered. "There's always someone looking for help among the well-off. It won't be glamorous work, but it will help pay the bills."

Dinah agreed, and to be sure, William returned home a few days later with several offers of employment. A number of homeowners and merchants around town needed domestic work done, ranging from laundry to cleaning to cooking, as well as taking care of children. The pay was paltry, even for the early 1800s–twenty-five cents per day. But with William and Dinah needing to scrape by for a living, a quarter each day was better than none at all.

The next morning, Dinah walked to work with her husband leading the way. When she returned home that evening, she proudly held two capped bust dimes and five large draped bust cents in her hands. She admired the female representations of liberty on each coin, perhaps a symbol to herself of her new-found freedom. Even then, it represented a small wage. But in Dinah's mind, holding it represented a revelation. At age twenty-one, Dinah received her first payment for her work. Holding actual cash she could use to buy goods represented an entirely new experience.

"Don't get too excited," William cautioned her. "That won't go far when we have to eat."

"It will go farther than what we'd have if I wasn't working," Dinah answered optimistically, a fact William could not deny.

Dinah understood William's admonition, but it failed to diminish her enthusiasm. She was a free woman whose efforts had value.

In a short time, Dinah had developed her own list of customers, all impressed by her hard work, dedication, outgoing personality, and yes, deference to their "authority." It took some time for Dinah to learn how not to live as an indentured servant. But Dinah also realized quickly that as an African American woman, even though she had gained her freedom, many still regarded her as a second-class citizen.

Nevertheless, Dinah built a rapport with certain families around the town of Reading and soon became a regular employee in more than a dozen homes.

"How was work today?" William would typically ask Dinah as they both settled in from long hours of labor.

"It was very good," Dinah replied. "I worked at the Ritter's house today. They are fine folks and are very kind to colored people."

She paused. "But their son is quite the rascal. You have to keep an eye on him every minute. If you don't, he'll be up to no good in no time and you'll spend the day cleaning up after him."

William and Dinah chuckled and sat down to a simple meal. A few minutes later, William got back up and retrieved a bottle of cheap whiskey and poured himself and Dinah a glass.

"Let's have a drink together," he said. "We both need it."

For a long moment, Dinah's mind flashed back to her childhood days at Gabriel Hiester's farm, and the beatings his drunken slaves endured when they didn't *"behave"* themselves. She fought back those thoughts as best she could.

Dinah picked up the glass tentatively. "Are you sure it's alright?" she asked. "I've seen bad things happen when people drink too much. Old Mr. Hiester used to whip his slaves half to death after they drank."

"It's fine," William said confidently. "It's good for what ails you. A glass of whiskey always makes the day better. And you won't get drunk on one glass. You just have to learn not to drink too much at one time."

The young couple toasted and drank together, a ritual that would soon become a daily habit. Sometimes, one glass became two or more, but not on this day. Soon thereafter, the hour ran late, and they retired for the night, only to awaken the next morning for another day of work.

CHAPTER 17
THE FACE OF SEGREGATION

1815

On most days, Dinah went about her workday without incident. The families who hired her typically exhibited cordiality, and those who did not she avoided as best she could. She labored long and sometimes hard hours, but being a free woman somehow made the days more palatable.

However, Dinah quickly received the reminder that "free" did not mean "equal." Pennsylvania may have abolished slavery, but segregation still reigned in the minds and hearts of many. Schools, hotels, bars, hospitals, restrooms, parks and other facilities often restricted African Americans. Restaurants regularly had separate windows and counters for black customers. A few years into the future, in 1838, Pennsylvania voters ratified a new state constitution restricting the right of voting to *"white freemen"* only. This prohibition remained in place until after the Civil War, when the ratification of the Fifteenth Amendment of the United States Constitution in 1870 made such practices illegal. Pennsylvania may have outlawed slavery, but it still treated its African American residents as something far less than citizens with equal rights.

Dinah had spent nearly all her life on the farms of Gabriel Hiester, Jacob Seltzer, and Major Samuel Jones, so she may not have been as acutely aware of these standards as others. One day, she finished her work early on a warm, muggy day. She had emptied her battered canteen filled with water hours before, and her throat burned with thirst. She still had quite a distance to travel.

As she walked home, she spotted a diner on the corner of the street. The eatery was small, barely large enough to hold only a few stools at the counter and two tables. She checked her pockets and ensured she had enough coins to purchase a beverage. Without thinking, she opened the door to the business.

The three white patrons stopped their conversation in mid-sentence, turned, and glared at her. A few seconds later, the owner of the establishment came out from behind the kitchen door and spotted Dinah.

"Hey!" he said with venom. "No niggers inside. There's a window in the back. We'll serve you there. You should know better.

"Damn niggers," he continued, "you can't teach them anything."

Flush with both anger and humiliation, Dinah fled the diner and ran toward her home as fast as her legs carried her. Flashbacks of her worst days as a slave seared through her mind. Her throat could wait.

By the time she arrived at the rented room, Dinah breathed heavily and sweated profusely. She leaned on a chair, her body shaking, trying to calm down. Eventually, she took a long drink of water, slumped onto a chair, and allowed herself to settle.

When William arrived home hours later, Dinah tried to recount the episode calmly but ended up shaking in spite of herself. She paced around the room, trying to corral her mixed emotions. William came up and held her tightly.

"We colored folk have to put up with a lot," he said. "You have to be careful. It may not be fair, but it's the only way we can survive. You'll learn what you can and can't do. I'll help you as best I can."

Dinah held William closely.

"It doesn't make sense," she said. "The Bible tells us we are all made in God's image, and white people claim to love the Lord. But they hate His face when it's not white like them."

William had no answers. He knew intimately what Dinah said and felt, but he was in no position to change the world. That would need to come from forces more powerful than himself in a time far different from the one in which they lived. Even then, the struggle would continue.

After this episode, Dinah quickly learned what to avoid and where she might receive a more friendly reception. Despite the vituperative insults she sometimes received, Dinah remained steadfastly outgoing and engaging in her quest for work. Years of indentured servitude had built a shield inside her that did not allow racist negativity to derail her efforts, at least not for long.

But somewhere inside, they always hurt.

CHAPTER 18
LIFE AND DEATH

1817

"Push mama, push," the midwife exhorted Dinah as the expectant mother lay sweating on the bed, both exhausted and in pain.

"Lord Jesus Almighty," Dinah screamed, "I am pushing. What more do you want me to do? I'm trying as best I can."

"The baby is almost here," the midwife assured her patient. "I need you to keep pushing. Push as hard as you can, mama."

"This must be a girl," Dinah said through her panting. "A boy would never dillydally like this and cause her mother such aggravation . . ."

Another scream of agony interrupted Dinah's pained missive as the baby inched forward.

Dinah looked up to the ceiling as she tried to manage this torment. The midwife and her assistants had frantically transformed the residence to accommodate her delivery. William and Dinah's small dwelling in Reading now served as a birthing room. When Dinah went into labor with her first child, William quickly left for the midwife and returned with her and some local friends to assist. Then, he situated himself outside the house and paced nervously waiting for news. Childbirth was a woman's affair in the early Nineteenth Century.

Towels and water quickly filled the makeshift delivery area. Dinah lay with her legs spread, while the midwife and her assistants worked feverishly. Childbirth in this era held tremendous risks for both the mother and the child, and the midwife used all her skills to bring them both through the delivery safely. The only painkiller Dinah received was a shot of whiskey. The alcohol had little effect as labor progressed, though she eventually received another dose or two.

Sometime later, Dinah gave birth to a daughter as she predicted. After a brief discussion, William and Dinah named her Sarah.

●　　●　　●

A few weeks later, Dinah held Sarah in her arms, rocking her in a futile attempt to calm the infant. For days, Sarah had run a high fever accompanied by diarrhea and vomiting. Dinah tried everything she could to heal her daughter's illness, but her collection of home remedies ranging from cold compresses to lard to sweet oil failed to ease Sarah's symptoms.

"Oh, my poor girl," Dinah said gently cradling her, "I wish I could make you feel better. I pray to God for your recovery."

But nothing worked. Sarah became more and more ill, growing weak and lethargic. She refused to eat and developed a dry cough. William and Dinah summoned a local doctor, but lacking antibiotics or modern testing equipment, he could offer little relief.

Sarah's life slowly slipped away over several days until she no longer breathed. Dinah watched her baby die, then held her tight, singing softly to her long after she was gone. A tear ran down Dinah's face. Eventually, she and William prepared Sarah for burial. Both were sure their daughter would soon meet the Lord. They had lost their child's innocent life far too soon. William and Dinah barely had time to be parents.

●　　●　　●

Having children proved a mixed blessing for a family in the Nineteenth Century. Death rates for children were incredibly high. The child mortality rate in the United States in 1800 was 462.9 deaths per thousand births. For every thousand babies born, more than forty-six percent did not live until their fifth birthday. In addition to stillbirths, diseases such as smallpox, diphtheria, measles, meningitis, scarlet fever, whooping cough, and cholera claimed the lives of many children. The development of vaccines to prevent many of these life-threatening illnesses lay far into the future. Death showed no preference, whether the child be black or white, rich or poor, though poor families typically suffered the most with substandard hygiene, nutrition, medical care, and housing.

In addition, for families living on the edge that required two incomes to survive—especially African Americans paid notoriously low wages—a child represented a serious financial challenge. In most cases, the mother left the workforce for some amount of time. This was true for Dinah until at least some of the older siblings had grown enough to watch their younger brothers or sisters.

William and Dinah ultimately had eleven children together. Only four lived to adulthood. Those who survived childhood were John, who eventually moved to Newark, New Jersey; Hannah, who married and soon became a widow, ultimately also living in Newark; Silas William, who seems to have left town and was *"roaming about the country"* never to return; and Mary Ann, whose marriage essentially ended when she became disabled and moved back with Dinah. Mary Ann remained with her mother until the end of Dinah's life and appears to be the only one who remained close to her mother.

Little information exists about the children who did not survive to adulthood. The Bethel A.M.E. Baptismal records show a daughter, Morgan, baptized in 1836.

For Dinah, the early days of motherhood represented a challenge for which she found herself totally unprepared. Babies waking hungry at every hour of the day and night and fussing for no obvious reason proved the least of Dinah's concerns. She had no nursemaids or housekeepers to help as she recovered from giving birth. No extra food came into the house just because an extra person now lived there. Illnesses, as Dinah well knew, could claim a child in an instant. Plus, she had the same internal fears of every African American mother of the time: the threat of their children kidnapped and sold into slavery or assaulted to "keep the colored people in line." Dinah rejoiced each day she woke up with her children alive and well.

With Dinah hardly having a relationship with her own parents, she had little guidance in her own life in how a parent should love and raise her children. Because of this, Dinah had to learn on her own. Motherhood proved just as much a journey of discovery as ev ery other aspect of her life. William may have tried to help as much as he could, but he had to redouble his workload when his wife could not bring home an income.

Some days, Dinah had more success than others. A little more than a year later, as she heard her young son crying, Dinah stopped her chores and looked over to the crudely made crib.

"Now stop your caterwauling, John Clark," Dinah said, not so gently as she might have, "I will feed you in a moment." In answer, the infant howled once again even louder, defying his mother's admonition.

In a few minutes, Dinah calmed the child, and both mother and son settled into their normal routine. For at least some time, feeding and changing her children as they entered the world consumed Dinah's days.

For every birth, baptism, and death, Dinah had someone record the event in the Bible she received as a wedding gift. Every so often, she had them add a recipe or some other piece of sage advice she had received.

"It's no matter that I can't read it," she said. "Someone will after I am gone."

It's difficult to define the Clark family bonds. Outside of Mary Ann, Dinah provided little detail regarding her children. She said that she *"had all my children christened,"* and that *"my children have been kind to me,"* hardly the rousing endorsement of a proud parent.

As adults, John, Hannah, and Silas William did not appear to remain regularly in touch with their parents. Perhaps this served as a reflection of Dinah's own early years, when she never had the opportunity to build any sort of relationship with her parents. In truth, she could barely remember her mother and father and did not know their names. Dinah may have thought she had completed her parental duties once her children reached an age where they could fend for themselves. Alternatively, this apparent alienation may have simply resulted from William and Dinah's constant need to work to support their family, leaving little time to socialize or travel. No doubt her children eventually had lives and families of their own. The challenge and the expense of traveling in the 1800s may have created a natural separation that was never overcome.

Or maybe Dinah's words simply did not reflect the bond she had with her children, a closeness she kept quiet and to herself. For as outgoing a personality as she demonstrated, Dinah maintained a cache of concealed information. She only hinted at some secrets and never revealed others.

CHAPTER 19
JOHN ADAM

1820

At some point shortly after their marriage, William and Dinah Clark moved to a farm owned by John Adam. No doubt they came to that decision based on a combination of factors, including their efforts to raise children in their small living quarters, William's debt, and the need for constant work.

In some level of irony, this move returned Dinah within only a mile or two east of where she was born and raised on Gabriel Hiester's farm. That thought likely did not bring positive memories, but she pushed those aside and moved outside of Reading once again. Though never forgotten, her life with Gabriel Hiester and her other slaveowners remained in the past and Dinah was determined to keep it there.

History records the owner of the farm as John or Jack and his last name as Adam or Adams. Though he went by "Adam," his children used "Adams" as their surname. The name likely evolved throughout the Nineteenth Century, a common occurrence as immigrants integrated themselves into the fabric of the United States.

The John Adam farm stood within walking distance of the Bern Reformed United Church of Christ founded in 1736. That structure served the congregation for nearly two centuries until a new church was built in 1917. John Adam married Elizabeth Frederich and together they had eight children: Louisa, John, Aaron, Joann, James, Esther, Richa, and William.

William Clark worked for John Adam during his time there, primarily clearing wood in heavily forested land. For Adam, this accomplished the dual goal of generating an income selling lumber while claiming additional land for farming, an ongoing task in the early days of Pennsylvania. According to Dinah, William *"cut wood on the farm for Congressman's Schwartz's furnace."* The identity of *"Congressman Schwartz"* has proved somewhat elusive. The most likely candidate was a man named John Schwartz, who served as a major in the War of 1812 and later worked in the manufacturing of iron products in the Reading area. His father, Phillip, served in the Revolutionary War and endured the army's encampment at Valley Forge. Schwartz, a Democrat, won election to the thirty-sixth Congress in 1860, many years after Dinah lived on the John Adam farm. Schwartz's time as a public servant was short-lived–he died prior to the end of his first term. Perhaps Dinah had heard of John Schwartz's election to Congress later in life and included that designation in her description.

While Dinah likely bore several children during this time, she also seemed to have found work when available. She claimed she *"went out as far as ten miles in the country and came back in the evening"* to work, a scenario that appeared to describe her living situation on the Adam farm. If true, however, Dinah spent much of her day traveling. Assuming she walked rather than journeyed by horseback or carriage, a ten-mile hike would typically would have taken two to three hours each way.

•　　•　　•

One warm, sunny day in October, William returned to the small cottage he and Dinah called home. He had finished his work early that day and the sun still had several hours before its descent for the night. He walked through the door and smelled a stew cooking on the stove. Dinah sat on a rocking chair, working feverishly with a needle and thread. She appeared frustrated with the progress, or lack thereof, she had achieved.

William greeted his wife, then looked more carefully at her task.

"What are you up to now?" William asked.

"That boy of yours, Silas, he done tore his pants again, this time climbing a fence," Dinah said curtly. "I can't tell you how many times I've had to sew his breeches, and yet he still finds new ways to put a hole in them. I'll never understand how boys can act the way they do. They're all but unmanageable, even as adults."

Dinah gave a quick look and a sly smile to her husband.

"He is an active child," William acknowledged. "But you know, he belongs to you too."

Dinah made a dismissive noise and continued with her work.

"He's got your wildness," Dinah said. "That didn't come from me. I was raised not to ruin every piece of clothing I owned. Only boys have that God-given skill."

William soon recognized this was an argument he could not win. "Anything I can do to help?" he asked, changing the topic.

"Besides giving that Silas a good talking to?" Dinah asked, then further considered the offer. "Stir that stew. It's not done yet, but I don't want it to burn. I'll be finished here in a few minutes unless he comes in here with a new pair of torn pants. I wouldn't put it past him."

William did as instructed. "Boys will be boys," he said under his breath, softly enough to ensure Dinah did not hear him.

She did anyway but ignored the comment.

Boys should act more civilized, she thought.

After dinner, William and Dinah allowed themselves a few minutes of respite, sitting on well-worn rocking chairs outside their home. They both filled their pipes and enjoyed a smoke along with a glass of whiskey. By now, the sun had travelled well to the west and sat just above the tree line in the distance, creating an explosion of color. One of the most dramatic aspects of Pennsylvania's nature was the kaleidoscope of colors as the leaves of the trees change colors in the fall, and William and Dinah now witnessed this annual event in all its glory.

Chestnut oaks, scarlet oaks, and black oak trees displayed a range of yellow and red leaves, while sugar maples offered a few orange tones. Red maples added scarlet to the mix, while birch trees offered their own variation of yellow and orange. The couple sat silently, enjoying the natural beauty of the spectacle. Finally, Dinah turned toward her husband.

"And here you are, cutting all this down," she scoffed. "What will this world be when you're done?"

"Now don't you worry none about that," William said. "More trees will grow."

"God will provide," Dinah said, "and my husband will keep cutting them down as fast as he can." Dinah chuckled and reached over and took her husband's hand. "It's fine. God can grow them faster than you can cut them. At least let's hope that's the case."

"What am I ever going to do with you?" William asked sarcastically and leaned over, giving his wife a soft kiss on the cheek.

•   •   •

The minister stood in the front of the small building the African American community used as a church. The young woman knelt down and placed her head above the font.

"I baptize you in the name of the Father, the Son, and the Holy Ghost," the minister recited solemnly as he doused the woman with more than a good amount of blessed water. He wanted to ensure his new parishioner would not be short-changed.

"Praise Jesus!" the congregation shouted joyfully. Another member of the church provided Dinah a small towel to dry her head as she stood up and smiled at her fellow parishioners.

By Dinah's own account, she joined the Bethel African Methodist Episcopal Church in Reading while living on the Adam farm. How often she attended services at the church is unknown. The fledgling place of worship stood a good ten miles away or more, a long one-way trip even in a horse and carriage, a luxury William and Dinah could hardly afford.

How the Clarks made the trip and how often remains unclear. Did they pool together with other African Americans and find transportation as a group? Perhaps. Maybe the Adam family proved benevolent and offered them a ride to church as they went about their own business in town. Unlikely at the time, admittedly, but possible. But Dinah held onto her faith in God throughout her life, and knowing her dogged perseverance, attended services as often as possible. William, no doubt, had no choice but to tag along.

"Are you ready to leave for church?" Dinah called to her husband on another day of worship. "The carriage is about to leave."

"Is it Sunday again?" William responded. "I could have sworn it was Sunday just the other day."

"Now don't you sass me," Dinah said with a smile. "If anyone needs a good church service, it's you. I've heard how you cuss when something doesn't go your way. You need to ask the Lord for forgiveness."

At this point, William surrendered the point. "I'm coming," he said. "Just let me get my hat."

CHAPTER 20
CELEBRATION

1830

William and Dinah's ten years on the Adam farm, while certainly eventful, remained relatively peaceful. Eventually, perhaps, John Adam ran out of trees for William to cut. Or alternatively, William and Dinah returned to the city on their own for whatever reasons made sense to them. But in any case, after a decade living in Bern Township once more, Dinah and her husband elected to return to Reading with their children.

"You leaving us without even saying goodbye?" Peg asked William. "That's just not proper."

John Adam employed Peg and her husband, Isaac, for both domestic and farm chores. They had worked alongside William and Dinah for as long as they lived on the Adam farm and had grown close. In many ways, Peg and Isaac represented the extended family the Clarks did not know.

"I would never think of such a thing," William stuttered, caught more than a little off-guard. "We leave next Saturday, so we still have nearly two weeks here. I certainly was going to get around to telling you."

"Hmmph, I bet," Peg said skeptically. "I'm pretty sure I've seen you a half dozen times in the last three days. No matter, that gives us plenty of time to give you a proper send-off. Next Friday night it is then. You and your wife will be there."

William had no choice but to accept.

The celebration began at nightfall, after the completion of the daily farm chores. Peg had organized a proper picnic, corralling tables, chairs, and blankets, having Isaac build a fire, finding lanterns, and preparing a sumptuous feast. William and Dinah arrived with their children and greeted the other residents of the farm, including members of John Adam's family. Several neighbors and friends, including the midwife who had delivered Dinah's children on the farm, had come to say goodbye.

Peg had overseen preparation of a fine feast, including wild turkey, cornbread, potatoes, and beans, along with a variety of puddings and pies for dessert. The crowd ate heartily, reminiscing about their various adventures with their departing friends.

"Now William," one said, "do you remember when you went to cut down a tree and came face to face with an angry skunk? I never saw you run so fast."

"Fast enough to miss that spray," William laughed.

"Not totally as I recall," Dinah added. "You smelled of high heaven when you got back. I sent you right back outside and told you to clean up and not come back until you didn't stink."

"She didn't let him back in the house for three days!" another partygoer cracked, eliciting a hearty chuckle from the crowd.

"That's no lie," William added, prompting more laughter and a soft smack on the arm from Dinah.

A female worker caught Dinah's attention.

"Dinah," she said, "how many times have we had to chase bats out of the attic in Mister Adam's home? We've worn out how many brooms?"

"They are scoundrels," Dinah agreed. "Those bats do seem to have a fondness for that attic."

"Silas," added a young woman, "I remember when you took your first steps. Look at you now, growing into a fine young man."

Silas stood as tall as he could to emphasize the point.

"Now if he could only keep his pants in one piece," Dinah whispered to her husband, eliciting an eye roll from William.

As the night grew longer, several guests pulled out a guitar and a drum and began playing a collection of Negro spiritual songs. Soon, the participants began singing along and clapping their hands, emoting a mix of sadness at seeing their friends leave and a wish for success and happiness in their future journey. The gathering sang the songs with all the sincere emotion they could muster, and the beautiful sound carried far into the night.

Nobody knows the trouble I've seen
Nobody knows but Jesus
Nobody knows the trouble I've seen
Glory, Hallelujah
Sometimes I'm up, sometimes
I'm down, ohh, yes Lord
Sometimes I'm almost
To the ground, oh yes, Lord.
Nobody knows the trouble I've seen
Nobody knows but Jesus.
Anybody knows the trouble I've seen
Glory, Hallelujah.

The group jumped from song to song, beginning to dance as the songs moved along and the pace quickened. William and Dinah walked through the gathering arm in arm, dancing, sharing memories, and accepting well wishes. The torches blazed in the darkness, the guests mingled in the soft light, and the sound of crickets and other wildlife filled the air. Fireflies offered flashes of light all around the celebration.

"We are going to be just fine," William said, snuggling close to his wife.

"I know we will," Dinah agreed. "We will go through life with our arms clasped together just like this, God willing."

John Adam himself pulled out four bottles of whiskey he had brought to cap the celebration. He filled glasses with a generous shot for each guest and raised his arm in toast.

"To William and Dinah," Adam said. "I always appreciated you during your time here. May you go on to joy and prosperity in the next phase of your lives. Reading Town will be lucky to have both of you, and we will always fondly remember you."

The group raised their glasses together and drank. William and Dinah accepted another shot, and then another. By the time the party ended, both had consumed more than their fair share of alcohol and stumbled back to their home. Their children had gone home earlier and lay fast asleep by the time their parents entered the door less than quietly.

Neither William nor Dinah said much as they collapsed on their bed. If they had hoped to get an early start the next day, powerful headaches and balky bodies hindered them in their goal. But they eventually overcame the aftereffects of the celebration and headed east toward the next chapter in their adventure. They looked at their future with a mix of hope and some trepidation. They had been out of the city for a decade and now needed to reestablish themselves as part of the heartbeat of the growing town.

CHAPTER 21
BETHEL A.M.E. CHURCH

1837

Pennsylvania may have abolished slavery, but segregation remained alive and ugly. African Americans faced systematic exclusion from many aspects of society. They typically attended their own schools and churches, shopped in their own markets, and found their own venues for entertainment. African Americans remained unwelcome in many venues and had to make do most times with shops and services far inferior to those catering to the white population.

Later in the Nineteenth Century, segregation even received support from the United States court system. *The "separate but equal doctrine"* established by the U.S. Supreme Court case *Plessy v. Ferguson* in 1896 legitimized racial segregation and allowed for separate facilities for different races as long as they were deemed equal in quality–a provision rarely, if ever, enforced. Perhaps the Supreme Court failed to make clear who made that determination. African Americans typically attended under-funded and poorly maintained schools and other facilities. The provision requiring "equal" establishments remained blatantly ignored and grossly violated well into the Twentieth Century.

Dinah found this exclusion most grating in the inability of African Americans to worship in a church of their own. She had adjusted as best she could to the other guardrails that limited her choices, but ever since childhood, religion had become a central part of her life.

If all of us are trying to find our path to heaven, she reasoned, *we should have a church that helps light our way. We deserve that as much as any man or woman.*

Ultimately, the African American community of Berks County finally committed to building a church of their own to serve the black residents. According to the Reading Branch of the NAACP, the first Bethel African Methodist Episcopal Church in Reading began in a log cabin on Franklin and Apple Street. Eventually, seven members of the church bought property at 119 North 10th Street in 1836 to build an authentic place of worship. These members included Samuel Murray, George Dillon, George Santee, Enoch Sanders, Jacob Ross, Isaac Parker, and yes, William Clark.

Always near poverty and in debt, William appeared an unlikely partner in this venture. But perhaps at Dinah's urging, he found a way to participate in this landmark occasion. Certainly, she would have encouraged that, likely even sacrificing what little they could provide to support such an important effort she held so near to her heart. Faith remained a central tenet throughout her life.

Other historical sources recognize Murray, Parker, Ross, and George Dillen (note the spelling difference) as the founders of Reading's Bethel African Methodist Episcopal Church. It's possible that Clark and Sanders remained lesser investors. Murray was most directly involved with the building's construction and the church remained closely aligned with the Philadelphia's Mother Bethel A.M.E. Church, a congregation founded in 1794 and the oldest A.M.E. church in the nation.

The Reading church has had its own storied history.

"Many preached from the pulpit but the ladies were responsible for organizing benevolent societies and mission circles, teaching classes in the large Sunday Schools attached to other congregations, as well as singing in the choir and providing a musical accompaniment for the Sunday services," according to the late Berks County historian Barbara Goda. Goda added that since most local organizations and societies remained segregated, the church provided an avenue for its congregation to provide community service.

Many individuals and families contributed to its creation. In whatever capacity, William and Dinah Clark did their part to make the facility a reality. The construction of the Bethel A.M.E. Church fulfilled one of Dinah's most fervent dreams. Dinah no doubt enthusiastically took part in the choir whenever possible.

"We need a church of our own," Dinah said to her husband at the beginning of the process. "The colored folks need a proper place to worship. I think we should help however we can to make this church a reality. It's important to us, it's important to our children, and it's important to all of us."

William may not have possessed the same religious zeal as his wife, but he realized he could not win this argument. Eventually, Dinah convinced William to be baptized in the church.

• • •

"Let us praise the Lord for bringing us this beautiful cathedral that honors His greatness," Reverend Dillon proclaimed to the congregation at the very first service in the new house of worship. "God has blessed us abundantly."

William sat in a pew next to Dinah, listening not quite so intently as those around him.

Humph, William thought to himself, *I don't recall the Lord chipping in to help pay for it. He might have opened his purse strings and rained some money down from Heaven if he thought this church so important.*

Dinah looked over at her husband as if she knew what he thought. He quickly caught her glare and straightened whatever appeared crooked on his face. He knew better than to incur his wife's wrath, especially during a church function. The service finished with a rousing spiritual in which the entire congregation joined with enthusiasm.

Wade in the water, wade in the water, children, wade in the water.
God's gonna trouble the water.
1 See that host all dressed in white,
God's gonna trouble the water.
The leader looks like the Israelite.
God's gonna trouble the water.

After the service, Wiliam and Dinah greeted their fellow churchgoers in a celebratory mood. Those in attendance included local prominent African Americans such as the Fry family, the Walkers, the Dorseys, the Sandersons, and many others.

"A wonderful service for a wonderful new church," Mr. Fry remarked. "This has been a long time coming."

"We finally have a place of our own," Mrs. Walker chimed.

"Let it be a symbol of our faith for many years," Mr. Sanderson concluded. "I hope my children, my grandchildren, and my great grandchildren can also worship here."

"It will be a wonderful sight to see our children baptized here," Mrs. Dorsey added.

At the time, Bethel A.M.E. Church stood as the only church in Berks County built using private resources from its congregation. Many who enabled the church's construction probably worked in Reading's booming iron industry nearby. The original church stood as a two-and-a-half story brick and stucco building with a gable roof.

Dinah lived long enough to see the church rebuilt in the late 1860s featuring a three-story brick tower with a pyramidal roof topped with a finial. The church received yet another remodeling in 1889.

"I don't recollect the names of all the ministers that preached in the Bethel Church," Dinah recalled many years after its initial construction. *"but Reverends Smith and Butler were among the best. Smith, in particular, was very kind and eloquent. He could move the congregation, and they took a liking to him."*

Soon after its construction, Bethel A.M.E. Church became the focal point of one of the most famous slavery cases to take place in Berks County. According to Goda, in February 1840, a group of Maryland slave catchers travelled to Berks County and began *"wandering about town for several days and examining all of the African Americans they could find."*

When they found a man they identified as *"James Turner,"* the slave catchers *"locked him up as a fugitive."* This action caused outrage across

Pennsylvania because it was *the first arrest of this kind in the memory of local residents."*

A trial followed. Jacob Ross, one of the church founders, testified that the slave catchers had in fact imprisoned a free man named Harry Jones. Jones had been a member of the Bethel A.M.E. congregation and had been living in Reading for approximately six years. He had recently married his wife during a ceremony at the church.

The judge ruled that the Maryland slavery law was not entered into evidence at trial and that he had no judicial knowledge of the legislation. *"Therefore,"* the judge wrote, *"there could be no legal proof that Turner or Jones owed service or labor to Cooley (his alleged Maryland owner)."* The judge freed Harry Jones, ending the slave catcher's quest.

The church's role in assisting slaves did not end there. It remained active in the desperate efforts of many African Americans seeking freedom from the horrors of slavery.

The church housed fugitive slaves, and the congregation supported the Underground Railroad. Slave hunters typically avoided searching for runaways in churches, which were considered sacred ground in the Nineteenth Century. By the completion of construction of the church, the Underground Railroad had become a sophisticated machine. The church itself included a chamber in the basement, commonly known as "The Pit," where runaway slaves could hide. Under one window at the front of the church stood a trapdoor, which concealed the crawl space large enough to hold twenty people. There, the church fed, clothed, and hid those in their flight to escape their past lives.

As early as 1786, George Washington complained that a *"society of Quakers, formed for such purposes"* had aided one of his runaway slaves. The enterprise continued to expand, and about 1831, became known as the Underground Railroad. This represented the same time period that steam railroads began to link the country, so it served as an apt moniker. Historians have never definitively discovered how the system got its name. However, many still adhere to an apocryphal legend that a slave catcher coined the term, when the runaway slave he pursued seemed to disappear as though he had escaped on a mysterious underground rail line.

However the Underground Railroad earned its moniker, it soon adopted railroad terms. "Stations" referred to the homes and businesses where fugitives would rest and eat. "Stationmasters" ran "Depots." "Stockholders" constituted those who contributed money or goods, and the designated "Conductor" handled the safe movement of fugitives from one station to the next.

Bethel A.M.E. Church established itself as a stop on the Underground Railroad nearly as soon as it opened. Some claim that Dinah Clark spoke about the church's role at the congregation's youth service.

"These poor colored folks have been slaves their entire lives," Dinah said. "They've been fed poorly, worked half to death, and whipped at their master's whim. I know. I lived that life. Those trying to escape will pursue freedom at all costs, and I don't blame them. Anything is better than what they have already endured. We need to help them however we can. They deserve to live as they see fit. They are human beings, not property to be bought and sold."

Dinah looked at each of the youth in front of her. "You all will face hard lives as colored people," she said. "But I pray to God that none of you ever have to experience the cruelty of slavery."

Bethel A.M.E. Church had many known allies in Berks County in the Underground Railroad system. Early abolitionists included the owners of Fleetwood's Kirbyville Inn, the Joanna Furnace, the Reading Furnace, and Scarlett's Mill. All provided safe havens for men, women, and children escaping from the bonds of slavery. The Washington Presbyterian Church joined the Bethel A.M.E. Church as religious institutions that served as way stations on the Underground Railroad.

The role of the Underground Railroad and its partners became both more critical and dangerous following passage of the Fugitive Slave Law as part of the infamous Compromise of 1850. One of the most controversial elements of the compromise, the Act required all escaped slaves be returned to their owner once captured. Even free states were required to comply with the law. The passage of the legislation contributed to the growing polarization across the country regarding slavery and served as yet another flashpoint leading to the Civil War. Many abolitionists openly defied the Act and juries refused to convict individuals charged under the law.

The Bethel A.M.E. Church congregation eventually moved to a new and larger house of worship on Windsor Street in Reading in 1974. The church's records have served as an important genealogical resource for African Americans attempting to reconstruct their family history.

For a time, the former Bethel A.M.E. Church building housed the Central Pennsylvania African American Museum. The National Register of Historic Places added the church to its list in 1979. The building eventually became a church once again, hosting the congregation of the Iglacia Pentecostal La Hermosa CLA.

•   •   •

Luck ended up being on the side of those who spearheaded the construction of the Bethel A.M.E. Church. Completion of the house of worship occurred just before The Panic of 1837, a financial crisis that led to a major depression that lasted into the mid-1840s. During that time, profits and wages fell precipitously, westward expansion stalled, banks failed, and unemployment spiraled upward. A bank run on May 10, 1837, led financial institutions in New York City to run out of gold and silver, leading to an economic collapse with both national and worldwide repercussions. President Andrew Jackson's decision to not extend the charter of the Second Bank of the United States severely limited the federal government's ability to regulate the nation's fiscal health, adding to the debacle. Had the founders of the church delayed in building the Bethel A.M.E. Church, construction may have never occurred.

CHAPTER 22
THE LIFE OF A SAWYER

1838

William and Dinah Clark held few career options, with Dinah's chances particularly limited. Most of her contemporaries worked as cooks, housekeepers, washerwomen, and nannies. They typically earned a paltry twenty-five cents per day, a low wage even by Nineteenth-Century standards. Dinah tried her hand as a whitewasher, a laborer who typically used a mix of lime and water to paint walls white but fared little better in her earnings and suffered severe skin irritation as a bonus.

Dinah always found work of some sort, but her family desperately needed additional income, and she felt compelled to find a better way to support her family. She discussed their financial straits with William one evening, when her husband suggested an unusual and novel solution.

"Why don't to learn to cut wood and become a sawyer like me?" he asked his wife. "There's always plenty of work around town. Everyone always needs wood, and they always have more than enough to cut. There are not that many sawyers around that don't work for the furnaces. I usually have more jobs than I can handle."

"And who is going to teach me that?" Dinah asked, knowing full well the answer.

"Well, I will, of course," William said assuredly. "You know, I've been cutting wood for some time now."

"Have you now?" Dinah asked jokingly. "I wondered what you did with those saws all day."

William smiled. "Now you're a strong woman, but sawing takes some practice," he cautioned. "You can't just go out and cut this way and that. You have to be careful, or you'll ruin the wood and hurt yourself. We'll get started tomorrow. You're a fast learner. I'm sure you'll pick it up."

"I better with a teacher like you," Dinah said. "An expert sawyer and handsome to boot." The two smiled, and William gave Dinah a quick kiss on the cheek.

The next day, after long hours of work, William returned home and set up a rudimentary station to teach Dinah the art of woodcutting. Sawyers provided a critical skill in an era where wood-fed fireplaces and stoves served as a major source of residential heating and cooking, as well as many commercial applications in addition to the iron furnaces. Residents also used coal, but wood often proved more economical and versatile for multiple uses. The introduction of manufactured gas in Reading did not happen until 1848, a decade later, and its expanded use depended on the time-consuming installation of underground pipes. Sawyers split wood to provide usable fuel, cutting everything from fallen branches and trees to boards, planks, and leftover timber from construction. Many homeowners always had extra wood available for cutting and useful repurposing.

Learning the craft, however, required both practice and strength. Dinah had experienced a lifetime of hard labor, so she was already stronger than at first appeared. But wielding the tools of a sawyer required some training and considerable skill and Dinah began her tutelage under the watchful eye of her husband.

The implements of an itinerant Nineteenth Century sawyer included an axe, a sawhorse, and a number of saws used to cut various types of wood. Larger wood-cutting commercial operations used a two-person pitsaw with one of the unfortunate sawyers standing in an excavated pit. Notoriously, the sawyer stationed in the pit received the worst of the day's wear. Fortunately for Dinah, the smaller jobs for which she trained did not require such an odious assignment, and she would typically work alone on flat ground.

While William had done his share of large woodcutting projects, his tutelage of Dinah focused on small jobs, where she could typically set up at the curb in front of the home and work from there. Sawing took significant exertion and required both endurance and patience. No one wanted wood cut crooked, jagged, or uneven.

A sawyer's life became one of balance and compromise. A practitioner needed to carry enough tools to complete a variety of work efficiently. There was no time to return home to retrieve a device the sawyer had failed or forgotten to bring. But at the same time, itinerant laborers had to keep their load light enough to travel. Sawyers often carried a sawbuck, a device to hold wood for easy cutting, on their shoulders as they traveled. The sawbuck comprised two "X"-shaped pieces of wood, joined by crossbars below the intersection of each "X". Sawyers cut wood by placing it in the "V" formed above the intersection of each "X."

Sawyers also carried at least one saw and usually more. A handsaw was a necessity, a thin but wide steel blade that cut on the push stroke. It allowed downward sawing on wood laid across a support such as a sawbuck. Sawyers might also carry a file to both smooth out rough surfaces and sharpen their blade as well as a chisel to loosen debris.

William gathered what tools Dinah needed, building a sawbuck from rough material and purchasing saws and other tools at bargain prices when he could find them. Fortunately for William, though perhaps not so much for the former sawyer, a man he had worked with on multiple occasions recently passed away and his tools became available. Again, to William's advantage, the supplies of a former sawyer had little value to anyone other than a current one.

William set up the equipment, explaining it to Dinah carefully each step of the way, making sure she understood how to arrange her workstation in order to work quickly and safely. Then he placed the saw in her hand.

"Do I saw now?" she asked.

"Just a moment," William said, holding her arm still until he felt she was ready. "Now I know you're more powerful than you look. But it takes more than strength to cut wood. Make sure you're balanced and firmly set."

"How hard can it be?" Dinah asked. "You've done it for years."

William shook his head. "Now don't you get sassy with me," he chided her with a smile. "You'll see what I mean."

She went about cutting the board in front of her. Part of the way through her attempt, the saw bowed and the cut became jagged, catching the teeth of the tool and jamming it. Dinah cursed under her breath, not loud enough for her Lord to hear, or so she hoped.

"Maybe a bit harder than you thought," William said flatly, a smile emerging on his face once again. He turned his head as he attempted to muffle a laugh.

Dinah flashed her husband a stern look, erasing his amusement. William continued to work with Dinah until she became familiar with the tools and the wood cutting process. She needed to increase her speed, but that would come with time and practice. After a few failed initial attempts, Dinah settled into a groove and became far more proficient in her efforts.

"You have the makings of a good sawyer there," William finally concluded.

"I had a good teacher," Dinah responded, "if not so patient and kind as he might have been. But he'll pay for that later."

At first, some customers showed some reluctance to hire a woman to do a "man's job." William assured them their skepticism was unwarranted. "She's as strong as most men," William said, "and she's had a fine teacher."

Not all were convinced, but enough people gave Dinah a chance to prove herself. Initially, Dinah worked with William if the job warranted her presence. There, she became William's de facto apprentice, further advancing her knowledge in real-life situations. On those days, William and Dinah worked as a happy couple, talking to each other and those passing by who stopped and observed the unusual sight of a female sawyer. For Dinah, the days moved far more quickly when could spend time with her husband while learning a new type of work. Dinah soon took a liking to life as a woodcutter. It was still a demanding job, but she enjoyed being outside and appreciated the better wages.

On one occasion, a middle-aged man stopped abruptly as he walked down the street and watched for a minute or more as the two sawyers worked. The man never said a word, only nodding when Dinah offered a "Good morning." Soon thereafter, he went on his way to his destination.

"Who would have thought I'd ever see a woman sawyer?" the man muttered under his breath. Dinah chuckled, hearing the comment despite the soft tone. The man proved not the last to observe Dinah's unusual line of work.

"Folks apparently have never seen a woman cutting wood," Dinah remarked after the fourth person stopped and watched her.

"Certainly none as pretty as you," William responded. "I think that's what stops them in their tracks."

Dinah smiled and gave her husband a wave. "Now you hush, now," she said. "You're embarrassing me. Though you are quite the charmer. But you save that until we get home."

William chuckled and went on with his work, occasionally glancing over at Dinah.

I'm a lucky man, he thought.

Not every job required two people, however, and clients would not pay for the extra hand. Dinah split her time between cutting wood and performing a variety of household tasks for families throughout the city at a much lower wage. But Dinah maintained her commitment and soon could cut wood as quickly and as accurately as most men—and even better than many.

By the time Dinah perfected her craft, she split two-and-a-half cords of wood in a day, a prodigious accomplishment. One full cord of wood measures eight feet long by four feet wide by four feet high, comprising one hundred twenty-eight cubic feet. For splitting approximately three hundred twenty feet of wood, Dinah earned one dollar and fifty cents per day.

"I liked sawing wood better than anything else I ever did," Dinah recalled. *"Sawing wood was a harvest to me. I always liked outdoor work better than indoor work."*

•   •   •

Dinah mastered the craft of a sawyer quickly and eventually found her new-found skill in great demand. While most jobs simply required cutting larger pieces of wood for heating and cooking, a few tasks demanded more precise work. Dinah prepared herself to handle any assignment, from simple sawing to creating more exact shapes and sizes.

Dinah soon learned to establish a routine to ensure both efficiency and accuracy. She secured the wood to her sawhorse with clamps, leaving sufficient room to work. If an exact size was required, she used a ruler to measure the wood and marked the spot with a pencil and square. While Dinah had never learned to read, her new job required that she perform addition and subtraction. Fortunately, she had mastered simple arithmetic years ago while completing household tasks and other assignments.

Dinah then placed her saw on top of the wood, slightly away from the cut line. Because saws do not cut along a one-dimensional line, a sawyer needed to be sure the finished product was neither too short nor too long. She angled the far edge of the handsaw toward the ground, slightly raising her elbow.

William taught Dinah to avoid too rigid a posture and emphasized she should resist the urge to hold the saw too tightly, both of which would make completing her job more difficult. At the same time, she ensured she did not hold the saw so loosely that it proved difficult to control and failed to cut on a line. The fine line between "too tight" and "too loose" eventually became second nature.

She held the wood in place with her left hand, keeping it a suitable distance from the saw to prevent an accident. Dinah started the cut, applying no pressure at first and then pulling back. She sometimes used another piece of wood to keep the saw from moving away from the line. Once the saw made a slight cut into the wood, she lightly pressed down and kept cutting through the lumber. She applied more or less pressure until she found the right level of force. She sawed smoothly, moving the saw back and forth, towards her body and then away from it. Occasionally, she leveled the saw on the cutline, making sure the cut remained straight. Dinah continued her sawing motion until the piece of wood was ready to break off. She slowed down and used less force at the end to avoid cracking the wood. She held onto the piece she was cutting to prevent the weight of the wood from breaking off in splinters.

Occasionally, too much sawdust accumulated, making it difficult to follow the line. Dinah stopped and brushed the sawdust away so it did not impede her view. Depending on the wood, the wind, and the type of job, Dinah also carried a pair of rudimentary goggles to prevent dust and wood chips from irritating her eyes. In short order, Dinah became as efficient or even more so as many sawyers who had worked the craft for years.

"And they say this is a job only men can do," she said as she worked. "I'll show them. Men aren't nearly as tough as they think they are and women are a good deal stronger than they believe. The Good Lord provides me with all the strength I need."

•   •   •

Dinah walked the streets of Reading with her sawbuck and her saws, moving from one home to the next as needed. She typically wore a bonnet, a blouse, and a long skirt. Her sawbuck hung around her neck with the bulk of the weight supported by her back. She carried an assortment of saws and other tools to use in completing whatever the assignment required. Dinah always ensured her clients were happy with her work.

But Dinah proved more than a competent craftsperson carrying her tools of the trade. Dinah allowed her outgoing personality and natural curiosity to win over friends and clients. She soon made many acquaintances across Reading and became a well-known personality.

"Good morning, Mrs. Jones," Dinah said, seeing the older woman walking down the street. "You're out quite early this morning."

"Don't you know it, Dinah," Mrs. Jones answered cordially. "I don't typically go out this time of day, but I have errands to run. You would think folks would be more accommodating to an older lady when they schedule such things. I'll likely be exhausted by supper time."

Dinah and Mrs. Jones shared a few more cursory comments, then both went about their way. Dinah had clients who needed work completed, and Mrs. Jones had shopkeepers waiting for her arrival. The sawyer met a few others along the way, always greeting them with a smile and a pleasant acknowledgement. She proved as good a salesperson as a laborer.

In truth, Dinah more than occasionally passed white people recalcitrant in their racist and segregationist views. She learned long ago she could do nothing to change their stubborn mindset. They would pick up their pace and hurry by her with only an angry grimace on their faces. Dinah soon learned to identify these folks and made a concentrated effort to avoid them as best she could.

Dinah's customers typically collected boards and planks and sometimes fallen tree limbs to be cut into firewood. Dinah set up shop at the curbstone. Soon, the female sawyer of Berks County had become well-known and received quite a measure of notoriety and admiration.

•   •   •

Dinah may have mastered the art of cutting wood, but she could not control the weather. One day in late summer, she completed her work and headed for home, a walk of nearly two miles. She packed her saws and mounted her sawbuck on her back, moving steadily past the homes and businesses of the city. Just like many late summer days, the weather proved hazy, hot, and humid.

A few minutes into her travels, however, the skies began to darken and appear ominous. Dinah looked up and hastened her pace.

"My Lord," she said to herself, "it looks like a storm is brewing. I hope I can make it home before it hits."

Dinah quickened her pace but still failed miserably in beating the storm. Thunder rumbled and lightning flashed, followed a few seconds later by a downpour of epic proportions. Dinah scampered as fast as she could, but encumbered by the tools she carried, she became thoroughly drenched as the storm continued. She gained a few seconds of respite under a porch roof every so often, but she resolutely continued on her path pelted by the rain every step. By the time she finally arrived home and safely escaped inside, water dripped from every piece of her clothing and tools. She found a towel to dry her face, then methodically laid out her tools to dry. She heard the storm abate twenty minutes or so later and the sun appeared shortly thereafter.

"Wouldn't you know it waited for me to find shelter before it stopped," Dinah muttered. "Sometimes the Lord has quite the sense of humor. I hope He's getting a good chuckle at my expense."

Sometime later, William arrived home from his day of work. Travelling from the other direction, he somehow had escaped the storm's wrath. He walked into his home only to find his wife and her belongings still drenched, water dripping on the floor. He looked at her curiously.

"Did you decide to take a bath with your clothes on?" he asked mischievously. "You know, we usually don't bathe until Saturday."

Dinah shook her head and rolled up her wet bonnet she had removed from her head. She threw it with some force at her husband, which he caught playfully.

"There," she said, laughing, "now it's your turn. You need it more than me."

CHAPTER 23
EDGAR ALLAN POE

1844

As internationally famous and renowned as author Edgar Allan Poe has become following his death, Poe spent much of his life barely scraping together enough money to survive. The author had hoped to be one of the first writers to earn a living with his storytelling, but that dream generated less-than-prosperous results. Nevertheless, Poe owns an undeniable legacy. He essentially invented the detective fiction genre and heavily contributed to the development of science fiction. The acclaim he has received after his death far outstripped the material rewards he garnered during his relatively brief life.

Poe's ongoing precarious financial situation may explain his delay in responding to an invitation to speak to a Reading organization that dubbed themselves the *"Mechanic's Institute,"* an educated group intent on continuing their lifelong learning. The Institute's Committee of Invitation had mailed correspondence to Poe at his residence in Philadelphia, inquiring about his willingness to speak to the group. At the time, however, a resident had to go to the Central Post Office and pay for the postage to pick up mail. Poe likely lacked the funds to retrieve the letter when it arrived. But when he finally did, he responded quickly to the invitation and gladly accepted the request for a March engagement.

Poe wrote:

"Gentlemen,

Through some accident which I am at a loss to understand, your letter dated and postmarked December 29 has only this moment come to hand; having been lying ever since in the Phila. P. Office. I hope, therefore, you will exonerate me from the charge of discourtesy in no sooner replying to your flattering request.

I presume that your lectures are all over for the season; but should that not be the case, it will give me great pleasure to deliver a Discourse before your Society, at any period you may appoint not later than the 9th instant.

With high respect

Yr. Obdt. St.

Edgar A. Poe"

By this time, Poe had already gained some level of fame. He published several stories, including *"The Gold-Bug," "The Fall of the House of Usher,"* and *"Murders in the Rue Morgue,"* in Philadelphia magazines, and he became one of the country's earliest short story practitioners. While the Committee originally proposed six different lectures, Poe's late response led them to agree on March 11 and 12 as dates for his presentations. Poe, however, would not speak on intrigue, suspense, and things that went bump in the night. His topic focused on American poets and poetry, far more esoteric than exotic.

The legacy of Benjamin Franklin served as the inspiration for the founding and naming of the Mechanic's Institute. Franklin considered himself a "mechanic" in his early years as a printer. "Ancient history" represented one of the most popular topics examined by the Mechanics Institute. In 1842, for example, they debated, *"was Coriolanus justified in leading an army against the city of Rome after he had been expelled therefrom?"* No document exists that recorded the attendance at such a robust event.

Poe, himself, had not led an exactly exemplary life. Born in Boston in 1809, Poe's father abandoned the family a year later and his mother died in 1811. Informally adopted by the Allan family from Virgina, he attended the University of Virginia but left after one year when his money supply ran dry.

He enlisted in the United States Army under an assumed name but failed out as a cadet because of both gambling and drinking. He then turned to writing, starting with poetry and later switching to prose. Trying mostly unsuccessfully to eke out a living as an author, he compounded his problems at age twenty-seven by marrying his thirteen-year-old cousin, Virginia, who came down with tuberculosis several years later in 1842.

It was soon after this point in his life that Poe traveled to Reading.

Early in the morning of the scheduled lecture, Poe left his Philadelphia home on Seventh and Spring Garden streets. His landlord, a plumber, was reportedly understanding and patient about the rent. Poe probably said goodbye to Virginia and Miss Clemm, a relative of his wife who acted as both nurse and housekeeper.

"I will be back the day after tomorrow," he told them, then looked at Virginia. "You will be in my heart the entire time I am gone. Miss Clemm will take good care of you while I am away."

Poe then gently pet the family cat on his way out the door. Whether the cat was named Pluto, was black in color, or wore an eyepatch is unknown, but Poe had recently published *"The Black Cat,"* a tale revolving around an individual's battle with alcoholism. That narrator began the story loving both his wife and animals but turned to alcohol and abused both spouse and pets. He initially spared only a black cat, Pluto. But in a fit of rage one evening, he gauged out Pluto's eyeball. The Poe family cat presumably avoided such a gruesome fate.

Poe wore a long, Spanish cape stylish at the time. He made his way to the Philadelphia and Reading Railroad, better known simply as "The Reading." The second-class fare on the train costs a little over a dollar. It entitled Poe to an uncomfortable seat on a hard bench.

The Reading was hardly a luxurious mode of travel. A small, wood-burning locomotive pulled the passenger cars, and the trip was infamous for its many stops along the way. The line constantly teetered on the edge of bankruptcy, though residents still considered it a travel wonder compared to previous modes of transportation between the two cities. Prior to The Reading, travelers endured a fourteen-hour trip made through a combination of canal boat and horseback or carriage. The Reading offered the same trip in four hours.

Poe arrived in Reading that afternoon and registered at the Mansion House Hotel, the city's most popular rooming spot for overnight guests on the southeast corner of Fifth and Penn Street.

The Mansion House had its own starry history. The first hotel ever constructed in Reading, its foundation traced back to the late 1700s. In Dinah's time, the Mansion House represented the largest and most well-known hotel in the city. Builders completed most of the original building in 1840, but the structure experienced significant expansion over the years. Besides the hotel, the Mansion House included a restaurant that hosted public events, a barbershop, and a billiard room. The first U.S. Telegraph Co. office opened in the reading room in the Mansion House in 1866. For many years, the hotel served as the center of day-to-day life in Reading and Berks County. Many prominent citizens from across the country patronized the Mansion House, including Theodore Roosevelt and Franklin D. Roosevelt. In 1914, former President Theodore Roosevelt addressed a crowd of over ten thousand from the hotel's balcony facing Penn Street as he sought a third term in office. That same year, Franklin D. Roosevelt, Theodore's distant cousin and then the Assistant Secretary of the Navy who would later be elected President, dined at the Mansion House while in the city to speak at the unveiling of the U.S.S. Maine anchor, still displayed in Reading's City Park.

In the early Twentieth Century, the hotel announced an ambitious renovation that would create a ten-story structure. Despite the owners completing some improvements, the centerpiece addition never became a reality. By the 1930s, the abandoned Mansion House fell into a state of general disrepair. In 1937, the owners razed the grand old building after determining the land was more valuable as a vacant lot.

But the Mansion House enjoyed its heyday when Poe arrived. After refreshing himself, Poe left the hotel on his way to find a late lunch and better familiarize himself with Reading. As he walked, he spied Dinah at a nearby curbstone cutting an impressive pile of wood. Poe stopped for a moment to observe the woman dutifully working at her craft. Eventually, Dinah looked up at the stranger and surveyed him quickly. She saw a small, thin man with a broad forehead, tanned complexion, and dark hair and eyes.

"I'm sorry to disturb your work, ma'am," Poe said apologetically. "I was merely admiring your skill with a saw. You are quite talented."

"Thank you, Mr...." Dinah paused and examined the man more closely. His haunted eyes highlighted the overall sadness she read on his face.

"Poe," he said. "Edgar Allan Poe."

"Thank you, Mr. Poe," Dinah said. "I appreciate your kind words. May God bless you."

Not able to read or write, Dinah did not know that Edgar Allan Poe had gained some measure of fame as a writer or that he would serve as a featured speaker at a prominent local event. Dinah greeted him as she would any other passerby.

Conversely, historians have scoured Poe's writing to divine his views on race, and the results have not been kind. Poe rarely depicted an African American in his tales, and when he did, they were typically either villainous or mad. Interestingly, many of Poe's most macabre stories may have found their roots in ghost stories told by an Allan family slave named Judith. Tradition holds that Poe listened to Judith's African American folktales by the night fire. Judith supposedly once told Poe that ghosts could spring from the earth and possess young boys who wandered in graveyards. The young Poe became so terrified that he refused to detach himself from his uncle's hip when passing a cemetery. If Poe's first exposure to horror came from African American folktales, his later fashioning himself as a Southern aristocrat offers more than a hint of irony.

Poe watched Dinah a moment longer, then tipped his hat. "You have a wonderful day, ma'am," he said and proceeded down the street. Dinah nodded and watched him as he walked away.

"The devil's be in him," she muttered to herself. "Seems like the spirits follow him somehow. I'll say a prayer for his soul. He needs it as much as any man."

Dinah looked up to heaven, mouthed a few silent words, then returned to work.

•　•　•

Poe's presentations that evening and the following day, most likely also held at the Mansion House, proved a rousing success.

"A poem deserves its title only inasmuch as it excites by elevating the soul," he said. *"The value of the poem is in the ratio of this elevating excitement... It is to be hoped that common sense in time will prefer deciding on a work of Art rather by the impression it makes – by the effect it produces -than by the time it took to impress the effect...The fact is that perseverance is one thing and genius quite another."*

Poe received repeated bursts of applause from the large and enthusiastic audiences. Virginia Poe would die in 1847. Edgar Allan Poe passed away in 1849 at the age of forty. His death occurred under bizarre circumstances, still the subject of debate today. Arguments persist whether Poe died of natural causes or unwittingly ingested some combination of poison or drugs. But long before he became the toast of literature and an inspiration to many writers and filmmakers who followed, Poe proved to be a hit in Reading.

CHAPTER 24
HINNERSHITZ ALLEY

August 1847

When William and Dinah Clark and their children left the John Adam farm after ten years, they moved back to what they thought was the familiar landscape of Reading. But Reading's significant expansion during that time transformed it from a town into a true city, making it unfamiliar to them. The population of Reading leaped from three thousand five hundred residents in 1813 to more than thirteen thousand in 1847 and continued to multiply through the years.

While industrial growth of iron and steel production initially spurred Reading's development, local industry shifted their focus to iron and steel fabrication as the upper Great Lakes region asserted dominance on the production side. The opening of the Schuylkill Canal and the Union Canal made Reading an ideal transportation hub and further stimulated economic and residential growth.

William and Dinah lived in rented homes for several years, both working throughout the city. While husband and wife labored hard to support their family, William had fallen deeply into debt. History does not fully explain why, but enough evidence suggests that both he and Dinah struggled with alcoholism. In addition, Dinah had been in and out of the workforce as she raised their children. Those factors, combined with the couple's efforts to support their family on low wages even for that time, likely represented a serious detriment to obtaining suitable housing.

"What are we going to do?" William asked Dinah one day. "If we buy a house, the creditors will take it as soon as they can. We can't let that happen. That would ruin us for good."

"I've heard Mister and Mrs. Boas talking," Dinah answered. "Mister Boas is important at one of the local banks. They're kind when they speak to me. Sociable too. Maybe I can ask Mrs. Boas if her husband might have a suggestion. He may have dealt these circumstances before."

Dinah had secured a number of domestic clients, and her friendly manner ingratiated her with many Reading residents. When she asked Mister and Mrs. Boas for guidance, she received valuable input and concocted a scheme to address her family's circumstances.

Eventually, Dinah bought a small log house on Hinnershitz Alley for two hundred dollars, the equivalent of about five-thousand five-hundred dollars in the 2020s. A provision in the deed prevented the seizure of the home by William's creditors.

Here's where things get a little murky. Based on the document dated August 3, 1847, filed at the Berks County Recorder of Deeds, Dinah deeded her home in trust to Enoch Sanders and his wife, Hannah. The relationship between William, Dinah, and Enoch remains somewhat unclear. Enoch received credit as one of the founders of the Bethel A.M.E. Church, reportedly preached there, and later became a prominent citizen in the city promoting the rights of African Americans. While it's tempting to think that his wife, Hannah, may have been Dinah's daughter, that assumption is clearly incorrect. Since the 1850 census lists Hannah as twelve years old and still living with William and Dinah on Hinnershitz Alley, Hannah would only have been nine years old in 1847. Furthermore, Dinah related later in her life that "*My daughter Hannah married a Mr. Deets, who enlisted in the army and died.*" Thus, that Enoch's wife and Dinah's daughter both carry the name "Hannah" remains a curious coincidence that can easily lead historians down a non-existent rabbit hole. The relationship between William, Dinah, and Enoch appears rooted in the friendships among the small African American community of the time and the bonds forged in the construction of the Bethel A.M.E. Church.

The accuracy of the 1850 census, by the way, can also be called into question, since it records Dinah as forty-eight years old. That would make her birth date about 1802 rather than the generally accepted 1794. But even Dinah acknowledged later that she *"did know how many"* years ago she had been born. In addition, the census lists Dinah as "Diana," the same name that appears in the 1847 deed to her home and later in city directories and even on her death certificate. Presumably, Dinah went by both names at certain points in her life. Alternatively, unable to read, Dinah perhaps did not realize that scribes substituted the more familiar "Diana" rather than her given name in various documents. There will always remain some uncertainty about the circumstances surrounding her family, her home, her life, and even her name.

While the relationship between William and Dinah Clark and Sanders may be unclear, the deed proves he did help them secure their home. Additionally, Sanders' mother, Sarah Harding, known throughout the community as "Auntie Hardy," lived with Dinah for a period of time, though the exact dates are unknown.

The home on Hinnershitz Alley, which ran east from Moss Street to Tenth Street between Washington Street and Walnut Street, sat less than a block from Dinah's beloved Bethel A.M.E. Church in the northeast part of the city. It was a simple home, built in a part of the town where residents were primarily African Americans. With the guardrails of segregation always prominent, many struggled financially and worked low-paying labor-intensive jobs. Admittedly, some broke those shackles and rose above the circumstances. But Dinah and her family did not constitute one of those fortunate few.

William and Dinah's home presumably resembled many other log homes of the day. Credit for bringing the log home to the American colonies belonged to the Swedes, who established themselves in parts of southeastern Pennsylvania in the mid-Seventeenth Century. They established several significant settlements as part of the New Sweden colony in Pennsylvania and Delaware and continued to oversee the land until William Penn claimed it under his charter. Swedish settlers typically built cabins from horizontally stacked, notched logs, with corner chimneys. Clay chinking filled the space between the logs.

The Log House on South Fourth Street in Reading, built in 1760, followed this construction pattern. The one-and-a-half story dwelling measured twenty-five feet by thirty feet. The builders chinked its pine logs with cut stone and mortar, and it features notch and saddle corner construction. Eventually the home of The Speckled Hen Cottage Pub and Alehouse, the National Register of Historic Places listed the building in 1979.

The Clarks likely lived in a home similar to this, with some of the sleeping quarters on the upper half floor. Dinah lived in this humble home for the rest of her life. She ultimately cared for her daughter, Mary Ann, who became disabled and remained with Dinah until her death.

●　　●　　●

William and Dinah sat peacefully on two chairs in their modest home on Hinnershitz Alley. Both typically worked six days each week, but on Sundays, they worshipped and rested, as did most of the rest of the Berks County community.

"Well, here we are," Dinah said contentedly. "An old married couple sitting by the fire resting our weary bones."

William chuckled. "We were very lucky to find each other," he said. "You've kept me in line all these years, even if you had to whoop me occasionally."

Dinah shook her head. "Now don't say such a thing," she replied with a chuckle. "Someone is apt to believe it and I'll be all over the news. Can you imagine what they'd say? 'Old colored woman jailed for thrashing her husband.' Wouldn't that be the scandal? We'd be the talk of the town."

"You're already quite famous as far as I can tell without being arrested," William said. "Even the white folks in town know you who are. They've never seen a lady cut wood like you can. 'A colored lady sawyer,' they say, 'whoever thought I'd see such a thing in my life.'"

Dinah waved her hand dismissively. "Bah," she said. "you're just jealous."

William turned toward his wife and smiled lovingly. "I am only ever proud of everything you've done," he said. "You are a remarkable woman."

"And don't you ever forget that!" Dinah said with a chuckle. "Lord knows where you would be without me. I've pulled you out of many a pickle."

"Ain't that the truth," William agreed. He had learned not to argue with his wife. Her will had proven as strong as her physical strength. While William had rescued Dinah from slavery, Dinah had served as the shiny beacon throughout their married life.

She packs more than most into that frame, he thought. *I am more fortunate than she will ever know.*

"Where are you off to tomorrow?" Dinah asked, interrupting his thoughts.

"I have to cut some wood at the Templin house," he said. "It's going to be cold. I guess I should count myself lucky. The colder the weather, the more wood needs cutting. They burn it like paper when there's a chill in the air."

Dinah smiled. "That's one way of looking at it while your hands freeze," she said. "It's the price of a good day's pay."

"What about you?" William asked. "Who are you sharing the news with tomorrow?"

"I have some work to do at the Jones house," Dinah replied. "A bit of wood cutting, but some chores too. Mrs. Jones is getting up there in years and needs some help around the house. She's not as spry as she used to be."

William chuckled softly. "That's probably true of all of us," he said.

Dinah chuckled in agreement. "I have to go a little later in the morning, because Mrs. Jones doesn't get out of bed so early anymore," Dinah added. "She likes to sleep in until daylight comes around. Can you picture that?"

"Imagine," William sighed. "Sleeping in. 'Till daylight, you say? I don't believe that's something I'll ever see."

William and Dinah fell silent. The two of them pulled out their pipes and filled them with tobacco, enjoying a smoke together as the day wound down. They shared a glass of whiskey and fell silent. Eventually, William moved his chair closer to Dinah's and extended his hand. His wife clasped it. After years of hard labor, neither had the soft palms of youth, but neither cared. The two closed their eyes hand-in-hand.

CHAPTER 25
DINAH AND HER CITY

1848

Dinah finished her work and packed her tools, her body spent from the busy day. She had toiled non-stop for hours, sawing wood and helping with domestic chores in several houses. For whatever reason, everyone in the city suddenly seemed flush with work they could not complete themselves. Dinah did not complain. For day laborers such as Dinah, that translated into steady work and a decent income. She could rest her tired body at home, knowing she supported herself and her family.

As she moved from home to home, she watched several groups of children playing outside. Some energetic youngsters chased after each other playing tag, while others covered their eyes in a spirited contest of hide-and-seek. A game called "stick and hoop" also proved popular, as participants used a stick to keep a large hoop rolling forward as long as possible. Some of the more skilled children rolled the hoop an astonishing length, while others still learning the skill struggled to keep the object moving just a few feet.

A different group of children threw their hoops to each other, using sticks in an attempt to catch them. Wooden or metal game pieces helped make this a popular children's activity in the Nineteenth Century. Children appeared to have no limit to their imagination in entertaining themselves. If they tired of traditional games, they invented new ones with their own rules.

"I wish I had half as much energy as they do," Dinah said to herself. "It's a wonder they can run from morning 'till night without getting tired. I used to be able to do that when I was a youngster. But back then, I had no time to play."

As daylight turned to dusk, Dinah began her journey home. She faced a walk of at least a mile. November meant the earlier arrival of darkness. The temperature hovered in the fifties, moderate for this time of year, but on this night, humidity hung in the air. As the light faded, Dinah walked through a dense fog, punctuated by the occasional streetlight. Occasionally, she took a few moments to study the city that had grown up around her. The town had an eeriness to it in the fog that it lacked in the light of day. Dinah walked on, deciding not to take too much time in this otherworldly environment.

Reading experienced an explosion of growth and subsequently converted from a borough to a city in 1847. Reading Iron Works had changed its name to Seyfert, McManus and Company and employed two-hundred-and-fifty workers in a rolling mill and nail factory on Seventh Street. The Henry Clay Anthracite Furnace sat southeast of the ironworks near the railroad, and the Franklin Foundry operated at Eighth and Chestnut Streets. Franklin had expanded to become a railroad car manufacturer in 1844. Other industrial shops included the Darling Foundry and Machine Shop at Third and Canal, the Union Canal Company, the Schuylkill Navigation Company, Jackson Rope Works at the foot of Bingaman Street, Reading Fire Brick Works at the end of Fourth Street, and the Lauer Brewery at Third and Chestnut located there since its founding in 1826. Dinah passed by many of these establishments, as well as homes both ornate and plain. Most of the city's residential development over the past thirty years occurred east of Seventh Street between Walnut and Chestnut, and south of Chestnut to the west of the railroad, primarily because people preferred to live near their place of employment. A significant part of the city's growth took place during the late 1830s and 1840s. Prior to 1837, scarcely anyone lived east of the railroad tracks. Dinah had witnessed significant changes in just a few years.

In 1840, Reading paved heavily used streets with hard white gravel as the municipality transformed itself more and more into an urban setting. By 1840, Reading contained one thousand three hundred and sixty-five buildings, of which seven hundred seventy-eight were built of brick, four hundred thirty-two were frame, and one hundred fifty-five constructed from logs. In 1847 alone, builders erected seventy buildings more than two stories high. Only fifty-six such buildings existed in the young city seven years earlier.

Minority groups played little part in the early development of Reading. Most immigrants who took up residence were Germans and found work in the industries, living in the newly developed areas. Eventually, a small community of free black families became established in the extreme Northeast, in the neighborhood of Tenth and Washington, through the 1830s and 1840s. William and Dinah Clark had been part of that growth. When Reading became a city in 1847, general development had just reached that section.

Dinah arrived home from her workday before her husband and began her tasks at home. Even though she had put in a full day of hard labor sawing wood and completing domestic chores, her house tasks remained. Dinah juggled preparing dinner with wrangling her children, laundering clothes, and straightening the house. When her children asked to play outside, she answered with her own brand of motherly care.

"Now don't you go gallivanting across the neighborhood," she admonished them. "You stay where I can see and hear you. It's dark outside, so you don't go far. I don't want to go chasing after you. If I do, I'm bringing the stick with me and you'll feel the end of it!"

Because Dinah had lost so many children, the ages of those who survived to adulthood varied widely. If the 1850 census was indeed correct, Hannah and Mary Ann still lived with William and Dinah on Hinnershitz Alley and would have been nine and thirteen in 1847. John and Silas, not listed in the census as residing at the Clark home, presumably had already left and lived on their own.

By the time William came through the door that evening, Dinah had a simple meal of pork and potatoes cooking in the oven. William put down his tools and wrapped his arms affectionately around his wife.

"Smells good," he said. "Almost as good as you."

Dinah smiled. "Now you stop that," she said, wriggling free. "We have no time for that right now and you don't smell as good as you might. You go clean yourself up and dinner will be ready shortly."

William kissed Dinah's forehead and did as he was told. He stoked the fire to keep the house warm and he and the children soon sat down to their evening meal. Before they ate, however, Dinah insisted they offer a prayer as a family dinner blessing.

Our Heavenly Father, kind and good,
We thank Thee for our daily food.
We thank Thee for Thy love and care.
Be with us Lord and hear our prayer.
Amen.

Afterward, the entire family cleaned their dinner plates and spent some time relaxing by the fire. Though William and Dinah had never learned to read, several of their children had received a rudimentary education as they interacted with other youngsters in the city. Hannah and Mary Ann read two of the small collection of books that had found their way into the Clark house. Their favorite was *Fairy Tales Told for Children, First Collection* by Hans Christian Andersen. Published more than a decade before, the book represented Andersen's first work in the fairy tale genre. While it may have appeared a simple accomplishment, that William and Dinah's children could read at all filled their parents with pride.

"The world may change one day, William," Dinah said softly.

"It may," William acknowledged, "though I don't know if we'll live to see it."

"If we don't," Dinah replied, "I pray that our children and our children's children will enjoy an easier life that we had. They deserve it."

William reached over and grasped Dinah's hand. "I'm sure they will," he said, "and it will be in no small part because of you."

While Reading's first public school opened in 1838, African American children in the city did not receive an equal education opportunity until 1854. The first public "colored school" opened that year, reportedly in the basement of the Washington Street Presbyterian Church on the northeast corner of Washington and Mulberry. But by then, nearly all the Clark children had reached adulthood, and a school did them little good.

CHAPTER 26
CHRISTMAS

1848

"Merry Christmas!" Mary Ann shouted before dawn lit the sky. "It's Christmas Day!"

Dinah awoke instantly. "Good Lord, child!" she admonished her. "The sun isn't up yet. I don't even get up this early for work on most days." But then the motherly instinct in her took control. "Merry Christmas, my child. We'll be out shortly. No looking in your stocking until we're there!"

At that point, William groggily opened his eyes. "Is it Christmas?" he asked.

"Go back to sleep, William," Dinah said. "When you wake up properly, you'll remember it's the blessed day our savior Jesus was born. You might even say a prayer thanking him for his sacrifice."

Christmas may not have been the commercial whirlwind in the mid-Nineteenth Century that it later became, but people across the world joyously celebrated the holiday. William and Dinah's household engaged in the Christmas festivities, though modestly, within their limited time and means.

Fortunately for the Clark family, many of their regular clients shared their Christmas spirit with small gifts. William and Dinah both came home with jars of jelly and preserves, fruit, nuts, candles, and elaborately decorated needlepoint. For the Clark family, these presents represented a tremendous bounty. As Christmas Day arrived, Dinah decorated their humble home with handmade decorations and strings of popcorn.

Neither William nor Dinah worked on Christmas. This day represented one of the few holidays they celebrated as a couple and as a family. Outside of Sundays, Christmas marked a rare time the Clarks took a day of rest.

Not that Christmas offered much true relaxation. Between children's presents, church services, and a holiday meal, the festivities never quite ended. If William and Dinah held any hopes of enjoying a calm, peaceful day, those dreams quickly evaporated. True to form, after the children awoke and rushed to their parents' bedside, they scampered toward the fireplace and impatiently waited for William and Dinah to arrive. When they finally did and gave the children permission to view their gifts, Hannah and Mary Ann each found their hung stocking stuffed with a small toy, a package of peanuts, a large shiny orange ready to eat, and several other treats.

"Just what I wanted!" ten-year-old Hannah said excitedly, inspecting the piece of fruit. "These are delicious."

In fact, oranges represented a coveted Christmas gift for children of little means in the Nineteenth Century. Expensive and somewhat rare, oranges also contained a significant amount of Vitamin C, a precious commodity for diets that did not always include fresh, healthy foods. Children's bodies likely craved oranges and the rewards they delivered. An orange proved to be a valuable and nutritious treat.

William and Dinah could not afford such a luxury for their children but provided them thanks to the generosity of one of their customers. The couple held hands as their children enjoyed their new-found treasures.

After a few minutes, William walked over to a cabinet and reached far into the back of one shelf. He pulled out a small package roughly wrapped in tissue paper. Walking back over to Dinah, he placed the package in her hands.

"Merry Christmas, my love," he said.

Dinah's eyes widened. "William," she said in honest surprise, "you shouldn't have. What a rascal you are."

"You deserve everything I could give you and more," he said.

"Well, that may be true," Dinah said jokingly. "But you still didn't have to get me anything."

Dinah slowly unwrapped the package and opened the box. Inside, she discovered a porcelain figure of an African American woman. Dinah marveled at the figure's beauty and intricacy. "William," she started, but her husband gently put a finger to her lips.

"I picked it because it reminded me of you," he said. "It was like you posed for it. Nothing could be more beautiful."

Dinah wrapped her arms around William. "I love you," she said softly. "Merry Christmas."

"I love you too," William responded. "Merry Christmas. I hope we celebrate many more together."

Following the emptying of the stockings and a small breakfast, the Clarks dressed in their best attire and headed toward Bethel A.M.E. Church to attend the Christmas service. In truth, their dress represented neither the latest fashion nor the highest quality. Sometimes mismatched and threadbare, the clothing served as the best the Clarks owned. Fine clothing did not rank as a priority when trying to feed and shelter a family on a limited income. No one at the church would notice or criticize their dress, since many African Americans shared the same difficult financial status. Even those of better means understood the struggles of their fellow parishioners. Before the Clark family entered the church, they passed a group of eight carolers, both male and female, white and African American, singing joyfully on this Christmas morning. For some, Christmas proved the one time of year where racial barriers fell.

"Joy to the World, the Lord is come!
Let earth receive her King
Let every heart prepare Him room
And Heaven and nature sing
And Heaven and nature sing
And Heaven, and Heaven, and nature sing."

William, Dinah and their children dutifully entered the church and silently took their seats in a pew toward the middle of the house of worship.

Soon, the minister, Reverend Scott, appeared at the pulpit and began the service, one filled with joy and great hope.

The service lasted a bit over ninety minutes and included Communion and a variety of religious Christmas hymns. Those passing the church would hear *Silent Night* and *Hark the Herald Angels Sing* sung loudly and passionately. Reverend Scott offered an uplifting sermon focused on faith and God's eternal rewards, taking longer than usual, likely inspired by the festivities of the blessed holiday.

"On the sacred Christmas Day, we gather in the warmth of fellowship and our hearts resonate with an ageless story, the story of a gift given to the world," the minister began his sermon, all in attendance listening with rapt attention. "Today, let us explore the profound meaning of Christmas.

"In the Gospel of Luke, we find shepherds in the fields keeping watch over their flocks. The angel of the Lord appears, and the glory of God shines around them. The archangel Gabriel crouched low so he could see clearly when enough shepherds had assembled to hear his grand announcement.

"Finally, the archangel proclaimed, 'Do not be afraid. I bring good news that will cause great joy for all the people. Today in the town of David, a Savior has been born to you; he is the Messiah, the Lord.'

"Upon hearing this angelic proclamation," the minister continued, "the shepherds hastened to Bethlehem to find Mary, Joseph, and the blessed child laying in the manger, the very son of God. They found Jesus, wrapped in swaddling clothes, lying in a humble feeding trough."

Reverend Scott continued, not missing a step in documenting the birth of Jesus and its importance to the salvation of men and women. He ultimately concluded his sermon, raising the congregation's sentiments to a fever pitch. Those in attendance proclaimed "Amen" and "Bless Jesus" as the homily reached its emotional end. The service concluded shortly afterwards, and the parishioners greeted each other warmly as they left, wishing each other a merry and blessed day.

The Clark family sauntered leisurely back to their home just down the block from the church. They spent a few precious moments soaking in the revelry of Christmas Day, ranging from the holiday greetings of neighbors to the carolers still singing in the distance to the occasional smell of fresh bread or pie wafting through the air.

Eventually, William and Dinah and the children entered their home. After putting away their coats, they properly reminisced about the fine church service, Reverend Scott's inspiring sermon, and the other families and friends they had seen. Then Dinah went about preparing Christmas dinner.

"What are we having, Momma?" Mary Ann asked.

"Now you make yourself busy and don't worry about what I'm cooking," Dinah said, not nearly as threatening as the words might sound. "You'll find out soon enough. And don't go ruining your appetite by eating all those peanuts. I'll call you and your sister when I need some help."

Dinah busied herself in the kitchen, starting a beef roast from scratch while pulling out a mince pie made the day before. Eventually, Dinah recruited Hannah and Mary Ann to help peel potatoes and stir what cooked inside the various pots on the stove. A few hours later, the Clarks heard Dinah's familiar "come for dinner" cry and hurried to the kitchen to enjoy the feast.

Dinah served her roast beef with gravy and potatoes, cream of peanut butter soup, chestnuts, cranberries, bread, and, of course, the mince pie. While the amount of food wasn't overly abundant, it represented a far greater feast than their usual meal. Everyone left the table with their stomachs full, basking in the afterglow of the Christmas season. The Clark family rarely had a day filled with nothing but presents, church, and good food. For Dinah, it represented the perfect holiday.

Following the Christmas meal, William and Dinah took a few moments to relax. After the couple spent some time sitting side by side on rocking chairs, Dinah stood and headed back toward the kitchen. "I best clean up," she said. "These dishes won't wash themselves and I have to get to work all the earlier in the morning. Some of these families leave quite the mess that needs to be straightened. Those folks who claim that they had a visit from Kris Kringle or Santa Claus, or whatever they call him these days, the children get all riled up. They near tear the place apart opening their gifts."

William followed her close behind. "Let me help with that," William said. "It's Christmas. You shouldn't have to clean up all by yourself."

Dinah turned and squeezed William's cheek. "Aren't you quite the sweetheart?" she joshed. "I'll make sure to give you the dirtiest plates. Don't you break anything or I'll smack your behind with the wooden spoon."

"Oh, now don't tempt me with such promises," William said. He and Dinah joined in laughter, then began their task.

William and Dinah cleaned the remnants of the Christmas meal together, occasionally playfully bumping into each other. At one point, Dinah threw some soapy water on William's face, laughing hysterically. William wrapped his arm around his wife, and Dinah rested her head on her husband's shoulder. A moment later, the couple continued their duties and ended the day, hand in hand, watching the fireplace and thanking the Lord for helping them find each other. Their children eventually joined them and together, the family sang a litany of Christmas carols.

"God rest you merry, Gentlemen
Let nothing you dismay,
For Jesus Christ our Savior
Was born upon this day,
To save us all from Satan's power
When we were gone astray:
O tidings of comfort and joy."

For the Clark family, Christmas served as a time for gratitude and celebration, no matter how modest their surroundings or the gifts they exchanged. It truly achieved its promise of peace and goodwill. On this day, perhaps more than any other, Dinah enjoyed and truly appreciated the freedom she had gained.

CHAPTER 27
MARKET DAY

1849

Working from nearly dawn to dusk six days each week hardly gave William and Dinah time to complete the necessities of life. However, shopping for food ranked as a critical need where Dinah needed to carve out time to feed her family, even if that meant taking a few hours away from employment. Occasionally, Dinah would free herself from jobs in the early morning hours to visit one of Reading's open-air markets.

Fortunately for Dinah and her family, the city had a long-standing history of fresh markets dating back to the original deed from Thomas and Richard Penn. The Penns ordered two fairs each year, on June 4 and October 22, though unfortunately this tradition did not survive into the Twenty-First Century. Markets arose from those events to serve residents on a more regular basis.

The Clerk of the Market erected as many stalls as necessary at the two markets on Penn Street, which operated weekly. The open-air markets on Penn Square enjoyed elaborate new facilities built in the 1840s that attracted significant crowds.

Francis B. Shalters, the owner-editor of the *Reading Times*, built the South Reading Market House, considered one of the finest buildings in Reading. The window on the north side resembled a rose, similar to those found in a cathedral. The iron columns supporting the first-floor porch were the original posts from the second market pavilion on Penn Square.

Dinah collected as much money as she had available and stepped outside on a warm, early fall day. She headed to the Penn Square market, only five or six blocks from her home. The facility was both convenient and all-encompassing, with the various vendors carrying nearly anything a household could need. Dinah carried two wicker baskets which she would fill with whatever groceries and other goods she purchased. Not all markets welcomed African Americans as customers, but this market, in such close proximity to the predominantly black neighborhood in east Reading, made an exception. Even then, however, some vendors served only whites. Dinah avoided those where she was unwelcome.

"Good morning, Dinah," a neighbor said. "Headed to market, I see."

"Yes, indeed," Dinah nodded affirmatively. "I have to get there before all the best produce is picked through."

The neighbor gave a knowing smile. "There's quite the crowd there today," she said, "but I'm sure there will still be enough left for you."

Dinah continued on her path, repeating slightly different variations of that conversation to multiple people on the way.

"Going to market, I see," one remarked. "Plenty of fruit and vegetables to choose from this time of year."

"How's the family, Dinah?" another asked. "They should eat well tonight, I would say."

"Beautiful weather," said yet a third passerby. "Enjoy it while it lasts. I'm sure it will turn cold before we know it."

When Dinah finally arrived at her destination, she found a bounty of fresh fruit, vegetables, meats, and other produce. Her visit to the market that day came near the end of the harvest season, and every vendor had filled their spaces to overflowing. The selection represented a shopper's delight. Residents bought as much as they could, some to prepare over the coming days and even more to preserve for the winter soon to arrive. Knowing that, vendors transported as much product as they could to sell to eager customers and looked forward to a profitable day.

Dinah scanned the pavilion, observing the crowd of shoppers haggling loudly with the many sellers. A trio of musicians had camped in the corner of the market, offering various popular tunes as entertainment and hoping for donations. Dinah took in the cacophony of noise with a deep breath and joined the throng, moving from space to space, checking the variety, quality, and cost of the items. Over the years, she had learned to haggle with the best shoppers.

"How much for the potatoes?" she asked one vendor.

"Three cents per pound," the burly man answered. "But I'll give them to you for two cents if you buy five pounds."

"I can always use potatoes," Dinah responded. "I'll take them if you throw in a couple of cloves of garlic."

"That sounds like a deal to me," the potato vendor said in agreement.

"The apples look delicious," she said to another.

"Thirty-five cents for a dozen," came the answer. "Just picked yesterday. You choose the ones you want."

Dinah looked at the vendor skeptically.

"I'll tell you what," the salesperson added. "I'll throw in an extra apple. Baker's dozen."

Dinah accepted the offer then moved on to the next stand.

"How much for coffee?" Dinah asked, continuing her journey down the long row of tables.

"Seventy-five cents a pound," the seller answered. "It's hard to come by these days."

"I'll have to pass," Dinah said reluctantly. "That's more than I can pay. We'll have to do without our coffee. Poor William will survive."

When no counteroffer came, Dinah continued on her expedition. She had a client whose husband ran a small shop where she could purchase coffee for less. Dinah continued shopping, buying beef at six cents per pound, milk at five cents for a gallon, and bread at six cents per loaf. She passed on sugar, which was an expensive luxury, but purchased flour. Crinkling her nose, she decided against the green beans, despite their attractive price. She still shuddered at the memory of picking beans as a child under the blistering sun in the open field.

"Someone else can eat those," she muttered. "They always leave a sour taste in my mouth."

Dinah passed by several vendors who gave her scowling looks. She recognized those merchants did not want her business. Fortunately, most of the sellers that day cared little about who purchased their goods, as long as the buyer had cash, and they made a healthy profit.

By the end of her journey, Dinah filled both baskets to the brim. She carried them low to the ground by their handles, balancing the weight of each as best she could. Hauling her saws and the other tools of her trade had provided her with more than enough strength and experience to tote two baskets of groceries.

Dinah had spent more than a week's pay purchasing food for her family. Now, she headed back the way she came to her home on Hinnershitz Alley. Even with her ability to carry a load, the return trip felt longer and took more time.

"Do you need help, Dinah?" a friend asked, seeing the weight of the baskets she carried.

"I'll be just fine," Dinah answered. "These are light compared to the sawbuck I carry to work every day."

"I suppose they are," came the response. "You have a wonderful day. I'm headed to market myself."

"Make sure they give you a fair price," Dinah said. "They like to hook you whenever they can."

"I'll take advantage of whatever bargains you missed," the friend answered. "But I suppose you may have picked them clean."

"I did my best," Dinah acknowledged. "But I think I still left a few for you."

By now, Dinah had nearly arrived home. She turned off Penn Street and headed north on Ninth, turning right onto Hinnershitz Alley. She could see her home from there. The Clarks would eat well that day and in the coming week.

CHAPTER 28
THE GREAT FLOOD OF 1850

September 1850

A massive storm system targeted Reading and southeastern Pennsylvania in September 1850, causing one of the most destructive floods in the region's history. Coming only two months after a July tropical storm soaked the area and caused flash floods that killed at least twenty people along the Schuylkill River, another storm claimed more lives and resulted in widespread damage to homes and businesses.

The heavy rain began on Saturday, August 31 and continued unabated for nearly two days. When William, Dinah, and their children headed for church on Sunday morning, a deluge of pounding rain greeted them as they left their home and began the short walk to Bethel A.M.E. Church.

"My Lord, William," Dinah exclaimed as she shielded herself from the onslaught. "If this keeps up, you're going to have to build an ark."

"It may be too late!" William answered. "We may get washed away before I finish."

"We best pray to God that He spares us," Dinah concluded.

The Clarks eventually arrived inside the church and joined the rest of the water-logged congregation. For once, even the children hoped for a service long enough to allow their clothing to dry and the storm to pass. But no matter how long the minister kept them that day, the heavy rain waited to provide yet another drenching.

By Monday, September 2, Reading had experienced the full wrath of the storm. Residents watched the Penn Street Bridge, built in 1815, sailing downstream after being struck by two out-of-control boats twisting along the engorged river flowing twenty feet above its normal height. Four other bridges also succumbed to the storm's destructive force.

Homes, stables, and shops could not withstand the raging waters. The residence of William Sands on Front Street between Franklin and Chestnut collapsed, killing three of his children immediately and sweeping his wife away. The next day, six miles below Reading, searchers discovered her body embedded in mud and rubbish in a cornfield.

The river uprooted and carried homes and businesses downstream. A pig sty holding over two-thousand hogs washed away, killing more than six hundred of the animals. The rest swam ashore, where rescuers dragged them from the water.

The storm claimed Krick & Ringer's workshop, along with timber for boatbuilding and their workmen's tools. Messers, Smith & Fox's Steam Saw-Mill and Planing Machine slid off its foundation and turned sideways on the road. The river carried Frees & Kissinger's storehouse on Water Street downstream, along with seven hundred bushels of salt. John Ritter's Lumber Yard became inundated with the entire stock of lumber carried away. Six feet of water at the Reading Gas Works left much of the city in darkness. At the Seyfert, McManus & Co. Rolling Mill, water stood eight inches high throughout the main building, flooding the storage vaults beneath the floor.

The floodwaters extended up Penn Street to Second Street. Streets on the south side of the city, in lower elevations and closer to the river, fared even worse. Both Franklin and Chestnut Streets were submerged up to Third Street, Bingaman Street to Fourth Street and other roads as far as Fifth Street. Many other buildings throughout the city sustained heavy damage and the destruction of property was rampant. At least eleven residents lost their lives, with more than one hundred buildings destroyed.

As Reading dried out, William and Dinah's skills as sawyers became a critical need. The water-logged wood remnants from damaged or destroyed buildings needed to be cut and hauled away, while construction to repair or rebuild structures required the preparation of new lumber.

"Now cutting wet wood is a little different," William instructed Dinah as they left for their first job.

"You don't say?" Dinah said, allowing a bit of sarcasm to escape in her tone. "I'm sure you will teach me the proper way to do it. You know, I've never sawed wood before."

"I hear the sass in your voice," William said.

Dinah nudged up against her husband. "Go ahead," she said. "I'm just joshing with you."

William shook his head. "Wet wood can be easier to cut because the fibers swell and it doesn't take as much effort to slice through," he explained. "You also get less sawdust and chips. But you have to be careful about splinters and tears. It might be harder to cut a straight line."

"My guess is they'll haul away most of this wood to burn anyway," Dinah said. "So a straight line might not be so important."

"I'd venture to say you're probably right about that," William agreed. "Just be careful."

"I always am," Dinah said. "I had a good teacher. He seems good at reminding me of that."

For the next several months, the two sawyers worked long, hard hours as they made their small contribution to rebuilding the city of Reading. Though they were paid well – earning more than their usual salaries - neither wished for such a catastrophe to strike again. The cost of life and property was far too high. The price the city and her fellow residents paid particularly affected Dinah.

"William," she said one day, "I think we should donate some of the money we're earning to the church so they can help those folks who lost so much in the storm."

William looked at his wife as though her head had exploded. "You know," he tried to argue, "we can certainly use the money ourselves. We barely scrape by on most days."

Dinah nodded knowingly. "That may be true," she agreed. "But we are scraping by. Some of these people lost everything they had. They are far worse off than us."

William began to speak, then recognized the resolute expression on Dinah's face. He knew he would not change her mind. "Well then," he said, "I guess we'll be making a donation to the church. Help those in need. Had that in mind all along."

William looked up to Heaven with a smirk.

I hope you're pleased, he thought, sending a message to the Lord, who chose not to answer. William, however, thought he gleaned a smile in the clouds.

CHAPTER 29
'LIJ

1850

"About 21 years ago my brother 'Lij, who was then roving about the country came to see me at Reading. He didn't say where he came from or where he was going."

Dinah Clark in 1871

By her own account, Dinah had two brothers and a half-sister. She knew little about them and assumed *"they were sold out."* Clearly, owners discouraged their slaves from forming close ties with any family members.

But Dinah saw *"Lij,"* presumably short for Elijah one more time, long after she left the Hiester farm. Dinah just finished cleaning up after her midday dinner, a tradition she maintained on Sundays following church services. After eating his meal, William had gone out to complete some chores and visit with a friend. The girls played outside. Dinah worked leisurely, enjoying the solitary quiet.

She heard a knock on the door, a rare occurrence at her Hinnershitz Alley home.

"Now who in the world could that be?" she said and opened the latch. "William shouldn't be getting home just yet. And in any event, he doesn't knock, not unless he's had too much to drink and knows he deserves a whooping."

Dinah opened the door and inspected her visitor. Outside stood a middle-aged African American man, perhaps a few years older than her.

"Can I help you?"

"Dinah?" the man asked. "Dinah Clark? Used to be Dinah Bell?"

"Yes," she answered suspiciously, studying the man carefully. "How did you know that?"

"Don't you recognize me?"

"No, not at all. Should I?"

"Yes," the man finally said, "because I'm your brother, Dinah. I'm 'Lij."

Dinah took a moment to absorb this unexpected information. "Elijah?" she said. "Good Lord above, why, I haven't seen you in, what . . ."

"About forty years," 'Lij said. "Forty long years. We were still very young."

"Oh, my goodness," Dinah said, and the two siblings gave each other a long embrace. "Come in, let me get you something to eat and drink. You shouldn't be standing out there in the cold."

Dinah served some biscuits and coffee, and the brother and sister engaged in a long conversation about the years since their separation. "I haven't seen you since Mister Seltzer bought me," Dinah said. "What became of you after that?"

'Lij paused, considering his answer. "Soon after you left, I took off from the farm and made sure they never found me," 'Lij said. "I've been travelling ever since. I try not to stay in one place for too long. It's safer that way."

Gabriel Hiester placed an advertisement in the *Aurora General Advertiser* in 1806 offering a twenty-dollar reward for a runaway named *"Lish."* He described Lish as *"about twenty-five years of age,"* more than a decade older than Dinah, but still within the realm of a possible sibling. Whether 'Lij and Lish represent the same person, history remains silent. More than likely, they are different people, especially since the advertisement describes Lish as a *"mulatto,"* but the possibility still remains. The early Nineteenth Century had no genetic testing available.

"Where have you all travelled?" Dinah asked.

"Everywhere I can," 'Lij answered, somewhat evasively. "I've been all throughout the northern states and even Canada. I don't go into the South, though. The South is no place for a colored man. I was a slave once and I have no desire to be one again."

"What brings you back to Reading, of all places, after all these years?"

"Well, old Gabriel Hiester is long gone, so I suspect no one is looking for me anymore," 'Lij said with a smile, "and I wanted to see if I could track down any of my family. You were the only one I found."

"How in the world did you find me?" Dinah asked. "I was sold, I married, I changed my name, and I've moved I can't count how many times."

"No matter all that, you aren't hard to locate," 'Lij laughed. "Everyone knows the colored woman sawyer who cuts wood all across the city. You are the talk of the town."

Dinah smiled with some embarrassment, then considered all those from her childhood she had not seen in decades.

"I lost track of everyone as soon as I left the farm," Dinah admitted. "I had no time to worry about finding them again and no way of doing it if I could. I'm glad you made the effort. Where will you be going to next?"

"Oh, here and there," 'Lij said, maintaining his air of secretiveness. "It's getting colder, so likely not any further north until spring. Those winters in Maine and Vermont are wicked. I've had snow nearly up to my neck more than once. But I always find somewhere to go. People need extra hands for the fall harvest, so I reckon I'll be busy soon enough. But I won't stay around here much longer, just in case."

'Lij visited Dinah for several hours, but indicated he needed to leave well before nightfall. Where he planned on going and how he would get there—by foot, by train, by canal boat, or by horse—'Lij would not say.

'Lij met Hannah and Mary Ann and the three joined in an animated conversation. The girls had never met a real aunt or uncle before now and remained fascinated by 'Lij's many travel adventures and anecdotes. William finally returned home an hour after 'Lij had arrived and they exchanged pleasantries.

"I never met anyone before now who knew Dinah when she was a child," William said.

"Oh, she was a rascal, that one," 'Lij said playfully. "Always in some sort of trouble. I bailed her out many a time. Had to go looking for her more than once."

"Well," William concluded. "That hasn't changed. She's still the same."

"Now William," Dinah said. "Don't you be telling no tall tales to my brother."

The three laughed. Eventually, 'Lij said he needed to leave for his next destination, wherever that may be. Before he left, he hugged his sister tightly.

"Now you take care of yourself and keep me in your prayers," he said. "I'll be all right wherever I end up."

A few minutes later, 'Lij slipped out the door and down the path of Hinnershitz Alley. Dinah lost sight of him as he approached Tenth Street and turned right toward Penn. She never saw him or any of her other siblings again.

CHAPTER 30
THE DEATH OF WILLIAM CLARK

1851

William Clark rose early for work as he usually did and left home at dawn. This day, however, ended far differently than any other. He never returned to Hinnershitz Alley. In an instant, Dinah's life changed dramatically.

In 1850, the census worker listed William as a sixty-one-year-old laborer. Just like Dinah, he was marked as unable to read or write. This was the same census that listed Dinah Clark as "Diana," age forty-eight. As with many other enslaved or indentured people where official documentation was scarce or non-existent, we will never know the full truth of their lives. Dinah's and William's ages may or may not have been correct.

William, presumably sixty-two or sixty-three by now, had performed hard labor his entire life. Combined with whatever other vices his body endured throughout that time eventually took its toll. William had suffered physical ailments over the past several years, reportedly badly enough to be disabled. But recently, he felt well enough to work once again.

Dinah was still home, preparing to leave for her own job, when she heard hard, desperate knocks repeatedly from her door. She opened it to find a young African American woman who lived a block over from her own home, heaving frantically with emotion.

"Dinah," the woman blurted between deep breaths, "your husband is laying on the road. I don't think he's breathing. Come quick."

"Oh Lord help me," Dinah answered in sudden distress and looked up hoping for his intercession. "I'm coming, William. Wait for me. I will be right there."

Dinah shot out of the house, leaving the door open behind her. She ran as fast as she could and found her husband two blocks away, lying flat on his back, his tools splayed on the ground around him. She bent down and shook him violently, with no response.

"What are you doing, William?" Dinah asked desperately. "You promised you would be home for dinner. You can't be sleeping in the middle of the street. You have work to do. You're causing quite the ruckus laying here like that. Look at the crowd you're drawing."

William did not move no matter how hard Dinah tried to rouse him. After a few minutes where William remained unresponsive, Dinah's mind finally wrapped itself around the realization that her husband had died.

"Oh William," Dinah said despondently as her body wilted beside him. "You have left me all alone. What will I do without you? You set me free and ever since, I have been by your side. We have always depended on each other to find our way."

Dinah sat next to the body of her husband and openly wept. A few folks came by to offer support, but she proved inconsolable. It took some time before Dinah finally composed herself enough to stand up and consider the next steps. Suddenly, her world felt much more chaotic and uncontrolled. She somehow needed to pull herself together. She could not continue to lie in the street with her dead husband making a spectacle of both of them. Nothing would bring him back.

As she slowly stood, Dinah realized she had to worry about both the immediate present and the not-too-distant future. She had to provide a proper burial for her husband even with little money to spend. Looking further, William had served as the primary breadwinner for the Clark family. Dinah would now have to shoulder that burden herself, redoubling her efforts as both a laborer and a homemaker.

Before Dinah could consider all the consequences of William's passing, she needed to take care of William's last rites. As it turned out, that became a somewhat tumultuous affair. Dinah could hardly afford a proper funeral and burial, so she found a white board and delivered it to George Durell, a nearby painter. She asked that a poem be painted on the board, and an attorney, John Richards, who had his office on the floor above the painter, obliged.

"Here lies the body of William Clark;
His soul was white though his skin was dark;
And when the Arch Angel cries: Who's there
He'll find him right side with care."

"Now Dinah," the attorney said. "This is too small for a headstone. I'll work with Mr. Durell to have a larger one made."

Richards fulfilled that promise and worked with Durell to complete a larger board. The painter added some decorative lines and set it aside to dry. Both John Richards and George Durell appeared to have acted in good faith.

Dinah eventually placed the board at William's grave at her beloved Bethel A.M.E. Church's graveyard on Tenth Street. The board remained there for some time, but not without attracting a level of controversy. Dinah may not have recognized the inherently racist tone of the poem as perceived by some viewers. Other African Americans, however, did and brought it to her attention.

"Some of the colored people said that they never heard of a piece of poetry like it on a gravestone," she recollected later, *"and made some ugly remarks about it."*

Either the comments swayed Dinah's opinion or perhaps, unable to read, she never fully understood the words on the board in the first place. In any case, Dinah soon pulled the board out of the ground in the graveyard and took it home.

"I'll put this board where it deserves," she said angrily and started a fire in her stove. "Let's see what that John Richards thinks of this. It's not fair that he takes advantage of a poor colored widow like this."

Dinah shoved the board into the stove, allowing it to burn. She used the fire to make that day's dinner for her and her daughters.

"I didn't think it was very nice of John Richards putting those words on," she concluded. *"I told him that if he didn't repent for every letter that he put on that board he would go to hell."*

Dinah's odyssey with William Clark's burial, however, ultimately had a happy ending.

"Old Mister Stricker made a nice marble head-stone for me," she said, *"for which I paid him two dollars, and he put on the age of my husband, and the time he went to Heaven."*

·   ·   ·

Williams' death marked a life-changing event in Dinah's life. William had pulled Dinah from slavery and had been her constant companion since she became a free woman. In addition to cutting wood himself and carrying coal for clients, William had taught Dinah how to work as a sawyer. He had provided many of the tools she needed to survive. Despite whatever vices William may have possessed, Dinah owed much of what she knew to her husband.

"You left me too soon, William Clark," Dinah would often say. "I could always depend on you to walk alongside me wherever I would go. Now I must travel alone until I see you again one day in Heaven."

After William's untimely death, Dinah intensified her efforts to support herself and children. She could no longer take time off rationalizing that William's work would cover their bills. She accepted any jobs available, including performing housework as well as the heavy labor of whitewashing, carrying coal and, of course, cutting wood. The tasks of a sawyer remained her favorite job, and she wandered from the shopping district in center city to the homes of her well-known clients where she sawed and split kindling to use for heating, cooking, and baking. Though she never sought fame, she became a fixture on the streets of Reading.

CHAPTER 31
A SINGLE MOTHER AND WORKING WOMAN

1852

Dinah had little time to grieve. Her family needed to be fed and other expenses paid, whether or not she had the money to pay for them. For the first time, Dinah stood as head of the household in every way. She could no longer lean on William for support.

Dinah accepted any type of work offered if she could fit it into her schedule. Her pay varied with the task performed, but she always expressed gratitude to her clients. Her friendly demeanor and hard work, along with her unusual profession for a woman, earned her the respect and confidence of people across the city.

"Good morning, Mrs. Buch," Dinah began a typical day. "What can I do for you today?"

"Nice to see you again," her client responded. "There's so much to be done here. These children are hellions."

"I understand that," Dinah responded. "Seems to be the job of children. I had challenges with my own when they were younger. When they misbehave, they don't seem to listen no matter how loud you yell. But when it comes to dinner, their hearing is clear as a bell."

"I have no idea where it comes from," Mrs. Buch continued. "They must get it from their father's side. I've been told he was a bit wild when he was young."

"Most men are," Dinah said, providing what reassurance she could. "Let's see if we can get things back on track. How can I help?"

Mrs. Buch led Dinah through the home, and together, the two women conquered both the housework and the rambunctious children. Dinah would repeat a version of those events in various homes throughout the city, building both a reputation for hard work but also one of creating an easy rapport with those who hired her.

Dinah not only did jobs with her own customers, but she let William's former clients know she was more than willing to take on his work. Some accepted her offer, having heard of Dinah's skills from her late husband. However, others expressed the familiar refrain that a woman could not competently perform a "man's job." Slowly, however, Dinah erased those concerns and cobbled together enough assignments to support herself and her family.

"They don't think I can cut wood the way a man can," Dinah muttered in defiance. "I'll show them a man would be hard pressed to keep up with my pace."

Later in life, Dinah expressed her gratitude to the many Reading residents who provided her the opportunity to maintain her humble lifestyle.

"A good many of the people of Reading have been kind to me and helped me along," she said. *"There is Mrs. Judge Banks, Mrs. J. Glaney Jones (now dead), Mrs. Wm. McIlvain, Mrs. Jacob Schumucker, Mrs. Samuel Buch, Mrs. John Ritter (now dead), Mrs. Aaron Ritter, Mrs. Moers, the stonecutter's wife, Mrs. Isaac McHose, Mrs. Leinbach, the preacher's wife, Mrs. F.S. Boas, Mrs. Jacob Livingood, Mrs. Judge Hagenman, Mrs. Lauman, Mrs. Henry Van Reed, Mrs. Frank Whiskeyman, Mrs. Kitty Gehr, and other that I could name if you would give me a little time."*

Sometime along the way, Dinah's daughter, Mary Ann, married for a short time then eventually moved back in with her mother. Mary Ann had married David Brown, who ran a barber shop in town. However, Mary Ann became nearly blind and, at some point and could not regularly leave the house safely. Whatever happened between Mary Ann and her husband, Dinah never fully revealed. But no matter the circumstances, Mary Ann left

David Brown and returned to Hinnershitz Alley. Dinah attributed Mary Ann's condition to a form of cancer. Even if true, Mary Ann more likely also suffered from diabetic blindness or a similar condition.

"My daughter Mary Ann has had scrofulous cancer in her face and eyes eleven years ago, and she is nearly blind," Dinah explained. *"She suffers a great deal at night–more than a brute. She can't go out of the house and she is in very needy circumstances."*

Dinah also appeared to have taken a dim view of Mary Ann's husband and his lack of support for his daughter.

"Her husband has a barber shop somewhere in town, but business is slack and he can't support her as she ought to be supported," she said.

Other sources, however, did not take as unfavorable a view of Mary Ann's estranged husband. A *Reading Times* article in 1872, lauded Brown as a *"Tonsorial Artist . . .quite dapper in appearance, is excessively polite, and very voluble of tongue."* Clearly, Dinah did not share the same opinion.

Rain or snow, hot or cold, sun or clouds, Dinah worked six days each week unless the elements absolutely prevented it. That proved a rare occurrence. If Dinah could somehow make it to her appointed place of work, she surely did. Her will and determination became legend as she made her mark across the growing city of Reading.

Dinah continued to use the grandiose Mansion House at the peak of its glory as a beacon for her daily workload. Many of Reading's wealthier families lived in close proximity to this center city landmark, and much of Dinah's work fanned in every direction from that location. Though Dinah may have never actually entered the Mansion House, it served as a guidepost as she balanced her work and family obligations as best she could. In the process, she became a fixture in the city's landscape and perhaps the most well-known African American woman in the region.

CHAPTER 32
FROZEN

1852

Dinah had witnessed many cold winter periods throughout her life, and she had worked through most of them. But few stretches matched the days in the middle of January in 1852. Dinah awoke early and felt the chill permeate through the house. She fed the heating appliance to provide some much-needed warmth, but no matter how much she stoked the flames, the small unit failed to fully combat the frosty temperature.

"What in the world?" Dinah wondered. "Just how cold is it outside?"

She moved toward the front door, turning the latch lock and cracking it open. Immediately, a harsh wind blew both her and the door back, with a brutal chill pouring inside. Snow and ice swirled through the air and Dinah struggled to force the door closed once again.

"Oh, my sweet Jesus," she cried. "William must be testing the Lord's patience something awful. Didn't I tell him in life he needed to listen to God's will? He better listen harder before we all freeze to death."

Despite the frigid conditions, Dinah still prepared herself to work that day and boldly face the severe winter conditions. She slowly ventured outside toward her intended destination. But even Dinah's resolve could not overcome nature's fury. Howling winds blew across the city, making sub-zero temperatures even more intolerable. A mixture of snow and sleet whipped the landscape, stinging the faces of anyone who dared to venture outside. Dinah soon realized that even if she reached her job site for the day, she could accomplish little work. The storm had virtually paralyzed the city.

Reluctantly defeated, Dinah turned and returned home. By then, Mary Ann had awoken and lay under a blanket in a semi-panic.

"Momma, it's so cold," she wailed. "I can hardly stand it."

"Yes, it is freezing, my child," Dinah acknowledged. "And it's far worse outside. I'm not going anywhere today. We're going to have to button up as best we can and stay warm. The cold goes right through your bones."

January 1852 sent a blanket of frigid temperatures across the northeastern United States. Residents in Delaware reported temperatures that dipped to minus twenty-five degrees Fahrenheit. The Delaware River reportedly froze over, allowing residents to walk over a body of water usually used as a major shipping channel. If the Delaware had frozen, surely tributaries such as the Schuylkill River that bordered Reading experienced the same fate.

Except for the most critical emergencies, outdoor work came to a grinding halt. The freezing water prevented firefighters from effectively combating even dangerous fires. Many homes lacked proper insulation, so residents struggled to keep warm even indoors. Streets and sidewalks became blanketed with ice that stubbornly did not thaw.

Despite these obstacles, Dinah ventured outside and headed to work whenever possible. She really had no other choice. Potentially sitting out weeks of frigid weather leaving her with no income did not constitute an acceptable option. Perhaps the only nod she gave to the severe weather was that she performed mostly indoor domestic chores. Those didn't pay as well, but it provided at least some level of income.

"I'm going to pray the Good Lord stops being angry and sends us warmer weather," she told Mary Ann. "I told your father to stop annoying Him. I know how William can be. I lived with him for years."

"Do you really blame Poppa for this?" Mary Ann asked doubtfully.

"Of course I do," Dinah said. "Who else would be up there that could cause such a stir? I'm going to pray as long and as hard as I can and tell William to behave himself in between my prayers."

"Well, if you think that helps, Momma. There's not much else you could do anyway. I don't think even you can control the weather."

Dinah glanced over at her daughter, a tear welling up in her eye.

"I miss him so, your father," Dinah said. "There are days I still stare at that front door and expect he'll be walking through it at any moment, prop his saw in the corner, and wrap me in his arms."

"I know, Momma," Mary Ann said. "I miss him too. He was a good husband and a good father."

God eventually heeded Dinah's petitions, not regarding returning William's return, but in providing more temperate conditions. Dinah proclaimed a prayer of thanks the day she mounted her sawbuck on her shoulders once again. Wood had grown in short supply as the city's residents burned anything they could to keep warm. Dinah's talents as a sawyer were never in higher demand. For Dinah, it served as the only benefit to the frigid temperatures she and Mary Ann endured in that long winter.

CHAPTER 33
WILLIAM LEE

June 1853

Not surprisingly in her travels, Dinah Clark attracted the attention of other men following the death of her husband. Dinah may have grown older and a life of hard labor made her less lithesome than in her younger years. But her outgoing personality and her fearlessness in crossing traditional boundaries of race and sex surely drew notice.

Dinah eventually met a man named William Lee, who labored in the local iron industry. Perhaps he worked as a sawyer, much like Dinah and her late husband. It's likely both William and Dinah felt the pangs of loneliness. They quickly developed a relationship and married soon thereafter. Perhaps too soon, as it turned out, because things did not go as planned.

·   ·   ·

"Now that we are married," William Lee said to Dinah in a harsh tone, "You listen to me and me alone. And to start, those children from your first husband have no need to come around here. We don't need them anymore."

Dinah looked at her new husband in utter astonishment. "They're my children too!" she said defiantly. "I bore each and every one of them. I know that for a fact. I was there."

"That don't matter none," William said. "You are married to me now and I am not the father to any of them. What happened before is of no consequence to me. You do what I say. I'm the boss of this house."

Dinah had taken much throughout her days on Earth, but this proclamation drew a line she would not cross. She had lived this life before and had left it behind. Dinah had promised herself long ago she would never go back. She stood up straight and glared and William.

"I was a slave once," she said with conviction. "I will not be a slave to no man again. If that's the way you feel, you can be the boss of yourself. It sounds to me like you need a stern talking to anyway. If you can kick yourself in your rear end, that may help, though I doubt you have enough sense for it to do any good."

Dinah turned and walked out the door and returned to her home on Hinnershitz Alley. William Lee never saw her again.

•   •   •

Most details of Dinah's second marriage have disappeared from history. *The Berks and Schuylkill Journal* reported on June 25, 1853, that *"Dinah Clark, widow of William Clark of Reading, married William Lee of Birdsboro Ironworks. David Medary, Esq., alderman of Reading, officiated."* Undoubtedly, Dinah felt the financial burden from the loss of her first husband and perhaps found this marriage a potential path to a more comfortable life.

But something turned amiss quickly. Dinah never changed her Clark surname (or if she did, quickly turned it back) and the marriage dissolved almost immediately. Later in life, she had little to say about these events in her life.

"I married a second time," she recalled. *"My second husband, whose name was Leo, didn't like my first husband's children, and he and I couldn't agree, and so I didn't live with him."*

Was *"Leo"* a nickname based on William Lee's last name, one that differentiated him from Dinah's first husband, William Clark? Likely, but another small detail that remains a mystery. William Lee represented only a brief moment in Dinah's colorful life. It was a moment, however, that showed her devotion to her children and her commitment to stand on her own. Slavery had irretrievably damaged and strengthened her at the same time. She used that resolve she had gained to survive and move through life's challenges. She would never turn back.

CHAPTER 34
THE TOWN NEWS

1855

Dinah arrived at the stately home on Walnut Street, her sawyer equipment slung over both shoulders. She had worked for the Kline family for several years and they had always treated her kindly. Dinah saw an uneven but substantial pile of wood of various shapes and sizes already stacked on the curb waiting for her to perform her handiwork.

Mrs. Kline stepped out of the house and walked toward Dinah as she set up her woodcutting equipment.

"Good morning, Dinah," the plump middle-aged woman said. "It's good to see you again."

"Likewise, Mrs. Kline," Dinah said, smiling. "Looks like I have quite a bit of wood to cut today."

"Indeed, and there's more in the back that we haven't even brought out yet," the homeowner said. "You know Mr. Kline. Always involved in some project or another. I swear he wastes more wood than he uses. I'm still not sure if he ever finishes any of the things he starts."

Dinah nodded, sharing a smile with Mrs. Kline. "Men will do what they do," she said. "You can't change them, no matter how hard you try."

"No denying that," Mrs. Kline agreed. "What is new with you?"

"Not much with me," Dinah answered. "Life is slow in Hinnershitz Alley. But in this town, there's always a buzz. Hard to keep up with all the news with everything going on."

"Really?" the woman asked, clearly inviting elaboration. "What have you heard?"

"Well, you know that new construction on Washington Street?" Dinah continued. "I hear they will be building a new hotel, with all the latest accommodations."

"You don't say?" Mrs. Kline said. "I thought there were quite enough hotels in town already."

"You would think so," Dinah agreed. "But the city officials say this is a growing town. Everyone wants to come to Reading and do business. Or at least that's what they claim. I do see more people on the street these days, that's for certain."

Mrs. Kline chuckled. "I suppose that is true," she agreed. "I haven't seen Mrs. Templin in quite some time. Have you? I know you've worked for her on occasion."

"Yes," Dinah said. "I saw her just the other week. It's no wonder you haven't met up with her recently. She has a fierce case of the gout. Can hardly walk. I had to help her up the steps. She suffers terribly and has to raise her foot every time she gets inside and sits down."

"Oh, that's too bad."

"And her grandchildren don't help things," Dinah continued. "Their momma brings the twin boys over. They're quite the rascals. Run all over the house tearing things up along the way. Never pick up after themselves, no matter how often you tell them."

"I'm sure Mrs. Templin doesn't appreciate that," Mrs. Kline said. "I know she likes to keep her house very tidy."

"Yes, she does," Dinah said. "I believe her gout goes all the way up to her face when those two arrive. She turns all red. I clean up as best as I can before I leave on most days. But as fast as I straighten up one room, those children rip apart another. I hope their mother gives them a good talking to when they get home, but if she does it doesn't seem to do any good."

Mrs. Kline smiled. "I'm glad my children are passed that stage," she said. "What else is going on about town?"

"Let me see. Did you hear about the new shop on Fifth Street?"

"No," Mrs. Kline said. "Tell me all about it . . ."

Dinah and Mrs. Kline went on for some time. A bit later, Mr. Kline looked out the front window and watched his wife and Dinah continue their conversation. "Now what could those two spend so much time cackling about?" he asked himself and shook his head. "I guess Dinah provides all the gossip. My wife always likes to be in the know, and Dinah seems to be the best reporter in town."

Mr. Kline turned and went about his chores. "That's all the better for me," he reasoned. "If she's talking to Dinah, she doesn't have time to check to see what I'm doing." Mr. Kline had many more projects that would waste much more wood. Dinah always had steady work as long as he possessed time, tools, and lumber.

Later that day, Dinah had moved onto a smaller job when another of her acquaintances stopped to greet her.

"Good day, Dinah," Mrs. Rushton said. "I hope you are doing well."

"I am, thank you," Dinah replied. "I'm always appreciative of the work, you know that."

"I'm always thankful for your help," Mrs. Rushton replied.

The two ladies exchanged pleasantries for another minute or two when Mrs. Rushton changed the subject. "Did you hear about poor Mister Gaston?" she said. "He had a stroke the other day and can't speak or walk. He's laid up in dreadful distress."

"Oh, that is a terrible shame," Dinah said. "He's a very nice man. I've done work for him on several occasions. I will keep him at the top of my prayers."

"He needs them," Mrs. Rushton said. "The doctors don't know if he'll ever recover. I'm sure his family will appreciate any good thoughts."

The two spent a few more minutes ruing the bad luck of Mister Gaston before turning to other points of interest. Dinah cataloged Mister Gaston's condition in her memory. It served as one more tidbit of a compendium of information she maintained about the city and its inhabitants. She had learned that skill early in her life. As Dinah worked through the streets of Reading, she relayed a collection of anecdotes, ranging from personal accounts to true news about progress in Reading. Through her years, Dinah developed many relationships and proved as reliable as and often faster than the daily newspaper in conveying the growing town's happenings. Many of her acquaintances in Reading valued her nearly as much for her knowledge of current events as they did for her ability to cut wood at a prodigious pace. Despite her inability to read or write, Dinah earned a reputation for her intelligence as much as her ability to complete hard work. She proved time and again that she was much more than at first appeared.

"It's a wonder the newspaper doesn't hire her," more than one husband said to his wife. "She knows more than all of their reporters put together."

"They probably would if she wasn't a colored woman," the wife replied. "You know how they are about such things."

"That's true," the husband acknowledged. "This town probably isn't ready for that."

By now, Dinah was in her sixties yet showed no signs of slowing down. She believed her faith in God and her dedication to her family kept her strong and vibrant. Dinah had no plans to age gracefully. She continued her daily life throughout the city, cutting wood and sharing information in equal parts.

CHAPTER 35
NINETEENTH CENTURY MEDICINE

1857

Dinah arrived at the Schmucker residence just after dawn fully ready to begin work on the impressive pile of wood awaiting her. Boards and tree limbs, broken furniture and leftover construction materials all lay in a pile. Dinah figured this would make up a full day's work. In fact, she would have to hustle to complete the task in that timeframe. The Schmuckers would have more than enough wood to burn when she finished.

The young couple had two small children, a girl and a boy, with yet another on the way. "Mrs. Schmucker has her hands full," Dinah said, and she laid down her equipment and set up her workstation. "I'm glad those days are behind me. I can't fathom chasing children around the house anymore."

As Dinah proceeded, the door burst open, and Mrs. Schmucker ran outside and looked desperately at the sawyer. "Dinah!" she cried, "Please come inside. My poor Nathaniel is dreadfully sick with a fever. I need your help."

Dinah did not hesitate. She dropped her tools and followed the young mother into the well-kept home. In the parlor, she found the five-year-old boy lying on the sofa, shivering under a wool blanket with sweat dripping from his forehead.

Dinah pulled down the blanket and inspected Nathaniel more closely. She saw a bright red rash covering much of his body. She touched it for a moment and felt a rough, sandpaper-like surface.

"This boy has scarlet fever," she said matter-of-factly. "You need to keep him warm and cover him with bacon grease."

"Bacon grease?" Mrs. Schmucker asked skeptically. "Are you sure that will work?"

"That's what I always did for my children," Dinah said. "Hopefully, he'll get better in a week or so if you keep after him. He's dreadfully sick, that is for certain."

"Will my daughter catch this?"

"I've never found scarlet fever to be catching," Dinah said. "Though I doubt the boy will want much company anyway. Best if she avoids him until he feels better."

While earnest in her assessment, Dinah may not have provided the most sound medical advice. Scarlet fever was indeed highly contagious and one of the leading causes of death in children in the Nineteenth Century. In addition, no definitive research has ever shown bacon grease to be an effective remedy. It's unlikely anyone has ever conducted such a study.

However, some strains of scarlet fever had demonstrated less potency as the century progressed, increasing survival rates significantly. Physicians at the time could prescribe little more than fluids to ease its symptoms. The development of antibiotics eventually provided doctors with an effective remedy, but fortunately, scarlet fever often heals by itself.

Mrs. Schmucker's husband arrived later that day and insisted on calling a physician, but in truth, he provided little additional relief, urging bed rest, sponging Nathaniel with cool water for the fever, and gargling with salt water for a sore throat. While the doctor confirmed Dinah's diagnosis, he deferred judgement on the efficacy of bacon grease.

Fortunately, Nathaniel recovered, though he smelled of breakfast for much of the next seven days. He resisted eating bacon for many months afterwards and showed a dislike for it throughout the rest of his life.

Dinah offered various medical advice during her interview with the *Reading Eagle* late in her life, much of it of dubious effectiveness.

"The best cure for scarlet fever is to keep the children warm and grease them with bacon," Dinah said. *"Scarlet fever is not catching—that is my idea. Small-pox, these are things that are catching. When I had the small-pox, I used a little*

sweet oil, and cold water out of the pump, and kept my face greased with hog's lard. Mumps and measles are easily cured. For the measles use saffron tea, and for the mumps take the children and rub their throats against the pigtrough. The doctors don't know much about these diseases, and in this respect the old women have the advantage of them."

Folk remedies served as common medicinal practices in the Nineteenth Century. Sarah Hardy, the mother of Enoch Sanders who supposedly lived with Dinah for a time, shared some of her own wisdom in a separate newspaper interview with her later in life:

"My children never had the scarlet fever. When they got the croup I prepared onion tea for them—made of onions and sugar and molasses boiled into a syrup. For measles I gave them sage tea and kept them warm, for mumps I rubbed them with goose grease, for the itch I boiled poison duck root in fat and greased the children with that, and for whooping cough I made tea of hornets' nests."

Those must have been interesting conversations between Doctors Clark and Hardy. Fortunately for all of us, the recipe for hornets' nest tea has not survived into the Twenty-First Century.

CHAPTER 36
THE PHOTOGRAPHER

1860

The art and science of photography was born in the Nineteenth Century and experienced rapid growth. Louis-Jacque-Mande Daguerre, a French artist and scientist, invented the first widely used photographic process called the daguerreotype. Introduced to the world in 1839, daguerreotype photographers spread quickly. By the 1850s, hundreds of artists offered lavish portrait studios in major cities throughout the United States. Daguerre's groundbreaking invention led his name to be one of seventy-two names inscribed on the Eiffel Tower during its construction in the 1880s.

Daguerreotypes offered both advantages and significant limitations. Photographers created their images on a polished silvered copper plate that offered incredible detail. But each image was unique with no easy way to reproduce them. Additionally, exposure times were extraordinarily long, requiring subjects to remain still throughout the capturing of the image.

Henry Fox Talbot and Frederick Scott Archer became early pioneers in developing new photographic processes. Talbot introduced his "calotype" process in 1841 that produced images on exposed paper. This process reduced the exposure time to "only" a minute or two for subjects in bright sunlight. The calotype negatives made it possible to produce as many prints as desired by simple contact printing. However, calotype prints tended to not have the pinpoint sharpness of daguerreotypes.

Archer's collodion process required photographic material to be coated, exposed, and developed within a short span of about fifteen minutes. This required the photographer to haul a portable darkroom if working in the field, a common site in the aftermath of battles during the Civil War. The collodion process used either a wet or dry form, but the dry form required significantly increased exposure times. Because those times could be several minutes long, the use of the dry collodion process was used almost exclusively for landscape photography.

By the beginning of the Civil War, paper prints had nearly entirely replaced daguerreotypes. Because of this, the Civil War became one of the first photographically documented conflicts in history and the most extensively covered war of the time. Coverage of the battles attracted a multitude of photographers, including Matthew Brady, Timothy O'Sullivan, Alexander Gardner, and George Barnard. Their work remains revered even today.

One of the lesser-known photographers was Charles A. Saylor, the first active photographer in Reading. When the Civil War commenced, Saylor left to document the conflict, and a partial collection of his work is displayed in the New York Public Library. Before and after the war, Saylor worked in Reading in various locations, primarily on or around Penn Street. He owned and operated the Chas. A. Saylor's City Gallery on the southwest corner of Fifth and Penn Streets for some time. Saylor moved again after that, to the southeast corner of Sixth and Penn Streets over the C.R. Heizmann & Bro. piano and music store (an ambitious entrepreneur, Charles Raymond Hiezmann went on to establish the Penn Hardware Works in 1877, which became a major manufacturing firm in the city). Saylor finally settled in the poshly named New York Gallery–clearly an attempt at borrowing the glamour of the nearby city — at 411 North Sixth Street and became a well-known portrait artist.

By the late 1850s, Dinah Clark had gained some measure of local fame throughout the city. Through some circumstance, perhaps by the intervention of one of her well-intentioned clients, she caught the attention of a photographer. Let's assume that the artist was Charles A. Saylor. The only photograph of Dinah known to exist appears to be unattributed.

Newspapers rarely employed photographers during Dinah's life. Nearly all illustrations were created through meticulously carved engravings. The interview late in her life included no photograph of Dinah, though her portrait accompanied a story printed nearly thirty years after her death. At some point, a photographer convinced Dinah to pose in front of a camera.

· · ·

As Dinah walked through the streets of Reading on her way home one warm afternoon, a smartly dressed young man in his twenties approached her. He took off his hat in greeting and quickly looked her over.

"Mrs. Clark, I presume?" the man said. "I've heard quite a bit about you. My name is Charles Saylor."

"Good day to you, Mr. Saylor," she responded cordially.

"I know this may sound unusual," Saylor continued, "but I was wondering if you might come down to my studio to be photographed."

Dinah looked at Charles Saylor as if he had just landed on Earth from the Moon. In fact, the *New York Sun* published a fictional series of articles in 1835 purportedly claiming discovery of life and an advanced civilization on the Moon. The incident became known as the *"Great Moon Hoax."* Dinah had heard of the commotion the articles had caused and wondered if this was some foul trick in the same vein.

"I can't imagine why anyone would want to see a photograph of a poor working colored woman, Mr. Saylor," Dinah said earnestly. "Even if they did, I would have no money to pay for such a thing."

"No, no, Mrs. Clark, you don't understand," Saylor added hurriedly. "I'm not asking for any payment from you. Just some of your time so I can capture your portrait."

Dinah paused and studied the young man, attempting to determine his true intentions. She could find no duplicity in his mannerisms. "You really want to take a photograph of me?" Dinah finally asked. "Why would you want to do a thing like that?"

"Indeed, I do," Saylor said in an enthusiastic tone. "I would like you to pose for a portrait for posterity. You've become quite well known here in town. Would the day after tomorrow suit you? Maybe come by my studio on your way to work and we'll photograph you with your sawyer's attire."

Dinah considered the offer while closely studying the photographer. He appeared earnest and well meaning, though in Dinah's mind, perhaps a bit mad considering his offer.

"I can do that," Dinah agreed. "I've seen your shop on Penn Street."

"That is wonderful," Saylor said. "Is nine o'clock too late? I know that may cut into your day, but it takes some time to set up my equipment."

"I will make that work," Dinah said. "Thank you."

As the young man walked away, Dinah continued on her way, shaking her head in disbelief. "What will they think of next?" she wondered. "Me in a photograph."

• • •

Dinah arrived at the appointed time and day. Saylor greeted her and spent several more minutes checking his camera. He finally positioned Dinah in front of a simple setting lacking any flourishes of his more ornate portraits. He wanted to capture the real Dinah – one that lived apart from the grandeur and opulence of the more wealthy and privileged residents.

Dinah wore a high-waisted skirt and a dark long-sleeved blouse with puffy arms. She had wrapped a tie around her neck, and her well-worn work shoes barely peeked out below her floor-length skirt. A rounded bonnet hid her hair, revealing only her facial features. Her unadorned face showed a woman in her sixties, one with a fierce, quiet internal strength. She had endured much and survived.

As a final touch, her sawbuck rested around her neck and stood behind her, supported by her back. Dinah could pose for a photograph and head directly to work.

As in most portraits of the time, Dinah did not smile. Historians suggest a variety of reasons for a lack of grinning faces on Nineteenth Century portraits, ranging from an epidemic of bad teeth, to long camera exposure times, to folks finding it unnatural to smile in front of a camera, to the mimicking of famous paintings whose subjects rarely smiled. Whatever the cause, Dinah's lips remain closed and her appearance as matter of fact as usual.

"Now this will only take a minute," Saylor told Dinah. "Hold as still as you can."

Dinah remained frozen in place, following directions exactly, an innate instinct she had learned long ago when her life was not her own. Saylor took his photograph, thanked Dinah profusely, and walked her toward the door.

"Now you stop by after work and I'll have a print for you," he said. "Everyone should have a portrait to be remembered by. Perhaps you can hang it on your wall at home."

"I will, Mr. Saylor," Dinah said, the whole time thinking it unlikely she would put a picture of herself in her living quarters.

Why do I need to look at myself? she wondered. *That's what a mirror is for.*

"Thank you for your time and your courtesy."

•   •   •

Dinah came home that day with a copy of the photograph taken by Charles Saylor. She showed it to her daughter with some measure of pride. Mary Ann viewed it as best she could with her poor eyesight. She also did so with a hearty dose of skepticism.

"Now what are we supposed to do with that?" Mary Ann asked. "Like I can't look at you anytime I want without a picture of you staring at me on the wall. Will the photograph check on me when you're not home?"

"Now you hush, girl," Dinah admonished her. "Some people in town thought it would be good if I had a photograph taken of me, so I obliged them."

"Well, I don't see why," Mary Ann said. "Where are they going to see it? They're not going to hang a photograph of you next to the white folks in town. And as far as I know, your picture isn't plastered on the post office wall yet. If it is, I'd go down there and turn you in."

"I don't know what they plan to do with it, but some people thought it important. You don't have to worry about it any longer."

"Well, I won't," Mary Ann said. "You enjoy looking at yourself all you want."

CHAPTER 37
THADDEUS STEVENS

1862

While history credits Abraham Lincoln with leading the fight to abolish slavery, in reality, Lincoln's views evolved over time. Legislators within his own Republican Party significantly influenced Lincoln throughout his presidency. Thaddeus Stevens, a member of the United States House of Representatives from Pennsylvania, became of one of the most vocal leaders of the "Radical Republican" faction and served as a fierce opponent of slavery and discrimination against African Americans. In many ways, Stevens earned credit for serving as "Lincoln's conscience" regarding emancipation. Only in the early Twenty-First Century did Stevens begin to gain the full respect he deserved.

Stevens was born into poverty in Vermont with a club foot that left him with a permanent limp. He moved to York, Pennsylvania in 1814 at age twenty-two to teach at the York Academy following his graduation from Dartmouth College. He continued studying for the bar and moved to Gettysburg in 1816 to open a law office. Stevens served on the Gettysburg borough council and in 1833 was elected to the Pennsylvania House of Representatives.

After accruing debt because of his business interests, Stevens moved his home and law practice to Lancaster in 1842. Soon, he became one of the most successful attorneys in the city and quickly paid off his debts. He also engaged the services of Lydia Hamilton Smith as a housekeeper. Described as a *"mulatto,"* Smith remained with Stevens for the rest of his life. Their relationship has served as the subject of much speculation.

Stevens became active in the Underground Railroad, both defending people believed to be fugitive slaves and helping to coordinate the movement of those seeking freedom. When workers renovated and restored his former home in 2003, they discovered a hidden cistern used to hide escaped slaves attached to the main building by a concealed tunnel. In that respect, Stevens and Dinah's beloved Bethel A.M.E. Church shared a common cause.

Voters in Pennsylvania's Eighth Congressional District elected Stevens to the United States Congress in 1848 and 1850. When the Thirty-First Congress convened in December 1849, he clearly stated his opposition to slavery when he spoke out against the Compromise of 1850 that allowed some United States territories recently gained from Mexico to become slave states.

"This word 'compromise' when applied to human rights and constitutional rights I abhor," he proclaimed.

When the Whig party refused to join him in seeking the repeal of the offensive elements of the Compromise, he left the party and did not run for reelection in 1852. In 1855, he joined the newly formed Republican Party and easily won reelection to Congress in 1858. There, he became one of the staunchest and most persistent anti-slavery voices in the country.

Once Abraham Lincoln won the presidency and the Civil War overtook the country, Stevens and others constantly pushed Lincoln toward a more forceful view regarding emancipation. As historian Fawn Brodie wrote: *"Lincoln seldom succeeded in matching Steven's pace, though both were marching towards the same bright horizon."*

As the war progressed and a Northern victory became inevitable, Stevens came to believe that slavery should not only be abolished, but that African Americans should gain a stake in the South's future by confiscating land from plantation owners and giving it to newly freed men. Even moderate Republicans rejected his proposal as too extreme, preventing its enactment.

•   •   •

In 1862, war raged between the Union and the Confederacy. While the Union had made a significant number of gains in the western states they would never surrender, the eastern theater had proven inconclusive. In the early days of the war, the Confederacy had shown much more resilience than expected. Abraham Lincoln would not release the Emancipation Proclamation, which declared all slaves in rebel states free, until January 1, 1863, though Thaddeus Stevens had promoted that view long before Lincoln's historic document.

Stevens had become a famous, if notoriously polarizing figure, serving as a leading voice for the abolition of slavery. In retrospect, Stevens served as Lincoln's well-lit beacon on the subject, constantly driving him further and further toward freedom and equality. For many northern abolitionists, Stevens stood as a heroic figure unwavering in his convictions. Southerners had a far less positive view of him.

While Stevens represented Lancaster in the United States House of Representatives, a man of his prominence and urgency of message never failed to travel beyond his legislative boundaries. Not surprisingly then, Steven took the short trip from Lancaster to Reading in the spring of 1862, perhaps to campaign for his seat but more likely to spread his anti-slavery message to a friendly audience. The Civil War raged just to the south, but Stevens remained solely focused and adamant in promoting his mission.

Stevens's rally took place at Penn Square at midday in the center of town and attracted a large crowd. Both African American and white citizens attended and warmly welcomed their speaker. Stevens took the stage with some difficulty, but as he peered out onto his enthusiastic audience, his voice found both vigor and vibrancy. His fervent zeal always allowed him to rise to the occasion.

"What an opportunity is presented to this Republic to vindicate her consistency and become immortal," Stevens said. *"The occasion is forced upon*

us, and the invitation presented to strike the chains from four million of human beings, and create them Men; to extinguish slavery on this whole continent; to wipe out, so far as we are concerned, the most hateful and infernal blot that has ever disgraced the escutcheon of man; to write a page in the history of the world whose brightness shall eclipse all the records of heroes and of sages."

The crowd applauded, encouraging Stevens to continue. He gladly obliged, needing little encouragement.

"Prejudice may be shocked, weak minds startled, weak nerves may tremble, but they must hear and adopt it," he proclaimed. *"Those who now furnish the means of war, but who are natural enemies of slaveholders, must be made our allies. Universal emancipation must be proclaimed to all. If slaves no longer raised cotton and rice, tobacco and grain for the rebels, this war would cease in six months. It could not be maintained even if the liberated slaves should not lift a hand against their masters."*

Stevens continued his address, becoming more animated and defiant, much to the delight of the crowd. The legislator considered this task a sacred mission, and he continued his discourse, buoyed by a receptive and enthusiastic crowd. Stevens was determined to achieve emancipation and, even after achieving that goal, he advocated for the expanded rights of freed African Americans.

In the middle of Stevens's speech, Dinah worked her way up the road to her next job. She changed her route in order to avoid most of those in attendance. She had learned to ignore events and happenings that would derail her work. But she paused momentarily and noted the large mixed crowd. That piqued her interest enough to focus on the dynamic speaker to which the crowd responded. She heard the shouts of "freedom" and "emancipation" circle through the audience.

"Emancipation," Dinah said to herself. "Fancy words. I wonder if I will ever get to see such a thing in my lifetime."

Dinah had bore witness to many lives affected by oppression. Besides her own experiences, she had seen firsthand the scars slavery left on those trying to escape. Individuals exploited and families separated and brutalized seared into her memory. She looked down at the scar Major Jones had left on her wrist. She involuntarily winced.

"It seems like such a dream to me," she said softly. "I've never seen a dream come true in my life. I can only hope the Lord sees the wisdom of such a thing and grants all the colored folks the freedom they rightfully deserve."

Dinah moved on, leaving Thaddeus Stevens and the enthusiastic crowd behind. She had work to do, and fancy speeches did not pay the bills. It would take three more years for the Civil War to be decided and "emancipation" to become more than just a fancy word. Dinah would be ready to assist those who needed aid when the time arrived.

CHAPTER 38
POWERLESS

1862

Every person has their flaws and weaknesses, and Dinah proved no different.

Significant evidence suggests that Dinah struggled with alcoholism throughout the years. Several historical guideposts suggest this proved an ongoing issue that disrupted her life on multiple occasions. More than likely, William Clark's untimely death created additional stress for Dinah, which made the lure of alcohol all that more enticing.

On March 13, 1862, David Brown posted a notice in the *Reading Times* that read: *"CAUTION – All persons are hereby cautioned against giving Diana Clark any liquor or money. Persons so doing will be dealt with according to law. DAVID BROWN"*

This takes some unraveling. David Brown had married Dinah's daughter, Mary Ann. But according to Dinah, David had abandoned her daughter when Mary Ann had gotten ill and became nearly blind. Remember, Dinah claimed Mary Ann's *"husband has a barber shop somewhere in town, but business is slack and he can't support her as she ought to be supported."* Clearly, Dinah did not hold her son-in-law in high regard. This notice may put that sentiment in a different light.

Whether David Brown's public pronouncement was motivated by a feud with his mother-in-law or genuine concern for her and his estranged wife, history does not say. But other evidence also suggests that Dinah battled a dependence on liquor for at least part of her life. Those who intervened received Dinah's eternal wrath.

John S. Richards, for example, enjoyed a diverse career. According to an article in the *Reading Eagle* extolling his legacy following his death, he was not only a long-time public servant but also one of Reading's greatest humorists and acknowledged wit. In addition, from an early age, Richard was an apostle of temperance. At age seventeen, he organized weekly meetings of the *"Young Men's Temperance Society of Morgantown,"* near Joanna Furnace. He remained a temperance advocate his entire life.

The *Eagle's* article lauded Richard's many accomplishments, as well as his oversized personality. Richards became the district attorney of Reading in 1849 and later mayor in 1854. In both capacities, he *"proceeded to put his ideas in reference to the liquor traffic in force. He saw that the law was complied with by the proprietors of hotels and saloons and furnished them with the names of persons to whom liquor was not to be sold under the penalty of proceeding against all violators with the view of having their licenses revoked."*

Among the names of Richards's *"Prohibited"* list was Dinah Clark, who was, according to the article *"an Amazon negress and a well-known character of the town, who sawed wood for the support of herself and invalid husband, and who was addicted to drink."*

Allegedly, when Dinah heard her name appeared on Richards's list, she *"invaded"* the office of Mr. Richards and *"demanded to know by what right he had to place such a ban upon her."*

The exchange reportedly became quite violent.

"She was in such a rage that before he could reply she had fired at him a heavy inkstand, a paper weight and other articles that she seized from his office table," the article continued. Knowing Dinah's long years of hard labor, her efforts undoubtedly had significant force behind them, if this indeed occurred.

• • •

"You son of a bitch," Dinah hissed at the object of her scorn. "How dare you sully my good name all throughout the town. I have worked hard to be an upstanding citizen, and you have no right to do such a thing."

"You are a drunk," Richards replied. "In fact, you're probably intoxicated at this very moment. You are an insult to God, and you should ask His forgiveness."

"I'll insult your God," Dinah answered. "My God knows who I am. You have no right to drag me through the mud. More than enough men have done that to me throughout my life. I will not allow you to be another one. I know what you're up to and it has nothing to do with how much I drink. You don't know who you are talking to."

"You should get down on your knees and pray," Richards answered. "Hopefully, God will have mercy and expel the demons from you."

"If you want demons expelled, I'll expel yours right now," Dinah said and moved aggressively toward Richards. "I will ask the Lord for forgiveness later, but first I'll give you the proper thrashing you deserve."

•   •   •

Deciding that discretion served as his best tactic, Richards fled his office while Dinah continued with her path of destruction. The newspaper claimed Dinah smashed the office furniture. When *the redoubtable 'Bully' Lyon endeavored to interfere, she seized the leg of a chair that she had broken and 'went for' 'Bully.' The latter got out of the way just in time.*

William "Bully" Lyon, by the way, served as a city detective and constable in Nineteenth Century Reading, earning a legendary reputation. Despite his conflict with Dinah, he had defied the Fugitive Slave Law and helped enslaved African Americans escape their owners. On one occasion, agents pursued a pair of runaway slaves to Reading, but the slave catchers lost the trail when Lyon turned them away. Lyon had safely hidden the escapees in the old jail cells at Sixth and Chestnut Streets. They remained concealed there in an unlocked cell until it was safe to resume their journey on the Underground Railroad.

None of that mattered to Dinah at the moment. She continued her rampage until *she had given full vent to her anger, when she then sauntered leisurely up Penn street.*

The Eagle pointed out that *"it was Dinah's husband, 'Old Bill Clark,' or 'Black Bill,' as he was commonly known for whom Mr. Richards wrote an epitaph which was printed on the board that was placed above the colored man's grave and which ran somewhat like this:*

Here lies the body of William Clark;
His soul was white, though his skin was dark,
And when old Gabriel asks: 'Who's there?'
He'll find Bill Clark right side up with care."

One might question the accuracy of this report. After all, the description of Dinah is of an *"Amazon negress and well-known character . . .who was addicted to the drink."* The objectivity of the report may be considered suspect, especially in an effusive article expressly written to praise Richards's life. In addition, the controversial epitaph on William Clark's gravestone isn't exactly the same as reported by the *Reading Eagle* in the interview they ran with Dinah. Then there's the obvious–if Dinah and Richards still both held a grudge against each other regarding the gravestone, that could have easily set off this chain of events. This likely also further explains Dinah's antipathy toward Richards even years after this alleged incident. Dinah clearly held grievances throughout her long life, and Richards remained on the top of that list.

But earlier, however, a similar public pronouncement, like the one published by David Brown, had been issued. While William Clark was still alive, advertisements placed in local newspapers by Enoch Sanders, the same Enoch Sanders who aided Dinah in buying her home on Hinnershitz Alley and who preached at Bethel A.M.E. Church, asked alcohol not be provided to Dinah Clark.

If William and Dinah struggled with alcohol, they found no shortage of availability in the city. Reading served as a hotbed of breweries and the introduction of beer-making coincided with the city's commercial and industrial growth. Serving as a center of trade, Reading boasted more than thirty taverns by 1762. Eventually, Reading's breweries ranked as some of the most important commercial manufacturers in the city. Reading became a brewing center as early as 1763. Years later, in 1826, Frederick Lauer established an ale and porter brewery at Third and Chestnut Streets and built a beverage empire over the next several decades. In 1886, the founding of the Reading Brewing Company led to the production of a lager that dominated beer production in Berks County for nearly a century before ceasing operations in 1976. Reading Premium Beer was eventually reborn, produced as a craft beer by Sly Fox Brewing Company. In Dinah's time, beer, wine, and whiskey were all readily available locally. A resident seeking a drink did not have to travel far.

Later in life, Dinah seemed to offer a love-hate relationship with drinking but claimed that she no longer imbibed.

"I used to drink liquor sometimes," she said, *"but I have given that up. Whisky sometimes strengthened me, and sometimes it did not. Liquor in its place is good; but out of its place it is not. A great many people are damaged by it and it destroys families."*

Dinah may have sworn off alcohol and her words suggest she had personal knowledge her drinking caused some damage along the way. But she did not give up all her vices.

"I smoke tobacco," she told the reporter. *"I think it is beneficial to me. Tobacco is good for some people and for some it is not."*

Dinah's tobacco use should not be a surprise. Smoking and chewing tobacco were common in the Nineteenth Century. The American Tobacco Company dominated distribution through the early Twentieth Century after acquiring the rights to a new cigarette rolling machine in 1881. This technology produced four hundred cigarettes each minute and allowed the company to gain a stranglehold on the market.

Dinah may have given up her whiskey, but she never gave up her smokes.

CHAPTER 39
THE EMANCIPATION PROCLAMATION

January 1863

In the midst of the Civil War, news of the Presidential Proclamation spread faster across the land than a shot from a rifle. Once and for all, Abraham Lincoln had clearly delineated the ultimate goal of the conflict.

"By the President of the United States of America:

A Proclamation.

Whereas, on the twenty-second day of September, in the year of our Lord one thousand eight hundred and sixty-two, a proclamation was issued by the President of the United States, containing, among other things, the following, to wit:

'That on the first day of January, in the year of our Lord one thousand eight hundred and sixty-three, all persons held as slaves within any State or designated part of a State, the people whereof shall then be in rebellion against the United States, shall be then, thenceforward, and forever free; and the Executive Government of the United States, including the military and naval authority thereof, will recognize and maintain the freedom of such persons, and will do no act or acts to repress such persons, or any of them, in any efforts they may make for their actual freedom.

"That the Executive will, on the first day of January aforesaid, by proclamation, designate the States and parts of States, if any, in which the people thereof, respectively, shall then be in rebellion against the United States; and the fact that any State, or the people thereof, shall on that day be, in good faith, represented in the Congress of the United States by members chosen

thereto at elections wherein a majority of the qualified voters of such State shall have participated, shall, in the absence of strong countervailing testimony, be deemed conclusive evidence that such State, and the people thereof, are not then in rebellion against the United States."

Now, therefore I, Abraham Lincoln, President of the United States, by virtue of the power in me vested as Commander-in-Chief, of the Army and Navy of the United States in time of actual armed rebellion against the authority and government of the United States, and as a fit and necessary war measure for suppressing said rebellion, do, on this first day of January, in the year of our Lord one thousand eight hundred and sixty-three, and in accordance with my purpose so to do publicly proclaimed for the full period of one hundred days, from the day first above mentioned, order and designate as the States and parts of States wherein the people thereof respectively, are this day in rebellion against the United States, the following, to wit:

Arkansas, Texas, Louisiana, (except the Parishes of St. Bernard, Plaquemines, Jefferson, St. John, St. Charles, St. James Ascension, Assumption, Terrebonne, Lafourche, St. Mary, St. Martin, and Orleans, including the City of New Orleans) Mississippi, Alabama, Florida, Georgia, South Carolina, North Carolina, and Virginia, (except the forty-eight counties designated as West Virginia, and also the counties of Berkley, Accomac, Northampton, Elizabeth City, York, Princess Ann, and Norfolk, including the cities of Norfolk and Portsmouth), and which excepted parts, are for the present, left precisely as if this proclamation were not issued.

And by virtue of the power, and for the purpose aforesaid, I do order and declare that all persons held as slaves within said designated States, and parts of States, are, and henceforward shall be free; and that the Executive government of the United States, including the military and naval authorities thereof, will recognize and maintain the freedom of said persons.

And I hereby enjoin upon the people so declared to be free to abstain from all violence, unless in necessary self-defence; and I recommend to them that, in all cases when allowed, they labor faithfully for reasonable wages.

And I further declare and make known, that such persons of suitable condition, will be received into the armed service of the United States to garrison forts, positions, stations, and other places, and to man vessels of all sorts in said service.

And upon this act, sincerely believed to be an act of justice, warranted by the Constitution, upon military necessity, I invoke the considerate judgment of mankind, and the gracious favor of Almighty God.

In witness whereof, I have hereunto set my hand and caused the seal of the United States to be affixed.

Done at the City of Washington, this first day of January, in the year of our Lord one thousand eight hundred and sixty three, and of the Independence of the United States of America the eighty-seventh.

By the President: ABRAHAM LINCOLN

WILLIAM H. SEWARD, Secretary of State.'"

When President Abraham Lincoln issued the Emancipation Proclamation, many across the country likely viewed it as more of a symbolic gesture than a genuine change. After all, the Battle of Gettysburg, the bloody three-day battle that most historians consider the turning point of the Civil War, would not be fought until more than six months after the proclamation was issued. Until that point, neither the Union nor the Confederacy could clearly claim the advantage. Ultimately, the battle that would in many ways define the future of the United States was fought less than one hundred miles from Reading and Dinah's home.

However, while the Emancipation Proclamation had little or no immediate effect on freeing slaves, its symbolic power proved incalculable. The Proclamation added a moral imperative to the Union's efforts and strengthened the North from both a military and political perspective.

In practical terms, the proclamation also allowed African American men to join the Union Army. Over the next two years, nearly two-hundred-thousand Black men fought against the Confederacy.

•   •   •

At the beginning of the war, most residents of Berks County strongly supported the Union and believed doing so upheld the Constitution of the United States. As soon as President Lincoln issued a plea for support among the Union states, Captain James McKnight and the Ringgold Light Artillery responded via telegram they would *"have ninety men, every one of them expecting to be ordered on duty for the U.S. Service before they leave their guns."*

The following day, the troop received orders to travel by train to Harrisburg as quickly as possible. Captain McKnight delivered more than he promised. He joined one hundred and one men who left Reading at six o'clock in the evening, making the Ringgold Light Artillery one of the first to leave their homes and arrive ready to serve. They had been training for such an eventuality since January 1861. When the attack on Fort Sumter commenced on April 12, 1861, the Ringgold Light Artillery stood ready to respond. A memorial to this intrepid group of men, some of the first defenders of the Union, was dedicated in Reading's City Park on July 1, 1901.

•   •   •

Reading also provided other important resources to the war effort. The Scott Foundry manufactured many of the famed "Rodman" cannons used by the Union Army. Owned by Seyfert, McManus & Company, the foundry formerly served as the Reading Iron & Nail Works. The firm also produced mortars and ammunition for the cannon.

Residents were keenly aware of the cannon production, since the foundry tested their cannons on a testing range near the "Big Reading Dam" on the Schuylkill River. The foundry fired cannon shells directly into the Klapperthal region of Neversink Mountain, where some of the concrete platforms remain. Local lore claims the name "Klapperthal" came from the noise created by the cannons being tested, though historians believe it more likely came from the German word that means "folded valley."

"What in tarnation was that?" Dinah asked in distress the first time she heard a cannon shot in the distance. "I pray to the Lord the rebels haven't come to Reading."

Soon, however, Dinah and the rest of the residents of the city learned to expect the sound of cannon testing in the folded valley. It's lucky for the

Union that the Confederates never attacked Reading, since they likely would have caught the entire town unaware, so accustomed did they become to hear the rumble of firing cannons.

An eight-inch Rodman Gun and forty Columbiad Shells symbolically guard the entrance of Reading's Centre Park, a display arranged by former Congressman Daniel K. Hoch, who had the cannon brought to Reading from an arsenal storage facility.

• • •

For Dinah, the Civil War remained mostly an abstract concept. But the conflict had one direct impact on her that required careful navigation–that, of all things, involved getting paid for her work.

With the outbreak of the war, official United States coins all but disappeared from circulation. Uncertain of the future, citizens hoarded coins in both the North and the South for the value of their copper, silver, and gold. Everyday commerce became increasingly difficult as making change was nearly impossible.

Several solutions of varying effectiveness emerged. In the North, many merchants purchased postage stamps and used them to make change. Naturally, purchasing stamps at the post office soon became more difficult as supplies quickly disappeared. In addition, the post office rarely bought back stamps from those who received them in commerce, and the stamps' gummed back often turned them into sticky piles of unusable paper. Not designed for everyday commerce, stamps failed miserably in their makeshift role.

Yet another solution involved the production of private scrip notes or coin-like tokens by various local merchants. Customers could redeem these notes and tokens for goods from the issuing merchant or, sometimes, at a local bank where the merchant held an account. By 1862, thousands of scrip notes and an untold number of Civil War tokens had created a chaotic financial situation. To impose some type of order, Congress passed the Stamp Payment Act, which essentially gave the Treasury the ability to print *"postage currency"*—essentially paper money -- to serve as fractional notes of less than one dollar. This fractional currency quickly became known as "shinplasters."

In Dinah's case, this monetary crisis proved challenging. More than once, she had to have a difficult and embarrassing conversation with her client.

"I'm sorry," she would say as she examined a piece of scrip given to her as payment. "This merchant doesn't do business with colored people. Do you have another way to pay?"

Fortunately, Dinah managed these circumstances mostly successfully throughout the war effort. She likely expressed relief with the introduction of fractional currency.

•   •   •

While Dinah didn't witness war directly, she saw many of its effects. She saw men leave and never return or come back missing an arm or a leg. Families wept and survivors often suffered.

"War is a messy business," Dinah said many times. "I pray to the Lord this scrimmage will end soon and the Union soldiers deliver a victory. The slaves have suffered long enough and should be free."

As Dinah walked through the town, she passed a familiar residence one day and met Mrs. Banks along the road. Dinah had known her for many years, and the two had become friendly. The woman appeared distraught as she peered worriedly down the street.

"Is everything all right, Mrs. Banks?" Dinah asked. "Can I do something to help?"

"Oh Dinah," Mrs. Banks said. "My son, Peter, has gone off to fight against the rebels. I don't know if I will ever see him again. One bullet and my boy could be gone forever."

Dinah could offer little insight into the future and had learned long ago to offer false hope. She was an exceptional sawyer and a fine friend, but a poor fortune teller. She provided what solace she could.

"He is fighting for a good cause," she said. "I am sure God will look over him. I pray He will bring him back to you safely."

Dinah tentatively put a hand on Mrs. Banks's back to offer comfort, a small but still bold gesture in the 1860s. Mrs. Banks looked at Dinah for a moment and Dinah pulled back. Then, Mrs. Banks wrapped her arms around her visitor. The two women held each other tightly for a long minute.

"Oh Dinah," Mrs. Banks finally said earnestly. "I do hope you're right."

The Civil War finally ended two years later, on May 26, 1865, resulting in a decisive victory for the Union. John Wilkes Booth had assassinated Abraham Lincoln a month earlier, on April 15, in Ford's Theatre. Law enforcement hunted Booth down and shot him less than two weeks later.

On June 19, 1865, Major General Gordon Granger freed the last slaves when he ordered the final enforcement of the Emancipation Proclamation in Texas. Juneteenth celebrations still recognize that event.

Dinah heard all this news and rejoiced. Against her own expectations, she had lived to see emancipation. She had prayed for many years that such a time would arrive.

CHAPTER 40
THE GREATEST SHOW ON EARTH

May 1863

The foreman greeted Dinah as she arrived at the site of her job, a busy location with workers moving in every direction performing a variety of tasks. The foreman had worked with her and even her late husband, William, for many years. He spoke over the cacophony of voices and tools put to good use nearby.

"I need you to set up here," the foreman said, walking her to a spot near a large pile of long boards. "You're the best sawyer I have, and I need to build a fence in two days. The show is coming to town whether we're ready or not, so this needs to be done no matter what."

Dinah nodded. "Thank you for the work, Mister Hopkins," she said politely. "I'll get right to work."

"Now Dinah," the foreman replied with a smile. "How many years have we known each other? I think you can call me Edward by now."

"Yes sir," she said. "I'll remember to do that."

Edward Hopkins shook his head, knowing he would never change Dinah's ways. "You let me know if you need anything," he said, then hurried off to direct the next artisan. He paused for a moment and looked back at Dinah. "There's a bonus for you if you get done early. And don't let any of these young brats give you any guff. You let me know if they do and I'll take care of them."

Dinah nodded and took a moment to take in the surrounding scene.

"I never saw such a commotion in my life," Dinah said softly as she set up her woodcutting station. By now, Dinah approached seventy years old, but despite the aches of age, she still served as good a sawyer as any who lived in and around Reading.

A growing throng of craftworkers of every sort surrounded her. Screams and shouts as people barked directions, often confusing and contradictory, permeated the air. The atmosphere seemed to threaten to erupt into chaos at any moment, but Edward kept a firm grip on the project's progress.

"How can you get anything done with all this caterwauling?" Dinah muttered but busied herself with her work. The circus was coming to town and a variety of workers had answered the call to help set up the grounds to accommodate the expected overflowing crowds. The circus proved a huge attraction.

The Civil War may have appeared an unlikely time to attend the circus, but the War Between the States failed to dampen the enthusiasm for one of the most popular spectacles of the Nineteenth Century. Nearly every United States citizen attended the circus at some point in time. Even President Abraham Lincoln attended the shows "under the big tent" to find a temporary respite from battle reports and other national priorities. Lincoln watched performances by the famous clown, "Yankee Dan Rice," and attended a show featuring the universally known little person, Charles Sherwood Stratton, better known as "Tom Thumb."

Dan Rice had become one of the most famous men in America, according to author David Carlyon, *"a talking clown, quipping spontaneously, booming out Shakespeare, singing about bloomers, feuding with Horace Greeley—and running for president."* As he travelled the country, Rice waxed poetic on politics, popular culture, and well-known celebrities of the time. He had created multiple fictions about himself, such as claiming he had served as the model for the patriotic image of Uncle Sam. Officially, he had not, but he did bear a strong resemblance to the figure when he wore a goatee and top hat. In fact, some historians wonder if Rice's famous image unconsciously influenced James Montgomery Flagg, the artist who created the figure, when drawing his images. Rice also said that Zachary Taylor had named him "Colonel" Rice and that he and Lincoln were good friends.

Neither were true. He also insisted that Queen Isabella of Spain expressed interested in his doing a European tour, even though at the time of his claim, Isabella was a mere ten years old.

Circuses travelled the countryside in both the North and South, despite the objections of evangelists who criticized the seediness and risqué aspects of the shows. During a time when social mores remained relatively rigid, the circus represented a mainstream form of entertainment that allowed audiences to experience the freakish and the fantastic in mostly acceptable ways. The circus was the equivalent of Hollywood and Broadway combined, with a bit of burlesque thrown in for good measure.

To be sure, the circuses of the mid-Nineteenth Century offered a far different experience than the one glorified at the height of the Barnum and Bailey Greatest Show on Earth. The circus overlapped with theater and minstrelsy in an adult-themed venue featuring near nudity with performers wearing skin-colored clothing, racy jokes, violence, and even politics. The circus environment outside the tent often included gambling, alcohol, prostitution, and occasional violence.

As a growing city and a major trading post in the Northeast, Reading attracted its share of circus events. Even in 1863, at the height of the war, with the Battle of Gettysburg soon to draw major factions of both the Union and Confederate armies, the circuses flourished. The *Reading Gazette and Democrat* ran an advertisement on May 9, 1863, promoting the Great National Circus and Model Show, featuring *"Mrs. Charles Warner, Formerly Mrs. Dan Rice."*

Say what?

Here's the short version of the story: Dan Rice unsurprisingly went through multiple wives. He divorced his first wife, Maggie, in order to marry a much younger woman. In return, Maggie started her own troupe, called *"Mrs. Dan Rice's Great Show."* Dan wasn't happy but had no choice but to allow it since that was indeed her name. When she remarried, Rice sued to stop her from using his name in the title of her show. Soon thereafter, audiences read *"Mrs. Charles Warner"* in fine print, *"formerly"* in even smaller print, and *"Mrs. Dan Rice's Great Show"* in large type. Dan Rice's name was larger than the name of any performers actually appearing in the show. When Maggie gave interviews to the local press, she mentioned she *"had been the wife of a somewhat famous clown."* No doubt that bit of shade infuriated her former husband even further.

The advertisement promised attendees *"A Genuine Circus"* with trained horses, performing mules, and *"other rare specimens of an animated nature,"* coming to Reading on Saturday, May 16. For an admission price of twenty-five cents, guests could attend a show at either two o'clock in the afternoon or seven o'clock in the evening.

The former Mrs. Rice herself promised to perform on a *"blind white horse"* and planned to introduce her daughter, Libbie, as well as many other acts. Perhaps the most notable of those was a Mr. George Derious, *"The Renowned Man Monkey."*

Dinah worked quickly, ignoring as best she could the raucous laborers around her. She represented perhaps the oldest artisan and one of the few women brought in to prepare for the event. Many around her could be her children or even her grandchildren. She had no interest in the circus. She had never attended one and her meager income could hardly afford such an extravagance. But she worked dutifully and produced more finished wood than many of those around her half her age.

"I don't understand the appeal of such nonsense," Dinah said to herself, ruminating on the spectacle for which she helped prepare, "but they pay well, so who am I to argue?"

Remarkably, a week after the Battle of Gettysburg, the *Reading Gazette and Democrat* ran an advertisement for another upcoming circus, this time Nixon's Cremorne Circus, held on Friday, July 17, and Saturday, July 18 in the afternoon and evening. The advertisement boasted of *"The Renowned Syro-Arabic Troupe of Male and Female Jugglers, Acrobats, (and) Contortionists."* The troupe included *"the first female gymnasts that have even appeared in America."* Madame Macarte's *"European Circus"* promised humor and entertainment to *"the most refined"* of audiences.

Unbeknownst to both audiences and organizers, the circus business would soon experience a radical transformation. In 1881, P.T. Barnum and James Anthony Bailey agreed to combine their competing shows to create Barnum and Bailey's Circus. Bailey added Jumbo, billed as the world's largest elephant, to the extravaganza. In 1909, the Ringling Brothers purchased Barnum and Bailey and eventually created The Ringling Bros. World's Greatest Shows and the Barnum & Bailey Greatest Show on Earth. Well into the mid-Twentieth Century, the circus remained a spectacle and much anticipated event.

Circuses redefined themselves as the Nineteenth Century came to a close. They softened their image and specifically catered to children. Even Dan Rice moderated his public personality and became known as Old Uncle Dan, losing most of his rough edge.

Dinah, of course, did not consider the present or future days of the circus and she dutifully cut wood to exact specifications. Near the end of several days of hard work, the location was nearly ready. As Dinah packed up her tools, she saw some of the circus animals being led into the tent. Horses and mules, as well as a few more exotic animals, walked by her. Nearly all followed those who led them without a fight. But Dinah thought she saw a soulful look of sadness in the eyes of several of the animals. Her mind flashed back to her younger days, when she did what was told but rarely experienced the joy of life and had no freedom. She felt some unspoken level of communion with these captive performers, many of whom suffered from maltreatment. Her eyes momentarily met the gaze of a passing stallion, and she felt the animal's pain. Soon thereafter, she left the premises and headed toward Hinnershitz Alley.

Dinah never attended a circus, even when she could afford to do so. She had witnessed enough caged torment in her life. In some way, Dinah shared the grief of the captive animals who did what they were told but had no control of their lives. She did not have to pay to feel that experience again.

CHAPTER 41
ENOCH SANDERS

1837 through 1876

One person who keeps appearing in the story of Dinah Clark is Enoch Sanders, the man who helped William and Dinah purchase their home on Hinnershitz Alley. Interestingly, Dinah never mentioned him in her interview late in life, and Sanders is a figure conspicuous by his absence.

In addition to his involvement in buying the Clark's house, Dinah knew Enoch through their ties with the Bethel A.M.E. Church, at the very least. After all, some sources listed both William and Enoch as members of the church's founding party, and Enoch reportedly preached at the church. Historians have also singled Enoch out as an early advocate for promoting the rights of African American citizens. But it appears Dinah's relationship with Enoch Sanders was uneven, tumultuous, and ultimately more than a bit frosty.

Remember, when Dinah purchased her beloved home on Hinnershitz Alley, she deeded it to Enoch and his wife. In addition, Sanders' mother, Sarah Hardy, known throughout the Reading community as "Auntie Hardy" supposedly lived with Dinah for some period. This could have been for several reasons, perhaps to help her following the death of Dinah's husband, or more likely, as part of Enoch's attempt to curtail Dinah's use of alcohol. Enoch posted an advertisement in the local newspaper admonishing residents and businesses to not provide Dinah with liquor.

Sarah Hardy proved to be quite the figure in her own life. She claims to have had two husbands and twenty children. She described herself as "*a bully"* at corn huskings, apple butter stirrings, and quilting parties, which represented the bulk of the social engagements of the day. *"We didn't have time to play and kiss as the young folks do now; we had to dance, which was often kept up all night,"* she told a reporter in her own newspaper article.

Enoch Sanders had a prominent career in Reading focused on his ongoing fight for racial equality. In fact, he became a key figure in that struggle.

On April 4, 1870, Sanders helped organize a march of two hundred individuals from Jochabed Lodge 1306 of the Colored Odd Fellows to Aulenbach's Hall on the 600 block of Penn Street. Braving sleet and freezing rain, representatives of the city's African American community marched with torches to celebrate the ratification of the Fifteenth Amendment two months earlier, which prohibited the federal government and every state from denying a citizen the right to vote based on race, color, or previous condition of servitude. Though the participants occasionally tried to set off fireworks, a steady precipitation thwarted their best efforts. The torch-light march culminated a series of events that day, beginning with the ceremonial firing of a cannon on a large rock formation called Leinbach's Hill overlooking the Schuylkill River. While the march organizers originally scheduled the cannon volley for dawn, the *Reading Eagle* reported the actual firing did not occur until ten o'clock because *"malicious individuals"* vandalized the cannon.

Notably, the Fifteenth Amendment did not apply to women. That had to wait another fifty years and followed an intensive women's suffrage movement until the Nineteenth Amendment granted them the right to vote in 1920.

In 1874, Sanders also helped organize a statewide equal rights convention at the Washington United Presbyterian Church at Washington and Mulberry Streets (the church later moved to the 700 block of North 10th Street). Speakers at the event called for uniform access to public transportation, hotel accommodations, and education. The Equal Rights League passed a resolution that said, *"The passage of the Civil Rights Bill is especially demanded by us, who suffer so much from the inhumanity of the American people, and the hesitancy to do this act of simple justice, and the failure of the last Congress to pass this bill is regarded by us as evidence of the low standard of civilization, which characterizes a large portion of the American people and is a concomitant of slavery."*

Unfortunately, African Americans had a long wait for the success of this initiative. The Civil Rights Act of 1964 did not become law until ninety years later.

In many ways, Enoch Sanders demonstrated true courage in his crusade to ensure the rights of African Americans. White supremacy spread its ugly head, and Reading did not escape it. In fact, founders of the *Reading Eagle* established the newspaper in 1868 partly to oppose passage of the Fifteenth Amendment.

Curiously, Dinah failed to mention Enoch Sanders in her interview with the *Reading Eagle* late in her life. As prominent a role as Enoch played in both Dinah's life – providing a means for her to purchase her home, preaching in the church she attended, serving as a prominent equal rights advocate in the community, and his mother living with her for a period of time - it's difficult to fathom that Dinah totally ignored him. That omission feels purposeful rather than accidental, especially considering the expansive nature of the article. Perhaps the *Reading Eagle,* if they still harbored some lingering resentment toward the passage of the Fifteenth Amendment, purposely cut Enoch Sanders out of Dinah's story. Or more likely, Dinah and Enoch parted on bad terms.

One can imagine Dinah being asked about Enoch Sanders and replying curtly.

"I don't have anything to say about him."

What happened? Most likely, Enoch's efforts to curtail Dinah's use of alcohol played a central role in their estrangement. Dinah may have placed Enoch in the same category as John Richards and David Brown, two others who publicly called her out for her drinking. Dinah inarguably held a vast reservoir of grudges she did not forget, and her antipathy toward those who confronted her was well documented.

One other less likely possibility revolves around Enoch's personal life. History does not offer any insights into the relationship between Dinah and Enoch's wife, Hannah. Perhaps they were close friends, perhaps not. But at some point in Enoch's life, circumstances changed, as evidenced by a short item in the January 8, 1894, edition of the *Reading Times*:

"Elizabeth, widow of Enoch Sanders, died at her residence, 124 Wunder street, after an illness of three weeks of grip. Her husband died eighteen years ago. One daughter, Mrs. Sophia Steele, of this city, survives."

Today, "grip" typically means influenza, but that may be the least interesting question regarding this brief passage when thinking about Dinah Clark and her relationship with Enoch Sanders. Whether through death or divorce, the marriage between Enoch and Hannah Sanders ended. Enoch remarried and had a daughter with his new wife. Perhaps this turn of events drove yet another wedge between Dinah and Enoch.

In any event, the relationship between Dinah and Enoch Sanders, two prominent Nineteenth Century African American figures in the city of Reading, remains confounding and entangled. Interestingly enough, they died only a few years apart.

CHAPTER 42
PAYING IT FORWARD

1866

"A good many of the freed (former slaves) came to Reading. Upwards of a hundred came at one time. I helped some of them carry their things from the depot."

Dinah Clark, recalling the days after the Civil War

They came on foot, by train, by boat, and by carriage. Men and women came, along with children, ranging from the elderly to the very young. They kept coming for months, all with their own stories of slavery, their sometimes treacherous travels, and their search for a better life. With the end of the war and new-found freedom for Southern slaves, many of those emancipated people fled north, away from the oppressive lives of their past. They travelled into an uncertain future, but one that escaped what they knew. Anything had to be better than hell, they reasoned.

Some of these freed slaves arrived in Reading and naturally gravitated toward the Bethel A.M.E. Church. The church's role in the Underground Railroad had become common knowledge among African Americans, and now refugees again searched for a sanctuary where they could start their new lives. The church and its congregation happily obliged. They had worked toward this moment for many years. They would not shy away now from those in need. To those who built and sustained the Bethel A.M.E. Church, God had answered many decades of prayers, and they joyfully opened the doors of their sanctuary.

Even though Dinah had now passed seventy years of age and began to feel the effects of her arduous life, she never hesitated to help those who now sought her aid. The memories of her days as an indentured servant still scorched her soul and left angry scars in her brain. That pain and abuse had happened many years ago, but she would never forget. She felt called to this moment. Anything she could do to help ease others into a new and better life would provide at least some small sense of satisfaction and solace. Dinah may never have been able to erase her own wounds, but she could make them less painful. She walked to the church whenever she had free time from her work schedule to provide both support and comfort to those who had come so far.

"What's your name, honey?" she asked a young woman as she picked up one of her well-worn bags of her possessions and walked with her into the church.

"My name is Peg," she answered. "I'm from South Carolina. I am so tired and so hungry. We have travelled so far."

Dinah gently put her hand on the young woman's back. "You're in Pennsylvania now," she said. "You never have to go back. Let's get you settled and find you something to eat."

The two women entered the church and Dinah helped Peg sit down in a pew with her belongings. "Now you stay right here while I get you some nourishment," Dinah said. "You need to build up your strength. Why, you're nothing but skin and bones. You have a whole life ahead of you and you need to be ready to embrace it."

Peg nodded, and Dinah scurried away, returning just a few minutes later with the promised meal. Peg hungrily ate a plate of escalloped eggs, a concoction of breadcrumbs, broth, hard-boiled eggs, minced ham, and crackers. She washed it down with a cup of lemonade. She soon brightened considerably, sitting back on the pew to allow her body to regain strength.

"Thank you for your generosity, Miss Dinah," she said. "You have been most kind."

"Now don't you worry about that," Dinah said. "I have been in your shoes. I just hope I can bring some comfort to your journey. You have a bright future ahead of you. You need to be ready for the rest of your life."

Dinah sat down next to Peg and spent a few more minutes with her. They spoke softly and earnestly, sharing details of their lives. Eventually, Dinah rose once again and headed back out of the church.

"There are others that need my help," she said. "I'll be back to check on you in a little while."

Dinah carried the bags of an older man named Abraham, and assisted a young couple named Isaac and Jane. The wife carried an infant son who had been born during their journey north. Dinah eyed the young boy, touching him gently.

"What's his name?" she asked.

"Freeman," Isaac answered quickly. "We thought it fit the times."

"Indeed it does," Dinah said. "This is a new day for certain and a joyful one at that. Your boy can remind you of your new lives when you look at him."

Dinah thought back to her own children, and those she had lost. She wondered if young Freeman would survive to adulthood.

I will keep him in my prayers, she said to herself. *Childhood is fraught with peril. You never know when sickness will strike a young one down. I hope young Freeman grows tall and strong and makes his parents proud.*

A short while later, Dinah came across a middle-aged woman who clearly struggled to continue. Dinah looped her arm around the stranger's and helped her into the church. Once the woman found a seat, Dinah checked her forehead.

"Oh, my Lord," she said. "You are burning up. Let me see what I can do to help."

Dinah's rudimentary knowledge of medicine combined Nineteenth Century knowledge with a collection of "old wives" tales and suspect practices. Between treating children with bacon grease for scarlet fever and saffron tea for the measles, Dinah's "cures" may not always have produced the relief she intended. Here, Dinah delivered a cool wet towel and willow bark, a treatment likely more effective than some of the other remedies she kept cataloged in her mind. Willow bark contains salicin, which has anti-inflammatory effects and works similarly to an active ingredient in modern-day aspirin.

The woman soon experienced some modicum of relief, and Dinah shifted her attention to others in need. The number of former slaves sometimes overwhelmed those available to help, but Dinah maintained her composure as best she could. She understood the fear, confusion, and uncertainty of the newcomers. They had left their tormented past but now arrived at an unknown future. They brought little or nothing with them except the clothes they wore and were uncertain where their journey would take them. Dinah remembered her own movement from one owner to the next as a young woman and her eventual freedom secured by her husband. All these travelers had left a tormented life but did not know what the next days and years would deliver. Whatever small measure of comfort Dinah could provide, she intended to offer to as many as she could.

Dinah soon came to the assistance of a young woman travelling alone. She had lost her husband and child when her former slave owner had split the family in a sale, and she did not know how to track them—or even if they still lived.

"What's your name, dear?" Dinah asked compassionately as she put her arm around the young woman's shoulders.

"Keziah," she answered. "I'm named after one of the daughters of Job."

"That's a beautiful name," Dinah said. "I know the story of Job. He was a man of great faith. My name is Dinah."

Keziah paused and looked at the woman helping her. "Dinah?" she asked with a voice of recognition. "Dinah Clark?"

Now Dinah stopped and looked over at her companion with surprise. "Why yes," she affirmed. "How in the world could you possibly know that?"

A smile crossed Keziah's face as she looked at Dinah with renewed pride. "You've well known among us travelers," she said. "We all hope to follow your path from slavery to freedom. I've heard your story over the campfire at night many times. The slave who became a sawyer."

"Oh honey," Dinah answered, somewhat flustered. "You don't want to follow my path. You have your own road, and I hope it's one easier and better than mine."

"That's not what folks say," Keziah responded. "They said you grew up a slave, suffered whippings from your masters, earned your freedom, helped other escaped slaves, and took on a job typically only done by men—and you outworked many of them."

Dinah chuckled. "Well, dear," she said, "some of that may be true, but the storyteller has glorified parts of that tale considerably. I can assure you I did not lead an easy life. I hope yours is a gentler path. Why don't we say a prayer together?"

The two women bowed their heads, and Dinah spoke first.

"Lord, now lettest thou thy servant depart in peace, according to thy word; for mine eyes have seen thy salvation, which thou hast prepared before the face of all people; a light to lighten the Gentiles, and the glory of thy people Israel."

Dinah and Keziah exchanged a few more words. Then Dinah gave Keziah a hug and suggested the church's pastor may have resources available to locate her lost family.

"I hope you can find your husband and son," Dinah said. "I'll pray to the Lord that you do."

Shortly thereafter, Dinah walked out of the church again in search of another freed soul to assist. By now, a woman in her seventies should have felt some fatigue, but Dinah shook off any tiredness. People needed help, and she committed herself to assisting as many as possible. She found the inner strength to continue on her mission.

"Imagine me, a hero," Dinah said to herself. "Who would think of such a thing? They'll bury me one day and no one will even remember my name."

If only Dinah knew.

CHAPTER 43
A FRAGILE BRANCH

1867

Late one summer afternoon as Dinah completed her work, Mister Armstrong, a gentleman who lived only a few blocks away, approached her as she packed up her tools for the day. Mister Armstrong worked as a tailor in town and had previously employed Dinah for a variety of tasks.

"Mrs. Clark," Mister Armstrong said, "I have an apple tree in my yard that has the blight. I'm afraid a storm could uproot it and cause quite a bit of damage. I was wondering if you had some time to take it down for me."

"I would be glad to help you out, Mister Armstrong," Dinah answered appreciatively. "I can come the day after tomorrow if that suits you."

"Thursday it is, then," he replied. They agreed on a price and how Dinah would cut and store the wood. Dinah promised to arrive early on the appointed day.

Dinah had completed similar tasks in the past and approached the job with typical determination. She had cut wood for Mister Armstrong for many years, and he treated her with respect and dignity. Even though Dinah had taken on fewer woodcutting jobs over the last several years as her aging body revolted against such arduous work, she always attempted to accommodate her longtime customers. She arrived at Mister Armstrong's home two days later, shortly after dawn, and set out her tools. Dinah examined the diseased apple tree that rose well over twenty feet in the air. The tree stood empty now, devoid of leaves or fruit, with its branches showing serious signs of degradation. Fortunately, with some care, Dinah could bring down the dead tree safely, ensuring no damage to any nearby homes and buildings. The job appeared a routine task, though navigating decaying trees always proved more challenging because of their unpredictable nature.

Dinah began her project that day by sawing off several low-hanging branches. She started a pile of timber she would cut into kindling and firewood. Dinah worked at a brisk pace, using her various saws to make quick work of her assignment. Age may have slowed her from her peak, but she still completed her task at an impressive rate. She labored for nearly three hours bringing down branches of various sizes, working her way up the tree.

"This tree is stubborn," she said to herself, "but not any more stubborn than I am."

As she continued her task, Dinah stood with one leg on her ladder and the other on the limb of the tree. She sawed diligently, battling with branches until they eventually gave way to her persistent efforts. But unfortunately, she maintained a precarious balance, and eventually, one branch she used as support proved not as sturdy as she hoped. It twisted under her weight and broke off. Dinah heard the branch crack and realized the pending calamity.

"God help me!" Dinah screamed as she fell. As if in slow motion, she felt herself toppling through the air, finally landing hard on her leg as she hit the ground.

"Oh, my Lord," Dinah said, writhing in pain. "That was not what I had planned."

After a few minutes as she recovered her senses, Dinah tried to get up without success. Pain shot through her leg and looking down, she could see a sizable cut. She pressed down on the wound with her dress to stanch the flow of blood and yelled as loudly as she could for help hoping someone would hear.

After some time, Mister Armstrong rushed out of his home and quickly viewed Dinah's plight.

"Mrs. Clark are you all right?" he asked, knowing full well the answer. "Oh, my goodness, clearly you're not. What happened?"

Without Dinah having to answer, he quickly reconstructed the event in his mind. Both Dinah and her ladder lay sprawled on the ground, with the wayward branch lying between them. Mister Armstrong pulled out a handkerchief and better covered Dinah's wound, putting pressure on the cut to slow the bleeding. He instructed Dinah to hold it firmly while he summoned the doctor. He then ran back inside and told his junior assistant to bring the local physician to the scene.

"And go as fast as you can," the tailor instructed the boy. "Poor Mrs. Clark is in a desperate state. I don't want her bleeding to death while we wait for you."

The assistant took off down the street at full speed. Still, by the time the boy arrived at the doctor's office and alerted him to the situation, and the doctor packed his bags and returned in his horse-drawn carriage, Dinah laid suffering for some time. Mister Armstrong had done what he could, but the poor woman clearly had sustained an injury far worse than the tailor could fix. His skill at mending clothes did not translate well to stitching skin and bones.

Doctor Collins took over from Mister Armstrong and examined his patient, still lying on the ground.

"What have you done to yourself, Mrs. . . ." the physician paused.

"Clark," she answered, "Dinah Clark. The branch gave way, and I fell from the ladder."

"Yes, I see," he said. "Let me examine this and determine what I can do to help you."

The doctor first stopped Dinah's bleeding, cleaning the wound and using some rudimentary stitches. "This is going to pinch," he warned Dinah.

Dinah winced as the doctor worked.

More than a pinch, she thought. *But not the worst I have endured in my life by far.*

Doctor Collins then tested Dinah's leg and soon found she could put virtually no weight on it.

"I don't think it's broken," he said. "But you certainly won't be able to walk on it for a bit."

The doctor helped Dinah sit down on a nearby bench and fashioned a rudimentary crutch from several pieces of wood. He then assisted Dinah in getting to her feet and standing.

"I'll help you to my carriage and take you home," the physician said. "You're going to have to stay off your feet for a week or two until you feel better. Give this time to heal."

Dinah reluctantly accepted the aid. As she slowly limped off the property with the help of the crutch and the doctor, she looked back at Mister Armstrong.

"Don't you worry about that tree," she assured him. "As soon as I am up and about, I'll finish the job for you."

"That tree isn't going anywhere, Mrs. Clark," Mister Armstrong replied. "It will be here when you're feeling better. Now you go take care of yourself and listen to what the doctor tells you. You don't worry about my backyard."

The incident laid Dinah up for the better part of two weeks, and she never fully regained strength in her injured leg. She soon learned that age possesses a wicked sense of humor, and that healing is neither as fast nor as complete in later years. Still, Dinah would not allow an accident to deter her. She returned to work sooner than she probably should have and as promised, finished taking down Mister Armstrong's tree, this time choosing not to rely on any suspect branches. She had promised him she would complete that job, and she remained determined to fulfill that vow. But she soon found herself not as nimble as she was in her youth.

The injury Dinah sustained affected her for the rest of her life, at least according to what she told the *Reading Eagle* reporter. The incident finally led her to give up woodcutting totally, the job she had enjoyed most of all throughout her life. Mister Armstrong's tree may have been the last wood that felt the wrath of Dinah's sharpened blade.

"About four years ago I cut down an apple tree for tailor Armstrong," she said. *"I stood with one leg on a ladder and with the other on a limb of the tree, when the limb twisted and hurt my leg. I think my rheumatism came from that."*

CHAPTER 44
WHAT SHE DID AND SAW

December 1871

"The *Reading Eagle* wants to interview you?" Mary Ann asked her mother. "What on Earth for? Did you rob a train or something and not tell me? I would have liked to see that if you did. Did you threaten the conductor with one of your saws? I bet that made him shiver."

"Now don't you be silly," Dinah scoffed. "The reporter told me I had an interesting life and wants to talk to me this afternoon."

"Well, I never heard of such a thing," Mary Ann said. "A newspaper wants to talk to a poor old colored woman who didn't commit no crime. Next thing you know, they'll be electing a colored man to Congress."

In fact, that had already happened. Joseph Rainey became the first African American legislator in 1870, representing South Carolina. Several other black candidates won seats the following year.

"Well, no matter what you think, the young reporter is coming to see me this afternoon," Dinah said. "You need to behave yourself while he's here."

"He's coming here?" Mary Ann said in a mix of wonder and distaste. "Well, I'm not going to let him see me. I'll find some place to hide. I don't want to talk to no reporter. I don't need my business splattered all over the newspaper. And I don't need to hear you spinning tales about things you probably don't even remember right in the first place."

"You suit yourself," Dinah said. "He doesn't want to talk to you anyway."

Mary Ann stood up and slowly found her way toward the kitchen. "I don't want to talk to him either," she said. "What is this world coming to? A newspaper reporter coming here. You'd think there would be enough news going on elsewhere that they don't have to talk to no silly old woman talking about things that happened before I was born."

"I heard that," Dinah said. "Now you hush."

Mary Ann smiled. "I love you, Momma. Now don't you go telling the world all your secrets. Some things are best left unsaid."

•   •   •

On December 23, 1871, the *Reading Eagle*, a daily newspaper serving Reading and Berks County, published a long interview with a then-elderly Dinah. At that point, she would have been about seventy-seven years old. The article appeared as a first-person recollection by Dinah recounting the story of her life, with the reporter adding only a brief introduction and a final thought.

While the *Eagle* did not attribute the article, one reference provides a partial identity of the reporter. In the 1872 *Reading Times* article regarding David Brown, the newspaper added that Brown was *"a son-in-law of Dinah Clark, whom our good brother Nicholson of the* Eagle *'interviewed' to the extent of two columns and a half some time since."*

At the time, journalism was a male-dominated profession, though some women did work covering primarily society news. Whether any women working in the *Reading Eagle* newsroom at the time depended on the progressivism of the newspaper. In any event, Mister Nicholson allowed Dinah to tell her own tale.

A shortened and summarized version of the interview, retelling Dinah's story and words in a more traditional third-person report, appeared in the April 14, 1907, edition of the *Eagle*. Dinah's story would make yet a third appearance in the *Reading Eagle* over a century later, when reporter Michelle Napoletano Lynch introduced Dinah to a new generation of readers on February 26, 2021.

Much of what we know about Dinah's life came from this interview. She left many gaps along the way and many questions remained unanswered, but her story remains a fascinating one.

"Dinah Clark–What She Did and Saw!

The Principal Events of her Individual Experiences no Longer Wrapped in Mystery and Uncertainty

One of the EAGLE reporters recently interviewed Mrs. Dinah Clark (formerly Miss Bell) with the following result:

A PLAIN RENDERING OF THE VOYAGE OF LIFE

I was born a slave many years ago–I don't know how many–on the farm of Gabriel Hiester on the Tulpehocken creek, in Bern township, Berks county, Pennsylvania. My parents' name was Bell; I don't know their first (Christian) names. They were both slaves. Mr. Hiester had eleven slaves, men and women. I had two brothers and one half-sister. I don't know what became of them but I suppose they were sold out. About 21 years ago my brother, Lij, who was then roving about the country, came to see me at Reading. He didn't say where he came from or where he was going.

I never went to school, and never learned to read nor write. The most I was taught was work. I used to hoe corn and potatoes, pitch hay and grain–I could stand aside of any man a-pitching hay–I took two rows in hoeing corn, and two swaths in raking and binding grain. I helped to spread dung, pick stones, and I carried lime out of the limekiln until sometimes my back was as raw as a fresh piece of beef. If I had as many dollars as bushels of grain I thrashed with the flail and carried into the granary, I would never want for anything more.

Mr. Hiester kept a barrel of whisky upstairs and made pretty sharp use of it himself. He gave liquor to the slaves who would sometimes get drunk in the field. When the slaves didn't behave themselves, they were taken in the large kitchen. The doors would be bolted and the slaves would have to go round like horses on a thrashing floor, and they would be whipped with cowskin as they came around, by persons standing in the corner.

We were fed rye bread as black as a hat, a few potatoes, and cheese mixed with water. You didn't see an ounce of butter on the table in two years. We drank rye coffee without milk.

Mr. Hiester was a good natured man when he wasn't intoxicated, and Mrs. Hiester was a splendid woman. She was very kind to the poor people.

There was a war many years ago (1812). I remember the scrimmage at Baltimore, and that is all I know about it.

When I was old enough to sit on a horse, I was sold for $100 to Jacob Seltzer, a farmer living on the Harrisburg turnpike, three miles this side of Womelsdorf. There, when the well was dry, I had to go two miles with the bucket to fetch water, and I had such poor shoes that I froze my feet. Sometimes the dog would put his nose in the water when I got back to the house, when the water was at once thrown away and I had to fetch another bucket full.

Mr. Seltzer sold me for a debt to Maj. Samuel Jones, who lives three miles from the Sinking Springs, in Heidelberg Township, where I lived until I was 21 years of age, when I received my freedom. Old Sammy Jones used to whip me with a cowskin, and I'll carry a mark on my wrist to my grave (shows mark of lash to reporter). Dr. Derry and Mr. Jones had together a large farm, a furnace, a grist mill and a store. Dr. Derry broke up Mr. Jones.

While at Jones's I married William Clark and we moved to Reading. We had eleven children. All died excepting four. Their names are John, Mary Ann, Hannah, and Silas William. John and Hannah are living in Newark, N.J., Silas William is roaming about the country, and Marry Ann, who married David Brown, a barber, is living with me in Hinnershitz's alley. My daughter Mary Ann has had scrofulous cancer in her face and eyes eleven years ago, and she is nearly blind. She suffers a great deal at night—more than a brute. She can't go out of the house and she is in very needy circumstances. Her husband has a barber shop somewhere in town, but business is slack and he can't support her as she ought to be supported. I think cancer springs from the cold. I don't know what is good for it. My daughter Hannah married a Mr. Deets, who enlisted in the army and died. I moved with my husband back to Bern township, where we lived on John Adams' farm ten years. My husband cut wood on the farm for Congressman's Schwartz's furnace. The rest of my life I lived in Reading. Here my husband used to saw wood, put in coal and do all kinds of work. He died about 20 years ago, and was buried in the Bethel church yard, on Tenth street beyond Walnut. He was a good, religious man, and was very kind to me. I got a nice white board and took it to George Durell, the painter, who had his shop in the basement of the house which is now the Savings Bank. I wanted some nice poetry put on the board, and Lawyer John Richards, who had his office up stairs, wrote these lines:

"Here lies the body of William Clark;
His soul was white though his skin was dark;
And when the Arch Angel cries: Who's there
He'll find him right side with care."

Mr. Richards said that my board was too small for a headstone, but that he would have a larger one made, which he did, and Mr. Durell painted the lines on it and stood the board in front of his shop to dry. The board was placed at the grave, where it stood for some time, when some of the colored people said that they never heard of a piece of poetry like it on a grave stone, and made some ugly remarks about it. I didn't think it was very nice of John Richards putting those words on, and I pulled out the board, took it home and burned it in the stove. I told him in the presence of William Coleman that if he didn't repent for every letter that he put on that board he would go to hell. I am not afraid of any man living. If John Richards dies as happy as my husband did, Heaven will be his home.

Old Mr. Stricker made a nice marble head-stone for me, for which I paid him two dollars, and he put on the age of my husband, and the time he went to Heaven.

I joined the Bethel church when I lived in the country. I have got religion, and I expect to land my soul safe in Heaven. God being my helper. I was christened. My children have all been kind to me.

I married a second time. My second husband, whose name was Leo, didn't like my first husband's children, and he and I couldn't agree, and so I didn't live with him.

When I became free and first moved to Reading this town was not any larger than Womelsdorf is now. I like Reading as an abiding place. The manners and customs of the people have greatly changed. The white folks are more kind and liberal than they were, and the colored people are more sociable.

Among the most influential colored persons in town are Hiram Fry and his son. The son is a very excellent young man. He would make a good lawyer and is well qualified to fill office. The Walker boys, and their mother and sister, are well thought of; as are also the Dorseys, Mrs. Hannah Sanderson, Mrs. Peter Kline, Mrs. Templin, Sarah Dillon, Aunt Peggy Bell, Grandmother Brown – and there are others, but I cannot name them just now. I think the colored people ought to have a new school house and a new teacher.

I don't recollect the names of all the ministers that preached in the Bethel Church, but Rev's Smith and Butler were among the best. Smith, in particular, was very kind and eloquent. He could move the congregation, and they took a liking to him. Smith is living and Butler may be dead. Geoge Dillon was one of the preachers, and so was Scott, Jeremiah Bury and John Cornish were local preachers. Rev. Mr. Wilson is our preacher now.

I have worked very hard, and had many ups and downs in life. Sometimes I was very poor, but I generally managed to have enough to eat for myself and family. Many a time I took my bag in the morning and went out as far as ten miles in the country and came back in the evening.

I used to wash, saw wood, put in coal, white-wash, and do all kinds of work. I got 25 cts a day for washing, and I used to saw and split two and a half cords of wood a day, for which I was paid a dollar and a half. I liked sawing wood better than anything else I ever did. Sawing wood was a harvest to me. I always liked outdoor work better than indoor work.

A good many of the people of Reading have been kind to me and helped me along. There is Mrs. Judge Banks, Mrs. J. Glaney Jones (now dead), Mrs. Wm. McIlvain, Mrs. Jacob Schumucker, Mrs. Samuel Buch, Mrs. John Ritter (now dead), Mrs. Aaron Ritter, Mrs. Moers, the stonecutter's wife, Mrs. Isaac McHose, Mrs. Leinbach, the preacher's wife, Mrs. F.S. Boas, Mrs. Jacob Livingood, Mrs. Judge Hagenman, Mrs. Lauman, Mrs. Henry Van Reed,

Mrs. Frank Whiskeyman, Mrs. Kitty Gehr, and others that I could name if you would give me a little time.

I quit sawing wood about ten years ago, and four years ago I was crippled with the rheumatism. I went from one doctor to another, and I tried a little of everything to have it cured. Dr. Collins gave me three bottles of medicine for a dollar a bottle, but it made me worse. I was recommended to a man living up Penn street. He came from Lancaster county, and I think his name is Homan. He gave me a pint bottle full of medicine for nothing. I took a table-spoonful of it three times a day and in a week I was cured. Such a man as he is very useful. About four years ago I cut down an apple tree for tailor Armstrong. I stood with one leg on a ladder and with the other on a limb of the tree, when the limb twisted and I hurt my leg. I think my rheumatism came from that. Excepting the rheumatism, my health has always been good. I used to drink liquor sometimes, but I have given that up. Whisky sometimes strengthened me, and sometimes it did not. Liquor in its place is good; but out of its place it is not. A great many people are damaged by it and it destroys families. I smoke tobacco; I think it is beneficial to me. Tobacco is good for some people and for some it is not.

The best cure for scarlet fever is to keep the children warm and grease them with bacon. Scarlet fever is not catching – that is my idea. Small-pox, these are things that are catching. When I had the small-pox, I used a little sweet oil, and cold water out of the pump, and kept my face greased with hog's lard. Mumps and measles are easily cured. For the measles use saffron tea, and for the mumps take the children and rub their throats against the pigtrough. The doctors don't know much about these diseases, and in this respect the old women have the advantage of them.

I heard of the emancipation and I was rejoiced at it. When the scrimmage commenced, a good many of the freed came to Reading. Upwards of a hundred came at one time. I helped some of them carry their things from the depot.

I think the EAGLE is a good paper. I never heard any of the colored people say the EAGLE did them injustice.

The happiest time in my life was when I was married.

• • •

We hope the citizens of Reading will take care of Dinah Clark, as she has worked hard enough to be independent. He who giveth to the poor, &c."

• • •

After the New Year, a middle-aged man in a suit and topcoat walked down Tenth Street and recognized Dinah from the newspaper article. As Dinah slowly passed him, he reached into his pocket and pulled out a well-worn seated liberty quarter and handed it to her.

"You have led a fine and difficult life," the man said. "I, for one, am proud you have been a part of our city of Reading. You have been a great contributor to our town."

"May God bless you," Dinah said and watched the man go about the rest of his day.

CHAPTER 45
THE UGLY SIDE OF HUMANITY

June 1873

Dinah Clark may have gained minor celebrity status in Reading and had many benefactors. However, human cruelty never rests, and Dinah witnessed enough of it, both from the country's institutions and from its citizens. That hard reality never ended throughout her life.

In a little documented event, the *Reading Times* published a brief report on June 18, 1873, that provided maddeningly scant detail:

"Dinah Clark, a well-known colored woman, made complaint yesterday afternoon in regard to one of her neighbors who has been maltreating her for some time. Dinah lives in Hinnershitz's alley. An officer was directed to inquire into the alleged grievance."

No other information regarding this conflict is readily available, so it's impossible to determine the cause or the length of the conflict.

It's easy to make snap conclusions regarding this incident. While slavery may have been the cause of the Civil War, the victorious North still suffered from widespread racism. An older African American woman, physically spent from decades of hard work but having earned some well-intentioned notoriety, would serve as an easy target for a hate-filled jealous neighbor. That a nearly blind Mary Ann lived in the same residence would only sweeten the punishment. Racial epithets and other verbal abuse may have escalated to vandalism and other forms of mistreatment.

Could the actions be based on a combination of jealousy and racism because Dinah had achieved some level of local recognition, which the neighbor felt was undeserved? Conceivably.

But some history may suggest that the dispute did not revolve around the color of Dinah's skin. First, in a segregated society that still viewed blacks as second-class citizens, it's unlikely the police would spend much time investigating racial abuse unless it had escalated to physical violence.

Perhaps even more telling, the area around Tenth and Washington Streets and the Bethel A.M.E. Church had originated as an African American community. This had occurred primarily in the 1830s and 1840s, about the same time Dinah and her late husband had purchased their home on Hinnershitz Alley. In the three decades that had passed since then, it's unlikely the demographics of that area had significantly altered. If someone wanted to launch a litany of racial abuse against their neighbor or neighbors, they might think twice about doing so in a community overwhelmingly made up of African American residents.

Still, a dispute based on racism is possible, but the little evidence provides few clues that would confirm or deny such a scenario.

Other possibilities remain as well. Perhaps this was a dispute around property, lifestyles, or simply two neighbors that had a long history of not getting along. That happens regularly, even today. Nearly every American has had some type of dispute with an unfriendly or arrogant neighbor that revolves around property lines, noise, unruly behavior, lifestyle, or a years-old perceived slight that grew over time.

Alternately, a younger resident may have taken pleasure in harassing two older, somewhat enfeebled women. By 1873, Dinah was approaching 80 years old and suffered from a growing number of physical maladies. She and Mary Ann could easily have been the subject of sharp-edged abuse by a younger resident who took pleasure in harassing those who could hardly fight back.

"Fly away, you old bats," could have been the starting point of a myriad of insults, growing more vituperative as time went on.

On the other hand, Dinah had a history of holding grudges. She had experienced disputes earlier in life with John Richards, Enoch Sanders, and

David Brown over her alleged overuse of alcohol, feuds she apparently carried to her grave. History suggests Dinah had a long memory when it came to grievances. Perhaps, the quarrel with her neighbor rested primarily on Dinah or even Mary Ann, either of whom may have become more combative and yes, even ornery, in their later years.

Lacking any additional information, any of these scenarios could have caused the complaint. Or perhaps it was something else entirely. We do not know the result of the officer's inquiry or even if the police actually followed up on the complaint. Again, the officer to which Dinah made the statement may have promised to look into the conflict, only to appease her in order to move on to other "more important" matters. Nor do we know if any official intervention ended the dispute. The entire episode remains one more mystery in Dinah's life. One can only hope that Dinah found peace in the last years of her life.

CHAPTER 46
HARRIET BEECHER STOWE

September 1873

In 1871, the West Reading Market House opened on the south side of Penn Street, just below Fourth Street. Business proved so good that soon after the successful launch, the directors of the business added an opera house to the front of the building above the market. Construction began, and the Grand Opera House Theatre celebrated its opening in September 1873.

The design of the Grand Opera House Theatre mirrored its name. A wide stairway led to its main entrance, enclosed by massive wooden doors. The facility's decorations were completed by a prominent Reading artist named Frederick Spang, whose paintings have been renowned both during and after his life. The auditorium at the Opera House Theatre seated about one thousand patrons.

When the theatre opened, the front of the parquet circle, the main floor of the theater, featured portraits of well-known celebrities, including acclaimed Swedish opera singer Jenny Lind. The head of Apollo rested above the proscenium, the arched wall separating the stage from the auditorium, and ceiling portraits included those of Mozart, Beethoven, and American Shakespearian actor Edwin Forrest as MacBeth. The stage's depth measured thirty-four feet with a twelve-foot apron. Performers reached backstage from the market house by climbing a spiral stairway.

The theatre opened September 12, 1873, with the spectacular production of *The Sea of Ice,* a melodrama adapted from the 1853 French play, *La Priére des Naufragés (Prayer of the Wrecked).* A concert program by the Reading-based Ringgold Band on the portico preceded the performance, and the local consensus deemed the opening *a grand success.*

A few days after the successful opening, one of Dinah's long-time clients, Mrs. McIlvain, searched her out and greeted her. Though Dinah's health had begun to fail her after a lifetime of hard labor, she still worked as much as she could. Now in her late seventies, however, Dinah's body had defied her best efforts, and she limited herself to performing domestic chores. As she had mentioned to the newspaper reporter two years earlier, she had left her sawyer days behind her. No doubt she missed them.

"Dinah," Mrs. McIlvain said as she met her on the street. "I don't know if you've heard, but the new Opera House opened just a few blocks away from you."

"I have seen reports of that," Dinah responded. "They say it's a very fine establishment."

"It is indeed," Mrs. McIlvain said affirmatively. "My husband and I attended the opening show. It is quite impressive, a wonderful addition to our city."

Dinah nodded in appreciation and started to go about her way.

"Dinah," Mrs. McIlvain stopped her. "I was wondering if you'd like to attend an event with me and Mr. McIlvain there."

Dinah looked at Mrs. McIlvain with a mixture of surprise and appreciation.

"Thank you for the invitation," she said. "But I can't afford such a thing. Besides, I would have to work."

"Oh Dinah, you misunderstand," Mrs. McIlvain responded. "We would like you to be our guest that evening. And don't you worry about missing a day of work. Mr. McIlvain and I will cover your wages that day."

Dinah still appeared skeptical. "I do sincerely appreciate that," she said. "But do you think I am allowed to attend? You know that may cause quite the ruckus."

Dinah may have been approaching eighty and had many white friends, but she remained keenly aware of the invisible but always present wall of segregation. She had seen her share of establishments that did not welcome African Americans into their premises.

But Mrs. McIlvain remained firm. "Now don't you worry about that," she told Dinah confidently. "I know the manager, and this is a special presentation. I'd allow that colored folks will be welcome to attend this event. I will see to it."

Dinah looked at her benefactor in sincere surprise. "You are very kind to include me," she said.

"It would be our honor," Mrs. McIlvain answered. "You have provided valuable service to us for many years and have always been a wonderful friend. We'll come around and pick you up in our carriage on Monday at about seven o'clock."

•   •   •

The performance Dinah attended on September 29, 1873, was indeed noteworthy. It turned out to be an appearance by Harriet Beecher Stowe, the author of more than thirty books, by far the most famous being *Uncle Tom's Cabin*. Beecher came from a very religious family and had been an ardent and outspoken abolitionist her entire life.

Stowe published *Uncle Tom's Cabin* in 1852 as the conflict between the North and the South began to become much more volatile, a boiling brew that eventually exploded into war less than a decade later. The book depicted the harsh conditions endured by enslaved African Americans and her words reached millions as both a novel and a play. The work became influential in both the United States and Great Britain, serving as a clarion call for anti-slavery advocates in the North and enraging slaveowners in the South. *Uncle Tom's Cabin* emerged as an immediate flash point, selling over three-hundred-thousand copies in the first year of its publication.

Stowe eventually traveled to Washington, D.C. to meet President Abraham Lincoln on November 25, 1862. Her own accounts of the meeting remained vague. She wrote to her husband that *"I had a real funny interview with the President."* An apocryphal account of the conversation claimed that Lincoln greeted Stowe with these words: *"So you are the little woman who wrote the book that started this great war."* Historians differ on whether

Lincoln actually said that, but in either case, the sentiment was not entirely wrong.

By the time Stowe appeared in Reading, she was sixty-two years old. She had agreed to give readings from *Uncle Tom's Cabin* as part of a nationwide tour. Dinah wore her best dress, which in truth, still paled among the rest of the attire worn by most guests in the audience. Though Dinah continued to work, she did so against all odds since she now had difficulty walking and suffered from failing eyesight. She received help to reach the second-floor theatre. As she surveyed the theater, she noticed a small section presumably reserved for African American attendees. More than a dozen people, many of whom she knew, already had secured a seat.

"I'll go find a seat over in that section," Dinah said softly to Mrs. McIlvaine.

"You'll do no such thing," the woman responded. "You will sit right here with us. If anyone says anything about it, I'll box their ears, believe you me."

Dinah timidly took her seat and, somewhat nervously, waited for the event to begin. She noticed several other African Americans seated throughout the theatre, an unexpected curiosity that piqued her interest. Little did she realize the speaker's reputation had encouraged the theatre's management to adopt a more lax seating policy for the event.

A few minutes later, the stage curtain opened, and Harriet Beecher Stowe appeared. Dinah never read *Uncle Tom's Cabin* or any other book. But as Stowe read the words, they reverberated in Dinah's soul.

"But now what?" Stowe recited. *"Why, now comes my master, takes me right away from my work, and my friends, and all I like, and grinds me down into the very dirt! And why? Because, he says, I forgot who I was; he says, to teach me that I am only a nigger! After all, and last of all, he comes between me and my wife, and says I shall give her up, and live with another woman. And all this your laws give him power to do, in spite of God or man. Mr. Wilson, look at it! There isn't one of all these things, that have broken the hearts of my mother and my sister, and my wife and myself, but your laws allow, and give every man power to do, in Kentucky, and none can say to him nay! Do you call these the laws of my country? Sir, I haven't any country, anymore than I have any father. But I'm going to have one. I don't want anything of your country,*

except to be let alone,--to go peaceably out of it; and when I get to Canada, where the laws will own me and protect me, that shall be my country, and its laws I will obey. But if any man tries to stop me, let him take care, for I am desperate. I'll fight for my liberty to the last breath I breathe. You say your fathers did it; if it was right for them, it is right for me!"

Stowe paused and looked out into the audience, resetting the scene in her mind.

"Unfortunately," Stowe said. "Many of our fellow human beings had to endure such torment in real life. The fictional book I wrote was based on the real suffering of colored men and women held as slaves."

She then continued with her reading.

"It was on his grave, my friends, that I resolved, before God, that I would never own another slave, while it is possible to free him," she recited, *"that nobody, through me, should ever run the risk of being parted from home and friends, and dying on a lonely plantation, as he died. So, when you rejoice in your freedom, think that you owe it to that good old soul, and pay it back in kindness to his wife and children. Think of your freedom, every time you see uncle tom's cabin; and let it be a memorial to put you all in mind to follow in his steps, and be as honest and faithful and Christian as he was."*

At the end of a rousing presentation that alternated between readings from Stowe's book and her personal anecdotes, the author read one last line from *Uncle Tom's Cabin.*

"All men are free and equal," Stowe concluded, *"in the grave."*

"I can only hope that we see the day when all men are free and equal during their living years," Stowe said. "The Union may have won the Civil War, but colored people still do not receive equal treatment across this country. That remains a disgrace, one that I hope and pray we one day will rectify."

Dinah unexpectedly felt powerful emotions as Stowe finished her presentation. She did her best to not show them, but eventually, a tear escaped from Dinah's eye as she recalled her many years of indentured servitude.

Gabriel Hiester, Jacob Seltzer, Major Samuel Jones, Dinah thought as each one flashed through her mind. A flood of memories overwhelmed her as she recalled her first twenty-one years.

"Are you all right, Dinah?" Mrs. McIlvain asked, seeing Dinah's distress.

"I am now," she said as she used a tissue to wipe away her tears. "I just needed a moment. Thank you for this. I will never forget your kindness."

.   .   .

The words of *Uncle Tom's Cabin* became so ingrained in the mind of Harriet Beecher Stowe that she wrote it a second time. Following the death of her husband in 1886, Stowe's health declined rapidly, and she began to develop symptoms of dementia. By 1888, Stowe started penning her classic book all over again, believing she worked on a new manuscript. She spent several hours each day with pen and paper, rewriting *Uncle Tom's Cabin* nearly word for word. She did this unconsciously from memory. She frequently drove herself to exhaustion working on a book she trusted was an original work. Clearly, the story and the language of *Uncle Tom's Cabin* defined the life of Harriet Beecher Stowe in many ways.

Harriet Beecher Stowe died in 1896, seventeen days before her eighty-fifth birthday.

CHAPTER 47
TIME REMAINS UNDEFEATED

1875

Dinah Clark may have lived a long life, but it was not an easy one, and that took its toll. From her early years as a child, she labored hard days that often stretched from dawn until dusk, six days each week. Losing William Clark at a relatively early age added to both her stress and her workload. She had gained some measure of local fame as a female sawyer, but that work proved backbreaking and arduous, especially as Dinah aged.

By the early 1860s, Dinah, in her late sixties, had mostly given up cutting wood, as she herself admitted. On one occasion, when she had returned to her work as a sawyer, the result had proved calamitous. After that, her body betrayed her and no longer allowed her to perform the work she so loved.

Her health continued to decline throughout the decade, and she blamed her ills on rheumatism. There may have been considerable truth in that, but it's likely she suffered from other maladies as well, considering the heavy toll on her body over the decades that included hard work, tobacco use, and alcohol.

That being said, Dinah did not give up without a fight, a trait that characterized her entire life.

"I went from one doctor to another, and I tried a little bit of everything to have it cured," she said. *"Dr. Collins gave me three bottles of medicine for a dollar a bottle, but it made me worse."*

One can only wonder what type of treatment Doctor Collins had fabricated. Physicians typically prepared medications since few pharmacies existed. Even if the concoction proved effective, these remedies usually treated symptoms rather than the actual disease. The ingredients for these formulas ranged from pain relievers such as opium and morphine to fever reducers such as willow bark and meadowsweet. The reliability and purity of such mixtures varied with the skill and knowledge of the practitioner.

The medical community had only begun to understand rheumatoid arthritis and conditions such as gout in the Nineteenth Century. Doctors typically treated rheumatoid arthritis with willow bark, which did at least contain its aspirin-like compounds. Its long-term effectiveness remained questionable.

Dinah did not surrender to her maladies, however, again showing her never-ending determination. *I was recommended to a man living up Penn street,* she continued. *He came from Lancaster county, and I think his name is Homan. He gave me a pint bottle full of medicine for nothing. I took a table-spoonful of it three days a day and in a week I was cured. Such a man is very useful.*

What magical elixir the man provided Dinah remains unknown. But Mister Homan, whether or not he was actually a doctor and with whatever secret formulary he devised, managed to provide Dinah some relief.

•　　•　　•

Dinah and Mary Ann sat outside their home on Hinnershitz Alley one day. By the mid-1870s, Dinah had reached more than eighty years of age and on most days, she felt every bit of it. Her body had revolted, and time now showed its patience. It preferred its victims to suffer gradually and slowly. Dinah had overcome many things, but even she could not defeat time.

A comfortable day in early October enticed the mother and daughter to enjoy a few minutes in the sun. The well-worn rocking chairs they used creaked noticeably as the two women soaked in the beauty of the early fall. The sun warmed their faces.

"What a couple of old ladies we are," Mary Ann finally said. "Neither of us can hardly see and you can barely walk. We sit outside and someone could saunter by and we wouldn't even take notice. They could steal our purse and just keep on their way, and later we would wonder where we put it."

"And yet by God's good grace, here we still stand," Dinah added. "Well, sit in any case."

The article in the *Reading Eagle* had added to Dinah's small slice of fame and had garnered a myriad of ongoing donations that supported her and her daughter. Some offered cash while others brought food. A handyman or two stopped by every so often to see if Dinah and Mary Ann's home needed any repairs. Many residents used the nearby Bethel A.M.E. Church—the church Dinah had given so much of her time and passion—to funnel aid to her. The nearby house of worship had once again proven her one steady and reliable lifeline.

Dinah rocked gently. Her mind wandered through her many years of life. "Back when I was getting whipped to an inch of my life by old Sammy Jones," she said, "I asked God why he made me suffer so. Why would he put me on Earth just to endure such a thing. It didn't seem fair. It didn't' seem right. I had done nothing to deserve it."

Mary Ann began to say something, but Dinah softly put a finger on her daughter's mouth to stop her.

"God told me He strengthened me so I could rise above my suffering and have the will to lead a better life," she continued. "I had to show folks I was more than a piece of property to be abused when the whim came over my owner."

By now, Mary Ann knew enough to allow her mother to continue her soliloquy. "So I stayed strong, I lived through many hard days, and the Lord brought me your daddy. He bought me my freedom. Then came our children, who were their own special blessings.

"Well, most of them, anyway," she added with a smirk.

Dinah paused for a moment and looked at Mary Ann. "Now don't you go asking which one was my favorite," she said. "You already know that answer."

Mary Ann smiled, and Dinah returned to her own inner reflections. "We didn't live a fancy life, and we were poor more often than not," she said.

"We weren't perfect by any means. I know God is going to ask me why I drank as much as I did, sometimes too much I will admit."

A smirk crossed Dinah's lips. "I may just ask him why he invented alcohol in the first place and see what He has to say about that. He likely won't appreciate my sass.

"On second thought, I best not aggravate the Lord more than I already have. He may turn me around and send me in the other direction. I surely wouldn't want that."

Mary Ann glanced over at her mother. "I'm pretty certain the Lord is going to have a long chat with you in any event!"

"Well, when he finishes with me, I hope to see your daddy once more," Dinah concluded. "I miss him so. Sometimes, it seems like we were sitting here just yesterday. And then I remember it's been over twenty years.

"Oh William," she said, looking up to Heaven, "you better be waiting up there for me. I don't want to find you charming some young, sweet looking thing. You're far too old for that and we went through too much together for you to cast me aside now."

Dinah and Mary Ann chuckled and fell into silence. Dinah filled her pipe and spent a few minutes smoking before she slowly worked her way out of her chair.

"It's time for me to make dinner," she said as she headed toward the front door.

"Momma, let me help," Mary Ann said. "You can't do it yourself anymore."

Dinah objected, then shrugged her shoulders. "Come on then, child," she answered. "Maybe between the two of us, we can make sure the stew gets into the kettle rather than on the floor."

CHAPTER 48
THE READING RIOTS

July 1877

By 1877, Dinah found herself in continuously declining health. She likely suffered from diabetes, heart disease, and high blood pressure, in addition to failing eyesight and arthritis from many years of hard work. Mary Ann, nearly blind with a variety of ailments, may have been in worse shape. Thus, the events of July 22 and July 23, 1877, shook the two women to their core, especially since the epicenter of the disruption took place only blocks from their long-lived Hinnershitz Alley home. They could easily hear the ruckus from their location, and Dinah repeatedly checked outside to ensure the safety of her family and the neighborhood.

"Let's pray they stay where they are," Dinah said to Mary Ann more than once. "We don't need any of those troublemakers in front of our house."

The "Cut" at Seventh and Penn Street–an excavated section of land constructed for use by the Philadelphia & Reading Railroad — served as the focal point for an ongoing labor dispute that exploded into bloody violence. The roots of the standoff traced back more than a year earlier, when in January 1876, railroads nationwide unilaterally imposed a ten percent pay decrease for all employees. Besides the salary reductions, the railroads withheld twenty-five cents from each employee each payday, described by the railroads as a *"bounty,"* with the withheld funds returned quarterly to employees who they determined had a *"clean record"*–a determination made solely by the railroad company using suspect criteria. When the railroad refused to restore the pre-1876 pay rates, tensions quickly escalated and became more and more confrontational, mushrooming to a climax in 1877.

When the Brotherhood of Locomotive Engineers staged a walkout in the spring of 1877, Philadelphia & Reading Railroad general manager John E. Wooten sent a letter to all engineers conditioning continued employment on withdrawing their membership from the Brotherhood. Predictably, this threat did not achieve its intended goal. Instead, it inflamed tensions even more and further emboldened the workers. The railroads continued to operate using other employees and outsiders, leading to physical confrontations erupting across the country.

While Reading had not been one of the initial sites of violence, the fact that the Philadelphia and Reading Railroad located its engine works and shops in the city made a clash all but inevitable. Conceived during a series of clandestine meetings at the Columbia House on Ninth and Penn Streets, the Brotherhood signaled the beginning of its campaign to disrupt train schedules and damage equipment with the blowing of tin horns. The siege of the Seventh and Penn Street Cut soon began.

"The Sunday Riot" started with the burning of a carload of shingles. The gathering crowd, sympathetic to the railroad workers' plight, soon joined in, setting fire to two cabooses, seven freight cars, and a watch house. When firefighters responded to the alarm, the crowd refused to let them through, at which point the fire chief less than reluctantly sent the crew home. The rioters then tore up the Philadelphia and Reading Railroad rail tracks, dumping charcoal on top of them.

The billowing smoke and raucous crowd soon captivated the attention of residents throughout the city.

"Who is making such a racket?" Dinah wondered. "Especially on the day of the Lord."

She eventually made her way to her front door and stepped out, quickly overcome by the noise and smoke in the distance.

"Oh my," she said in wonder. "It looks like the whole city is going up in flames."

"What's going on?" Mary Ann cried from inside the house and Dinah worked to better ascertain the ongoing events.

"You just sit right where you are," Dinah cautioned. "I think there's quite a bit of trouble a few blocks away on Penn Street. This is none of our business, and we should stay as far away as we can."

Dinah stood outside for a few minutes more, further trying to make sense of the disturbance. She soon saw a police officer she recognized for many years rushing toward the scene. He stopped and looked up at the elderly woman.

"You best remain inside, Miss Dinah," the officer cautioned. "There's quite a goings-on down at the railroad and it's likely to get worse before it gets better. The railroad and its workers are at each other's throats. It's been a long time coming. You go back inside and lock the doors."

Dinah nodded. "I will," she said. "You stay safe. I'll keep you in my prayers."

The officer nodded in appreciation and continued toward the scene of violence. He knew he would soon face the perils of a volatile and unpredictable situation.

Dinah turned to return inside the hopefully safe confines of her home only to find Mary Ann at the door.

"Momma, what's going on?" Mary Ann asked again.

"Now you get back inside," her mother scolded. "You can't see nuthin' anyway."

"Now Momma," Mary Ann objected. "That's just cruel."

"Not any crueler than getting hit in the head by something you don't even see coming," Dinah answered as she gently pushed Mary Ann further into the house and followed her inside, closing and locking the door behind her. "The smell of devilry is in the air. I fear there's much more terrible things to come before things get better. We should sit down and pray. We aren't going to be any good out there. Just two old helpless women getting in the way. I just hope the Lord keeps all the rabble rousers away from here."

The chaos continued well into the evening. Rioters eventually destroyed the Lebanon Valley Railroad bridge, which spanned the Schuylkill River north of Reading, setting it on fire. The bridge served as the primary route for passenger trains to Harrisburg. The wooden bridge burned brightly, flames shooting high into the night sky, providing an unexpected display for nearby residents.

But things did not end there. In fact, they worsened.

The next day, known as *"The Monday Riot"* turned even more violent. With local officials unable to raise a posse because of the overwhelming sympathy for the railroad workers, Philadelphia and Reading Railroad president Franklin P. Gowen appealed directly to the Pennsylvania National Guard for assistance. Approximately three hundred members of the Fourth Pennsylvania Volunteer Militia, all from outside the Reading area, arrived on scene under the command of General Franklin Reeder to restore peace and order. They failed miserably.

The members of the Guard marched along the railroad tracks to clear the path of strikers. By now, thousands of residents had gravitated to the area, further provoking the situation. The Guard's arrival only made matters worse, and a new and deadly tinderbox soon ignited.

One young bystander picked up a baseball-sized stone and hurled it as hard as he could at one of the newcomers. It hit the soldier on the shoulder hard enough to knock him into the man next to him and disrupt the march.

"Take that and go home," the bystander yelled. "No one wants you here. The railroad bosses are bloody thieves."

Others in the crowd followed suit, picking up stones and any other objects they could find and began throwing them toward the members of the Guard from either side of the cut. In planning their arrival, the Guard had not accounted for the unruliness of a crowd sympathetic to the cause of the strikers.

"Go home!" the crowd yelled.

"Tell the old bastard Gowen to pay his workers what they deserve!"

"Go back and suck your mother's teat!" one particularly foul voice cried. "I tried it once, and it's quite sour. I had to spit it out."

Rattled and bruised, several angry soldiers turned and aimed their rifles into the crowd. Without orders, they shot randomly, killing ten bystanders and wounding forty more, including five police officers attempting to restore order. The crowd dissipated in panic, causing even more chaos at the scene.

Federal troops arrived by Tuesday, July 24, establishing a semblance of stability and replacing the beleaguered state militia. Crews repaired most of the damage to the railroad damage within a few days. However, rail passengers to Harrisburg rode in wagons and coaches across the river until the completion of the rebuilding of the Lebanon Valley Railroad Bridge.

Inquiries, arrests, and trials followed, and the events of July 22 and July 23 received national news coverage, earning the name the *"Reading Riots."*

Fortunately for Dinah and Mary Ann, they remained inside and safe throughout the ordeal. They fervently prayed to God to keep them out of harm's way. On this occasion, the Lord answered their prayers. Hinnershitz Alley remained outside the zone of turbulence. But the skirmish killed or injured dozens of residents. Dinah said a prayer for each one.

CHAPTER 49
GOOD FRIDAY

April 11, 1879

By 1879, Dinah had reached her mid-eighties and struggled with both frailty and disease. She hardly appeared the strong, sturdy woman who had roamed the city of Reading sawing wood to support her family. But Dinah never lost her religious zeal, and during Holy Week, she attended services regularly as usual. Her weakened body would not stop the devout woman from attending church. The congregation at Bethel A.M.E. Church always knew to expect Dinah, especially during the blessed days counting down to Easter Sunday.

Mary Ann heard her mother opening the front door of their house before noon.

"Where are you going, Momma?" Mary Ann asked. "It's a little chilly out there today."

"I'm headed to Good Friday services," Dinah answered. "They start in a few minutes. I don't want to be late."

"You going to church again? Weren't you just there yesterday?"

"Yesterday was Maundy Thursday," Dinah said. "Today is Good Friday. It's Holy Week. You know that. I taught you better than to act like you don't know."

"Yes, I know that," Mary Ann said with more than a hint of exasperation. "I also know you're a sickly old woman and Good Friday services go three hours. Are you sure you're well enough? The minister doesn't want to interrupt his service halfway through to start a funeral procession."

"I'm just fine," Dinah huffed, waving her hand dismissively at her daughter. "Don't you worry about me. The Lord will take care of me. He always has."

"Well," Mary Ann concluded, knowing she would not change Dinah's mind, "I hope the Lord picks you up and wipes you off if you trip and fall on your face on the way there. And I hope He reminded you to wear a coat."

Dinah gave her daughter another cursory shake of her arm and slowly shuffled out the door, following the all-to-familiar path to Bethel A.M.E. Church. Her sight may not have been what it was in her younger days, but she knew the way by heart. By now, she used a hand-carved wooden cane to help her along. It took her some time to arrive, and a gentleman helped her to her pew when she finally entered the house of worship.

Reverend Davis had elected to conduct a liturgical service known as The Three Hours' Agony that commemorated the time Jesus Christ spent on the cross. Despite the insistence of some younger members of the congregation, the service's name did not serve as a comment on the time they were required to sit in the church pew. The solemn service centered on prayer, reflection, penance, and a series of homilies focused on the "seven last words" spoken by Jesus. In truth, most ministers interpreted the "seven last words" broadly, and the utterances made up many more words than that. More accurately if less poetically, preachers offered sermons on the seven last phrases Jesus voiced while on the cross, culled from the various Gospels. These sermons concluded with Jesus's last phrase, either *"It is finished"* or *"Father, into your hands I commit my spirit!"* depending on whether the minister followed the Gospel of John or the Gospel of Luke.

Dinah sat in prayer throughout the service, listening intently to the words of the minister and joining in song with the rest of the congregation.

"Were you there when they crucified my Lord?
Were you there when they crucified my Lord?
Oh oh oh, sometimes it causes me to tremble, tremble, tremble.
Were you there when they crucified my Lord?"

The congregation completed the hymn, and Reverend Davis prayed, starting with Psalm Twenty-two.

"My God, my God, why hast thou forsaken me? why art thou so far from helping me, and from the words of my roaring?

O my God, I cry in the day time, but thou hearest not; and in the night season, and am not silent.

But thou art holy, O thou that inhabitest the praises of Israel.

Our fathers trusted in thee: they trusted, and thou didst deliver them.

They cried unto thee, and were delivered: they trusted in thee, and were not confounded."

The minister paused, then offered a prayer. "Almighty god, your Son Jesus Christ was lifted high upon the cross so that he might draw the whole world to himself. Grant that we, who glory in this death for our salvation, may also glory in his call to take up our cross and follow him; through Jesus Christ our Lord."

"Amen," the congregation answered.

As the service continued, Dinah's mind wandered throughout the various stages of her life. She remembered her days as a youth on Gabriel Hiester's farm, her adolescence with Jacob Seltzer, and the dark stormy days with Major Sammy Jones. Dinah thought of her husband, William Clark, fondly, the man who freed her from slavery and stood by her throughout his life. She gave not a second of consideration to William Lee.

Then Dinah thought of her children, those she lost and hardly had time to know and those who had gone out into the world. She smiled at the many friends and acquaintances she had made as she travelled through the city for work. She frowned at the thought of the few with whom she had experienced a conflict and put those quickly out of her mind. For a woman born of little means, she had lived a memorable life. Not one anyone would remember, she knew, but one that suited her.

I think the Lord will approve of what I've done with the time I've been given, she thought. *I suppose I will find out soon enough. He'll be sure to let me know as I sit waiting for His judgement.*

The Good Friday service finally ended at three o'clock, commemorating the time that Jesus died. The congregation offered one more solemn moment of silence, confidently knowing He would rise again. Easter would serve as a time of celebration and represent a joyfully stark contrast to the somber tone of this annual ritual.

Those in attendance greeted each other warmly afterwards as they departed from the church. Many had known each other for decades and had helped build and grow this venerable house of worship. They had developed deep and meaningful relationships centered on their lives and their religion. Several of them offered to help Dinah walk home.

"Now don't be silly," she scoffed. "I live right down the street. You can see my house from here. If I wander off in the wrong direction, one of you can come down and set me straight."

As Dinah slowly left the church grounds and worked her way home, she paused and looked back at the familiar edifice one last time. Somehow, deep in her soul, she sensed this would be the last time she would visit Bethel A.M.E. Church while still alive. She would not share that feeling with anyone, especially not her daughter. But she knew her time had nearly arrived. She had lived a full life.

"I suspect I'll be joining you soon, Jesus," she said. "You just make sure you've left a place for me next to William."

CHAPTER 50
REST IN PEACE

April 12, 1879

"Momma?" Mary Ann asked plaintively as she approached her mother's bedside. Dinah typically woke up long before her daughter, but on this day, Mary Ann rose to a quiet house. She knew immediately something was amiss.

Though nearly blind, Dinah's daughter had an ominous feeling as she continued through the home. She knew her mother had been sickly over the last several months despite her best efforts to hide it and live as close to a normal life as possible. But her health had clearly declined at a precipitous pace.

Mary Ann inched closer to the bed, finally leaning down and touching her mother. Dinah's body was cold, and she was not breathing. Mary Ann tried to shake her mother awake, already knowing the uselessness of the gesture. Dinah had laid down to sleep the previous evening for the last time. The Lord had called her while she dreamed.

"Oh Momma," Mary Ann cried. "You've left me to be with my Poppa again."

After Dinah returned home from Good Friday services the day before, Mary Ann noted her mother seemed oddly at peace. At the time, she attributed it to a particularly inspiring church service, but now she realized Dinah recognized she was enjoying her last hours on Earth. Before she went to bed, Dinah approached her daughter.

"You take care, child," she had said. "I will always look over you and God will protect you."

Mary Ann looked at her mother curiously as Dinah took her in her arms and hugged her tightly.

"Are you all right, Momma?" she asked. "I'm going to be right here tomorrow."

"Yes, you will be, and so will I," Dinah answered. "I'll be just fine. Don't you worry about me."

Dinah then slowly strolled to bed and rested her weary body. Mary Ann thought about that conversation as she held her mother's body. She noted Easter Sunday would be the following day.

"Momma," Mary Ann said quietly, "you always said Heaven must be beautiful this time of year. I guess now you've found out. It's even more grand now that you're there."

Mary Ann paused and allowed a picture to form in her mind. There walked her mother, younger and again full of vigor, strolling with the angels celebrating Jesus Christ raising himself from the dead. Dinah wore a bonnet in her hair and flowers and ribbons flowed all about her. A sumptuous feast lay at the end of the long entrance way to God's great hall. Dinah smiled, the burdens of her life slipping away as she feasted in God's glory.

"I am feeling hungry," Dinah said to the angelic being beside her. "Can I sit down and have a bite to eat?"

"You can do whatever you want," the angel replied. "Would you like your husband to join you?"

"William?" she asked and then looked up and saw him standing at the other end of the room. She rushed toward him and wrapped her arms around him.

"I've been waiting for you a long time," William said. "Now we can spend the rest of eternity together."

Dinah held her husband closely. Her worldly concerns slipped away, and she stood in peace and happiness.

"Amen to that," Mary Ann whispered, as she allowed the image to dissipate. "You're in a better place now."

Mary Ann sat by her mother for some time, grieving. She eventually felt compelled to open the drawer on the small table beside Dinah's bed. There, she found the photographic portrait taken of her mother by Charles Saylor twenty years earlier. She looked at it with a smirk.

"Well, Momma," she said. "I guess I finally have reason to hang this on the wall."

•   •   •

Dinah Clark died on April 12, 1879. The official cause of her death was listed as Bright's disease, for which she reportedly suffered for more than five months. Bright's disease is an obsolete name for kidney disease brought on by diabetes, heart disease, and high blood pressure. Dr. Israel Cleaver attended to her. She had lived a long life, dying at eighty-four or eighty-five years old—her exact age unknown because of the uncertainty of her birth date. In either case, she had far outlived the average lifespan of Americans in the Victorian Age, which for women stood at slightly over fifty years old. In truth, however, that average remained significantly depressed because of the high child mortality rate, something of which Dinah was quite familiar.

Dinah Clark had gained much more fame than most African Americans—and especially African American women—in that time period, and the *Reading Times* included her at the end of 1879 on a list of notable residents who had died that year.

Dinah's small claim to fame extended even beyond the immediate Reading area. The *Lebanon Daily News*, serving a town thirty miles to the west, published a brief acknowledgement of her death on April 17, 1879, even graciously adding a few more years to her already long life.

"Dinah Clark, colored, died at Reading on Saturday, in her eighty-ninth year. She had lived in Berks county all her life, and was born a slave."

Her funeral ceremony was held at the church within footsteps of Dinah's home. In a testament to the barriers Dinah crossed, the *Reading Eagle* reported about two hundred people attended the service, approximately seventy-five of them white.

"Porter Dobbins, John Williams, John Steele and Henry Carey were the pall-bearers. The body was dressed in a white shroud and encased in a plain walnut coffin. In her hand was a lily and on her breast a white rose. The cortege went from the late residence of deceased, Hinnershitz's alley, to the A.M.E. Church, Tenth street, where Rev. Davis, the pastor, preached the sermon, after which the funeral proceeded to Charles Evans Cemetery, where the interment took place. The cortege came down Washington street to Sixth, where the cars were taken to the cemetery."

Outside the church, those passing by could hear the mournful sounds of the congregation in song.

> *"Nobody knows the trouble I've seen*
> *Nobody knows by Jesus*
> *Nobody knows the trouble I've seen*
> *Glory, Hallelujah*
> *Sometimes I'm up, sometimes*
> *I'm down, ohh, yes Lord*
> *Sometimes I'm almost*
> *To the ground, oh yes, Lord."*

Henninger's Funeral Home arranged her burial at Charles Evans Cemetery, located on Centre Avenue in the northern section of Reading. Dinah was buried in an unmarked grave on the Aaron and William Still plot. Aaron Still ran a well-known and respected barber shop on Tenth Street and during his lifetime, worked tirelessly to advance the rights of African Americans. He served as one of the vice presidents of the Old Reliable Club, a state political organization and was a good friend of Frederick Douglass. He reportedly arranged for several of Douglass's presentations in Reading. Aaron's son, William, served in the Civil War and followed in the footsteps of his father working as a barber. At the time of her death, Mary Ann was buried in the same location.

"I have got religion," Dinah told the *Reading Eagle* reporter years earlier, *"and I expect to land my soul safe in Heaven. God being my helper."*

• • •

Just as many other Northeast industrial cities, Reading experienced highs and lows since Dinah's passing. The development of the canal system and later the railroads made Reading an important nexus throughout much of the Nineteenth Century as goods and people traveled east to west and then back again.

Reading joined the burgeoning early automobile industry in the early Twentieth Century, becoming home to the Daniels Motor Company and the Reading-Standard Company. Perhaps the most famous Reading-based automobile manufacturer, however, was the Duryea Power Company, operated by Charles Duryea. By 1905, Duryea manufactured sixty cars a year, including the four-wheel-drive Phaeton that sold for one-thousand-six-hundred dollars. Duryea's legacy remains memorialized today in Reading by Duryea Drive, a windy, twisty uphill road he used to test the durability and refinement of his vehicles.

Reading continued to grow until the 1930s. By then, its population had blossomed to more than one-hundred-and-eleven thousand and it represented the seventy-sixth largest city in the United States. The city enjoyed a bustling downtown and a vibrant lifestyle for most of its residents.

But just as many other urban centers, Reading experienced a significant downturn from the 1940s through the 1970s. The strength of the railroads faltered, the manufacturing industry declined, and many residents migrated to the suburbs in search of single homes, backyards, and off-street parking.

The population did not again show growth until the 2000 census, driven primarily by the immigration of various Hispanic nationalities and the western movement of residents from the Philadelphia suburbs. By the 2020 census, the city's population had grown once again to over ninety-five-thousand residents.

Dinah's log home on Hinnershitz Alley is long gone.

CHAPTER 51
PLEASANT VALLEY

August 1970

Over four hundred years, the valley had undergone many transformations, and it stood on the verge of yet another. For centuries, the land stood pristine as a prime hunting ground for the Lenape. Running along the Tulpehocken Creek, the valley provided both fertile soil and a strong freshwater stream that sustained the tribe's livelihood in the southern part of their territory.

English settlers arrived in the Sixteenth Century. Besieged by disease and famine, the Lenape population decreased significantly by the time William Penn established the Commonwealth of Pennsylvania. The Lenape allied with the French during the French and Indian War in the mid-Eighteenth Century, but their influence receded following the resolution of that conflict. The British Empire now controlled the territory.

By the 1770s, the valley inexorably became settled by colonists as the European population expanded. On the hill above the Tulpehocken Creek, Gabriel Hiester built a home and began working the land. The American Revolution soon created the United States of America. From that point on, the ground served as a successful farming operation for two hundred years. Along the way, the owners that followed Gabriel Hiester added multiple outbuildings until the farm boasted more than a dozen structures, including a multi-level barn, two large pig stables, a chicken coop, an impressive butcher shop, a garage, and other sheds and storage facilities.

As time passed, the region around the farm became known as Pleasant Valley. Residents now affectionately knew the Tulpehocken Creek as "The Tully," and it served as a favorite fishing spot for them. Gabriel Hiester's mill became the Pleasant Valley Roller Mills, new establishments such as the Pleasant Valley Hotel opened, and the town of Obold that overlooked the valley eventually changed its name to Mount Pleasant.

In 1938, John Swope purchased the farm along the Tully and continued the land's agricultural tradition. During the late 1950s, John turned the operation of the farm over to one of his sons, and there Clarence Swope and his wife, Peggy, raised their young family.

The long history of the valley, however, would soon face a destructive turn. The U.S. Army Corps of Engineers had slated this region for construction of a dam, a development that would seize over sixty farms, hundreds of homes, and thousands of acres in the area. The dam would flood the meadow where the Lenape hunted, where Dinah Clark found temporary respite as a child, and where generations of families had lived and prospered.

•   •   •

By now, Pleasant Valley had become domesticated. Generations of farmers had turned much of the meadow by the creek into pasture for herds of dairy cows. The field showed the scars of recent history. Remnants of the Nineteenth Century Union Canal stood idle. The waterfall on the Tully, still known as Hiester's Dam, represented the last evidence of an elaborate hydro-powered system that ran the equipment at the Pleasant Valley Roller Mills through the 1800s and into the mid-Twentieth Century.

A picnic pavilion, outhouse, and stationery grill had been built along the Tully, and a Swope family gathering brought relatives from near and far every year. A pond had been constructed and stocked with fish.

The two oldest Swope children, twelve-year-old Joey and eight-year-old Ronnie clattered around the house and yard most of the morning while their mother worked in the kitchen and monitored their one-year-old sister, Michele.

"Joey," his mother said as he walked through the room, "can you take this box up to the attic?"

"Sure," he said. He snatched up the box and walked through the dining room into the back hallway that led up two flights of stairs to the third floor. The house had been expanded since Gabriel Hiester first built it, with an indoor kitchen, an additional bedroom, and a bathroom added once modern plumbing became available. An old massive coal boiler now heated the home, belching and consuming fuel at an impressive rate during the cold weather months. While the house maintained some of its elegant charm—the elaborate woodwork still decorated the living room, though somewhere along the line it had been painted an off-white–two centuries of hard use and technological advances had dulled some of its original luster.

When Joey arrived on the third floor, he placed the box on top of the others stacked along one wall. Before he went back down, he stopped and looked around the room curiously, something he had done many times before.

"I wonder why they cut this attic into three rooms," he said to himself. "Who would live up here? It gets hot as blazes in the summer and cold as hell in the winter. I guess I'll never know."

Joey spent a few more minutes exploring the attic, noting the slats still open on the wall facing east. He pondered if anyone ever "shot at Indians" as his family claimed. He ran down the steps, and soon, he joined Ronnie on one of their frequent explorations around the farm. Their father had finished the morning milking and fed all the animals. Clarence had taken one of their Farmall tractors into the fields to plant, pick, or cut whatever the crops demanded at the moment. The two boys now could claim some free time.

They skipped rocks in the Tully, wandering down to Hiester's Dam, which they called only "the falls," watching and listening to the water storm over the barrier. The boys knew nothing of the old millrace that had long disappeared, the mill having transformed to electric and other fuels before either of them had been born. They searched the decaying remnants of the Union Canal, then slowly picked their way back toward the farm buildings. Along the way, they dueled with fallen sticks and observed the various wildlife–from birds to groundhogs–that they encountered. Occasionally, on other excursions, they encountered a water snake but fortunately avoided any today.

"I hate snakes," Joey intoned, eyeing the ground carefully as they walked.

"Water snakes aren't poisonous," Ronnie chided.

"Don't care," the older boy concluded. "They're still snakes."

The sun climbed high, and Joey and Ronnie sweated in the late summer heat. They considered returning to the confines of the farm, where they could climb down the steps of the arch, the root cellar built two centuries earlier. Even now, that served as the coolest spot on the farm. The old house never had seen the sight of an air conditioning unit. But a slight breeze provided just enough relief to maintain their journey. As they walked through the meadow, Joey stopped and looked down, eventually reaching down and picking up a stone.

"Is this what I think it is?" he asked his brother.

Ronnie came over and examined the elongated, triangular object. "Looks like an arrowhead to me," he confirmed. "Dad has a collection he's found through the years. He can probably tell us more about it."

"I'll show it to him," Joey agreed. He paused and checked the sun's movement in the sky. "We should probably get back. It's time to milk soon. They'll be bringing the cows in from the pasture. Dad will give me hell if I'm not there to feed the calves."

"The cows are all the way in the back field today," Ronnie said. "We need to help them get across the road anyway."

With newfound determination, the two boys picked up their pace and headed back to the farm complex. Unfortunately, Joey didn't secure the arrowhead in his pocket. As he climbed the hill back to the farmhouse, the relic slipped out and nestled once again in the long grass of the meadow.

A few minutes later, Joey stopped and turned around toward the meadow. For a moment, he thought he saw a Lenape bowman down a deer. A second later, a young African American girl picked up the lost arrowhead and looked up at him.

"What the hell is wrong with you?" Ronnie asked.

Joey turned toward his brother, then looked back again. The meadow no longer showed any sign of activity or disturbance.

"Nothing," he finally said. "Seeing things I guess."

"Too much soda will do that to you," Ronnie cracked. "You have to quit drinking. It will rot your brain."

The two brothers continued on their journey toward the barn. By the time they returned to help with the milking, the arrowhead and its past lives had become long forgotten.

•　•　•

A few months later, the two brothers played outside, throwing a football back and forth in the yard. By now, fall had arrived, and they had exchanged their summer attire for jackets and jeans. The farm's hired hand, Adam, walked up to them, slightly agitated.

"Where is that goddam Clarence Swope?" he asked. "I have to get hay down, straw down, and I can't find him anywhere."

"He went out into the field hunting earlier this morning," Ronnie said. "He's looking for deer."

"He can clean his own goddam deer himself then," Adam said and stalked off. "I'm not helping."

Joey looked at his brother. "How is it that Dad goes out hunting but never comes back with anything?" he asked.

"I don't know," Ronnie asked. "Maybe he doesn't see any bucks."

"I don't even think he loads his gun," Joey said. "I think he just says he's going out hunting to get some peace and quiet. Probably walks there, lays down, and takes a nap. A deer could come up and smell him and Dad would never notice. He doesn't even like to eat venison."

Ronnie laughed. "I guess we'll see when he comes back."

Predictably, their father returned a little later with nothing in hand other than his rifle.

"See," Joey said, eliciting a chuckle. "Told you."

"What the hell are you two laughing about?" their father asked, eyeing his two sons.

"Nothing," Joey answered. "Nothing at all."

As a hunter, their father proved less successful than the Lenape and the Hiester family members who came before him. But perhaps he had achieved his objective, nevertheless.

Later that day after the sun had set, Joey and Ronnie lay on the bank in the pasture west of the farmhouse looking at the moon. Apollo 11 had landed on the lunar surface just a year earlier and Neil Armstrong became the first man to step onto a world other than Earth. Following an ancient tradition of which they were both unaware, the two boys concocted stories about the moon, envisioning what might occur in the future.

"Do you think we'll ever live up there?" Ronnie asked.

"Not likely," Joey answered sarcastically. "Turns out it's not made of cheese after all. Nothing to eat."

Joey and Ronnie lay there in silence for a few minutes, looking at the moon and the stars. They enjoyed a spectacular view, far from the lights of the city or any other obstruction that could dim the panorama.

"Soon, you know," Ronnie said. "We're going to have to move."

"Yeah," Joey answered sadly. "The farm will be under water. Everything we had here will be lost."

Joey paused for a moment.

"Pleasant Valley lost," he concluded softly.

•　　•　　•

The Swope family moved from Pleasant Valley the next year as the unstoppable flow of "progress" slowly overtook the land. Soon thereafter, the Corps of Engineers purchased the farm and demolished the Eighteenth-Century home and outbuildings. Less than a decade later, the Blue Marsh Lake flooded Pleasant Valley and all the history beneath it with sixteen billion gallons of water. Somewhere at the bottom of the manmade lake, the arrowhead still sits.

CHAPTER 52
THE READING EAGLE

February 2021

As Joe stepped away from his desk, his cellphone started ringing. He glanced at it quickly.

The *Reading Eagle*, he thought. *Now what happened?*

Joe had fashioned a long, successful career as a public relations professional. After spending ten years working at the college where he received his bachelor's degree, he had moved on to a regional natural gas and electric utility. He had been there for nearly thirty years. As he inched closer to retirement, the world had turned upside down with the COVID-19 pandemic. For nearly a year, he had worked from home, which perfectly suited him. He worked better alone, drawing in resources as he needed them. Working for a utility company for so many years, Joe had learned that much of his job focused on managing potential crisis situations. Whenever a reporter called, his internal alarm immediately took notice.

"Good morning, this is Joe Swope," he answered.

"Hi Joe, this is Michelle Lynch from the *Reading Eagle*," the voice on the other end of the line said. After a few minutes, Joe determined this call had nothing to do with Joe's job, but rather with his avocation as a part-time author. "I'm working on a story, and I think it has a connection to the farm you grew up on and wrote about in your book, *Pleasant Valley Lost*."

And that's how two lives, Dinah and Joe's, separated by sex, by race, by life circumstances, and by nearly one hundred and fifty years, somehow became intertwined. Although their lives differed greatly, the same land shaped both Dinah and Joe.

Dinah's life forced Joe to reconsider his view of the "old farm" as his family referred to it. To him, it had always served as the paradise lost of his childhood, the place where many of his fondest memories had seared into his memory. But for Dinah, the farm represented the first of the multiple rooms of hell she had endured in her early life. Joe would now always have the somber undertone of the lives that came before him. Albeit it in far different ways, their early days on the farm had prepared both Joe and Dinah to face life's challenges with strength and endurance.

Joe spoke to the reporter, but admittedly, at that point, could not provide much new information. In fact, he learned much more from the reporter than she did from him. A few days later, on February 26, 2021, Joe picked up his daily newspaper (yes, he still read the paper edition) and spotted Michelle's story.

"Itinerant sawyer Dinah Clark sawed her way to local fame in 19th-Century Reading.

Carrying a buck on her shoulders and saw in hand, the tall, strong Black woman was a familiar figure in the city from the 1850s until her death in 1879 . . ."

"You know," Joe said as he read further. "I should find out more about Dinah and her life. Hers is a story worth telling."

CHAPTER 53
LEGACY

Dinah Clark never read a book or wrote a letter. She never voted. If she ever travelled outside the confines of Berks County, she never mentioned it. Between the cost of travel and the ever-present veil of segregation, she likely remained in the Greater Reading area her entire life. Besides, she likely considered trains some mechanical beast from hell and vowed never to travel on such a contraption. Some in the 1800s believed that women's bodies could not withstand the speed of trains, which could reach fifty miles per hour, an unsubstantiated conclusion that may have spooked Dinah. This theory proclaimed that women's uteruses *would fly out of their bodies if they accelerated to that speed.* Apparently, according to this notion, men's parts were more firmly attached and not prone to such expulsion. Dinah probably said a silent prayer every time a train rolled by.

While Dinah engaged in a profession unusual for a woman in the Nineteenth Century, she made no permanent contributions to the craft. Indeed, alternative fuels and modern technology have all but reduced the job of an itinerant sawyer to a figure of history. Most people today would not even know the definition of a sawyer if asked.

Dinah Clark had her flaws. Yes, she probably drank too much and smoked too much. She had ongoing feuds with several prominent citizens and apparently held grudges for many decades. She was not one to forget any perceived transgressions easily.

Nevertheless, what Dinah Clark contributed to the world remains unforgettable. She rose from a childhood of poverty and involuntary servitude to build a life with her husband and her children. Dinah entered the "men's" world of work and succeeded. She helped build a church and provided runaway slaves a refuge. Later, she assisted freed former slaves and helped them start a new life as they travelled north. She shattered as best she could the racial barriers of the time and became a well-known woman in the growing city of Reading in the Nineteenth Century. The depth of her strength and endurance remains remarkable.

Dinah made enough of a mark that, even today, re-enactors portray her in events marking local history. When the *Reading Eagle* told her story to a new generation of readers in 2021, it provided new life to her near-forgotten tale. That story now lives in cyberspace, read by countless readers across the country and the globe. Her beloved home on Hinnershitz Alley is long gone and the original Bethel A.M.E. Church has been repurposed, but her legacy lives on. It's not hard to imagine Dinah Clark walking up the alley, crossing Tenth Street to attend church or travelling down Penn Street toward Fifth with her sawbuck across her shoulders on her way to her next job.

Dinah Clark crossed the bridge between slavery and freedom and broke through the barriers that divided the work of men and women. In her own humble way, she served as a trailblazing pioneer without ever knowing it. Reading and Berks County, and the world, are better for her life.

She deserves to be remembered.

"Make me a grave where'er you will,
In a lowly plain, or a lofty hill;
Make it among earth's humblest graves,
But not in a land where men are slaves."

"Bury Me in a Free Land"

Frances Ellen Watkins Harper (1825-1911), American abolitionist, suffragist, poet, and writer, and one of the first African American women to be published in the United States.

ACKNOWLEDGEMENTS

For my entire publishing journey, which now encompasses seven books, I have had the support of my family and friends. I am eternally grateful for their patience as they watched me tap the keys on my laptop, scribble ideas on a notepad on a plane, or recite story points into my phone, so I didn't forget them by the time I got home. My kids pretty much have accepted these quirks as typical "Dad" behavior by now. My significant other, Krysta, learned that I needed my hour or so every morning to write or edit. Many times, I got a "I'll let you wake up and write" message from her. I promise I made it up to her later that day! Thanks to all of you for your continued patience!

Sharpened Blade toes the somewhat tenuous line between fiction and non-fiction. We primarily know about Dinah Clark from a newspaper interview eight years before her death and a few other articles that mention her throughout her life. Those sources provide a broad framework but leave many gaps unanswered. The trick in constructing this book consisted of trying to envision what happened in the voids Dinah did not address within the context of what we know (sometimes as best as we can tell!). Dinah no doubt led a colorful life, likely far more textured than history has recorded. Hopefully, I've done it justice.

I've tried to mimic Dinah's speech as best as I can based on the *Reading Eagle* newspaper article that provides the best picture we have of the real individual. However, those familiar with the Nineteenth Century and the realities of slavery likely realize I have made a conscience choice to not use African American Vernacular English (AAVE) in Dinah's speech. AAVE makes up a variety of English-based dialects, which likely resulted when African American slaves in the South adapted the language spoken by first- and second-language English-speaking slaveholders from England and other European countries. This combination of languages from multiple nations represented a form of speech and communication more complicated in many ways than modern English. That complexity makes it both more difficult for the writer to write and the reader to fully understand. How much of AAVE northern slaves such as Dinah and her parents adopted remains a question that may depend on the specific geographic and family circumstances. For the purpose of telling the story more effectively, I've likely made Dinah's speech patterns more recognizable to the contemporary reader.

In a similar vein, Pennsylvania German – still better known by many as Pennsylvania Dutch – was almost certainly spoken by many of the immigrants that populated Berks County. I have personal experience with the use of Pennsylvania German many generations later since my father spoke it fluently, especially when he didn't want us to know what he said. For ease of reading, plus the lack of access to a reliable translator, everyone in *Sharpened Blade* speaks English.

I usually am pretty self-sufficient in researching my books, but this one called for a lot of help along the way. It turns out that writing about events in the Nineteenth Century required many "how did they do this?" inquiries that needed unexpected investigation. I had more than my share of "aha" moments as I wrote, and serendipity also played a critical role. Writing *Sharpened Blade* turned into a story by itself.

This book likely wouldn't exist without Michelle Napoletano Lynch. Working as a reporter for the *Reading Eagle* with a keen eye for local history, Michelle contacted me in 2021 as she worked on a profile of Dinah Clark. Michelle realized Dinah had been born on the same farm on which I grew up and highlighted in my first book, *Pleasant Valley Lost*. At that moment, I realized why the third-floor attic in the old farmhouse had been sectioned into three distinct rooms. Without that connection, the story of Dinah Clark would likely never have caught my attention.

Michelle later read a draft of the manuscript at my request to ensure I had not gone astray. Again, she provided valuable insight, as well as the copy of the 1847 deed to Dinah's beloved home on Hinnershitz Alley. Between what each of us gleaned, we finally deduced the mystery of the two Hannahs – Dinah's daughter and Enoch Sanders' wife. In addition, Michelle's sleuthing discovered the name of the reporter who interviewed Dinah, allowing Mr. Nicholson to earn his due credit.

Michelle also pointed me in the direction of several local Berks County historians who had documented Dinah's life journey in various publications.

Michelle's own discovery of Dinah Clark traces back to Berks County's pre-eminent historian, George M. Meiser, IX, and his wife Gloria Jean Meiser. Together, they have published twenty-five volumes of *The Passing Scene,* a compilation of photographs and text documenting the history of Reading and Berks County. Volume 12 of the series, published in 2000, provided a short history of Dinah and included her only known photograph. The Meisers credited Dennis Casner-Witwer of Spring Township for providing the photograph and Sandra Stief for completing valuable research assistance. This work eventually inspired the latest wave of interest in Dinah's story.

Thanks also to Lisa Adams, an archival assistant at The Henry Janssen Library of the Berks History Center. Not only is Dinah Clark's life sometimes shrouded in mystery, but her references to various people in her life were often obscure. Armed with nothing more than a couple of questions based on what I had gleaned, Lisa scoured the History Center's archives and found important information that I incorporated into the book.

The Berks History Center's magazine, *The Historical Review of Berks County*, also deserves mention. In particular, *"After the Tumult,"* Brian C. Engelhardt's article in the Fall 2024 issue served as the inspiration and provided most of the source material for the chapter on The Reading Riots, an event Dinah no doubt heard but thankfully one in which she did not take part.

Other writers who have researched the history of Berks County proved valuable resources. The late Barbara Goda, a high school history and social studies teacher for thirty years, wrote extensively about Berks County and the notable women throughout its history. Her work provided valuable information about Dinah Clark and Sarah Hardy, who appears briefly in this book.

Then there's Tracy Ball, the best-selling author of *Civil Warriors* and a number of other books. Tracy has written extensively about race relations, and I always trust her judgement to let me know when I have gone astray in my character depictions and dialogue. Tracy provided an extensive critique that helped embed more authenticity into the story, and I greatly appreciate her insightful input. She also called the book a "masterpiece," a compliment I'll accept even if she was using a bit of hyperbole. By the way, if you liked *Sharpened Blade*, read her books. You won't regret it.

Some details arrived at the most unexpected times. I was sitting with some of my kids at a Denny's Restaurant in Orlando in 2023 when we began a conversation with Gemini, an African American server. Gemini grew up in Texas and served in the military, and rued the fact that he couldn't wear his cowboy hat and boots in Florida because "everyone thought of the black cowboy from *Blazing Saddles*." Gemini had never visited Pennsylvania but told me he wished he could travel there because, living in the South his entire life, he had never seen the leaves changing in the fall (a comment that inspired one short scene in the book). As we continued to talk, Gemini somehow got to the subject of weddings and provided a detailed description and history of why African Americans jumped over a broom at their wedding ceremony. When I got back to where I was staying, I took detailed notes because I knew I had to include it in this book.

Gemini, by the way, had never married.

Another unexpected contributor was Sheila, a clerk in a gift shop at Caesar's Palace in Las Vegas. Again, our conversation shifted to this book and the custom of jumping the broom. She added an important detail–the recording of weddings, births, deaths, baptisms, and other important information in family Bibles that passed down through generations. Shelia recounted she had such a Bible, published with beautiful color illustrations that served as a valuable family heirloom.

In addition, there are vast online resources which proved invaluable as I navigated through question such as "how did a sawyer do their job?" to "what events took place in Reading in the 1860s and 1870s?" to "what are the symptoms of smallpox?" Anyone scouring my search history must be scratching their head by now.

Several sources proved particularly valuable. The *GoReadingBerks.com* site provided valuable material documenting the history of Reading and

Berks County. The archives of the various Reading newspapers through the ages, particularly The *Reading Eagle,* offered both news of the day and the history of the community. Newspapers long served as the first draft of history, and in that respect, they provided the only first-hand look at Dinah's life.

Every so often, I needed to solicit the knowledge of an expert. Not being a hunter, I tapped the experience of a long-time friend and family member, Chad Kershner, who had travelled the Pennsylvania hills in search of deer for many years. Chad helped me through the steps of gutting a deer in the wild. Living among the many hunters in the Commonwealth, I knew I best not screw that up.

While one might question some appearances of famous people in this tale, most are absolutely true. Edgar Allan Poe indeed received an invitation to speak in Reading by the Mechanics Institute, Harriet Beecher Stowe made a presentation at the Grand Opera House Theatre, and the elaborate circuses of the day traveled through Reading during the Civil War, however unlikely that may appear today. While I could not find direct evidence that Thaddeus Steven spoke in Reading, it's almost unfathomable to believe that he did not during the tumultuous times in his effort to spread his fervent abolitionist message.

Sharpened Blade represents book number seven in a remarkable journey that began much later in life than most authors. Black Rose Writing has served as both my publisher and an amazing partner. They've put up with me as my books have bounced through genres over more than a decade. Thanks so much to Reagan Rothe and the rest of the BRW team!

ABOUT THE AUTHOR

During a career that spanned nearly 50 years, Joseph J. Swope worked in both corporate and non-profit settings as a chef, a public relations professional, a photographer, and a university adjunct professor. He retired in 2024 and now claims he doesn't understand how he had time to work.

However, he has continued his lifelong dedication to writing. *Sharpened Blade: The Story of Dinah Clark* is Swope's seventh book, his literary efforts ranging from historical fiction and non-fiction, to horror, to a children's book, to fantasy and science fiction.

Swope lives in Reading, Pennsylvania, where he plays senior softball and is known for his cheesecake and five onion cream soup. He has seven kids ranging from 35 to 6 and two grandchildren.

OTHER TITLES BY JOSEPH J. SWOPE

NOTE FROM JOSEPH J. SWOPE

Word-of-mouth is crucial for any author to succeed. If you enjoyed *Sharpened Blade*, please leave a review online—anywhere you are able. Even if it's just a sentence or two. It would make all the difference and would be very much appreciated.

Thanks!
Joseph J. Swope

We hope you enjoyed reading this title from:

www.blackrosewriting.com

Subscribe to our mailing list – *The Rosevine* – and receive **FREE** books, daily deals, and stay current with news about upcoming releases and our hottest authors.
Scan the QR code below to sign up.

Already a subscriber? Please accept a sincere thank you for being a fan of Black Rose Writing authors.

View other Black Rose Writing titles at www.blackrosewriting.com/books and use promo code **PRINT** to receive a **20% discount** when purchasing.

www.ingramcontent.com/pod-product-compliance
Lightning Source LLC
Chambersburg PA
CBHW030020200726
48283CB00012B/703